## Praise for *Blue Birds*

### *Winner of the Virginia Library Association's 2016 Jefferson Cup for Young Readers*

"Composed in varying formats, the descriptive and finely crafted poems reveal the similarities the two girls share, from loved ones lost to hatred between the English and the Roanoke to a desire for peace . . . Fans of Karen Hesse and the author's *May B.* (2012) will delight in this offering."
—*Kirkus Reviews*

"A memorable account of a friendship that transcends culture and prejudice."
—*Publishers Weekly*

"An excellent historical offering . . . belongs on public and school library shelves."
—*VOYA*

"With two compelling main characters and an abundance of rich historical detail, Rose's latest novel offers much to discuss and much to appreciate."
—*School Library Journal*

"An imaginative historical novel with two sympathetic protagonists."

—*Booklist*

"Themes of fear and freedom will appeal to a wide audience."

—*School Library Connection*

"Using language that's both plain and exquisite, Caroline Starr Rose weaves history seamlessly into the stories of two girls with distinct backgrounds and voices. The crossing lives gave me a big world that lingered past the pages."

—Jeannine Atkins, author of *Borrowed Names*

"Rose has given us a complex story, a real and researched story, a story that, despite its roots in late-sixteenth-century America, feels contemporary. In bringing readers Alis and Kimi, Rose has not just brought us a distant era. She's brought her readers a way of sinking in with real questions about difference—and a credible suggestion that such differences might be overcome."

—Beth Kephart, author of *This Is the Story of You*

# JASPER AND THE RIDDLE OF RILEY'S MINE

Also by Caroline Starr Rose

*Blue Birds*

*May B.*

# JASPER AND THE RIDDLE OF RILEY'S MINE

CAROLINE STARR ROSE

G. P. Putnam's Sons

G. P. Putnam's Sons
an imprint of Penguin Random House LLC
375 Hudson Street
New York, NY 10014

Library of Congress Cataloging-in-Publication Data
is available upon request.

Printed in the United States of America.
ISBN 9780399168116
1 3 5 7 9 10 8 6 4 2

Design by Eric Ford.
Text set in ITC New Baskerville.

To Noah and Caleb,
with all my love

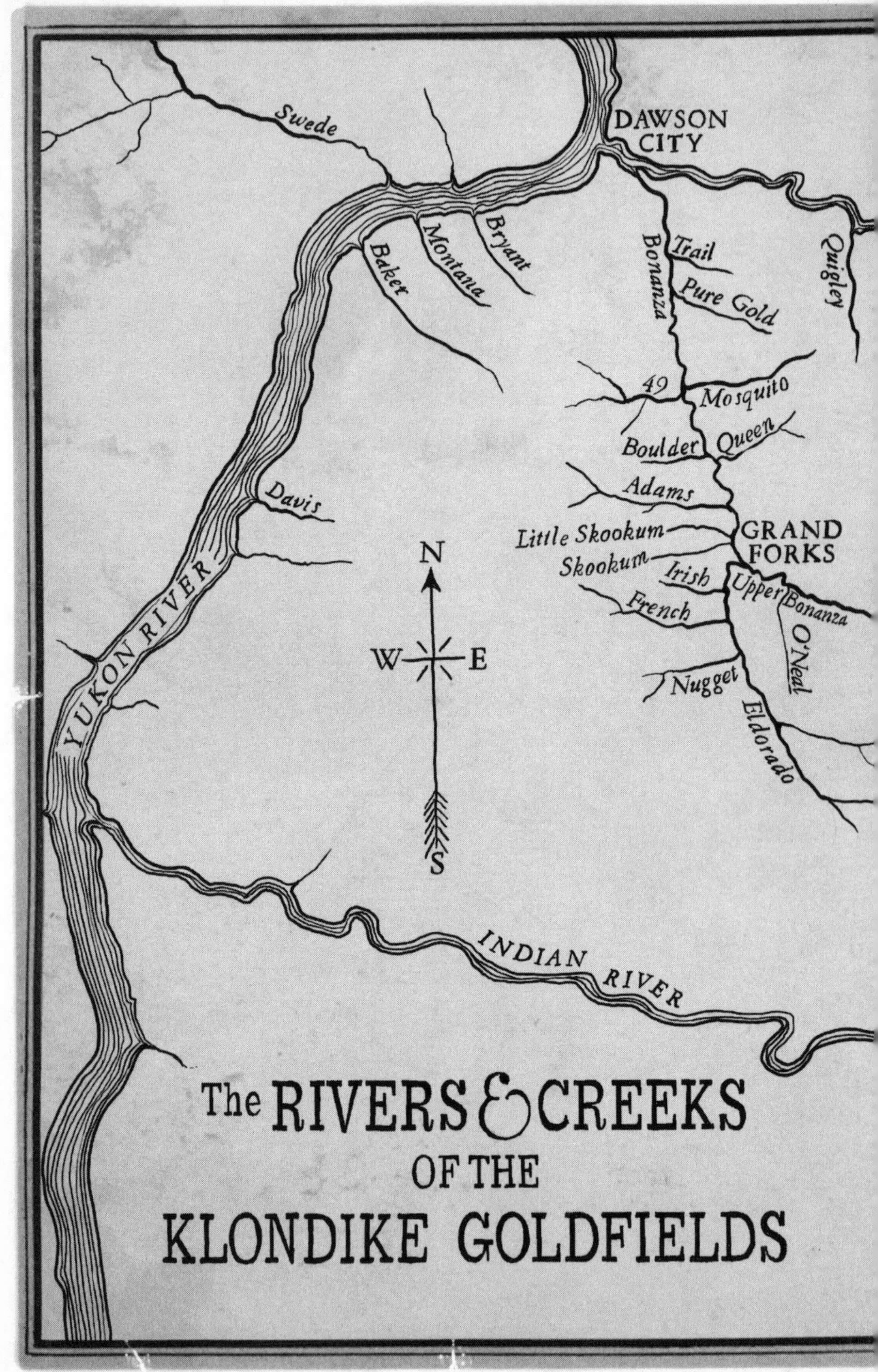

Swede
DAWSON
CITY
Bryant
Montana
Baker
Trail
Bonanza
Pure Gold
Quigley
49
Mosquito
Boulder
Queen
Adams
Davis
Little Skookum
GRAND
FORKS
Skookum
Irish
Upper
Bonanza
French
O'Neal
N
W
E
S
Nugget
Eldorado
YUKON RIVER
INDIAN
RIVER
The RIVERS & CREEKS
OF THE
KLONDIKE GOLDFIELDS

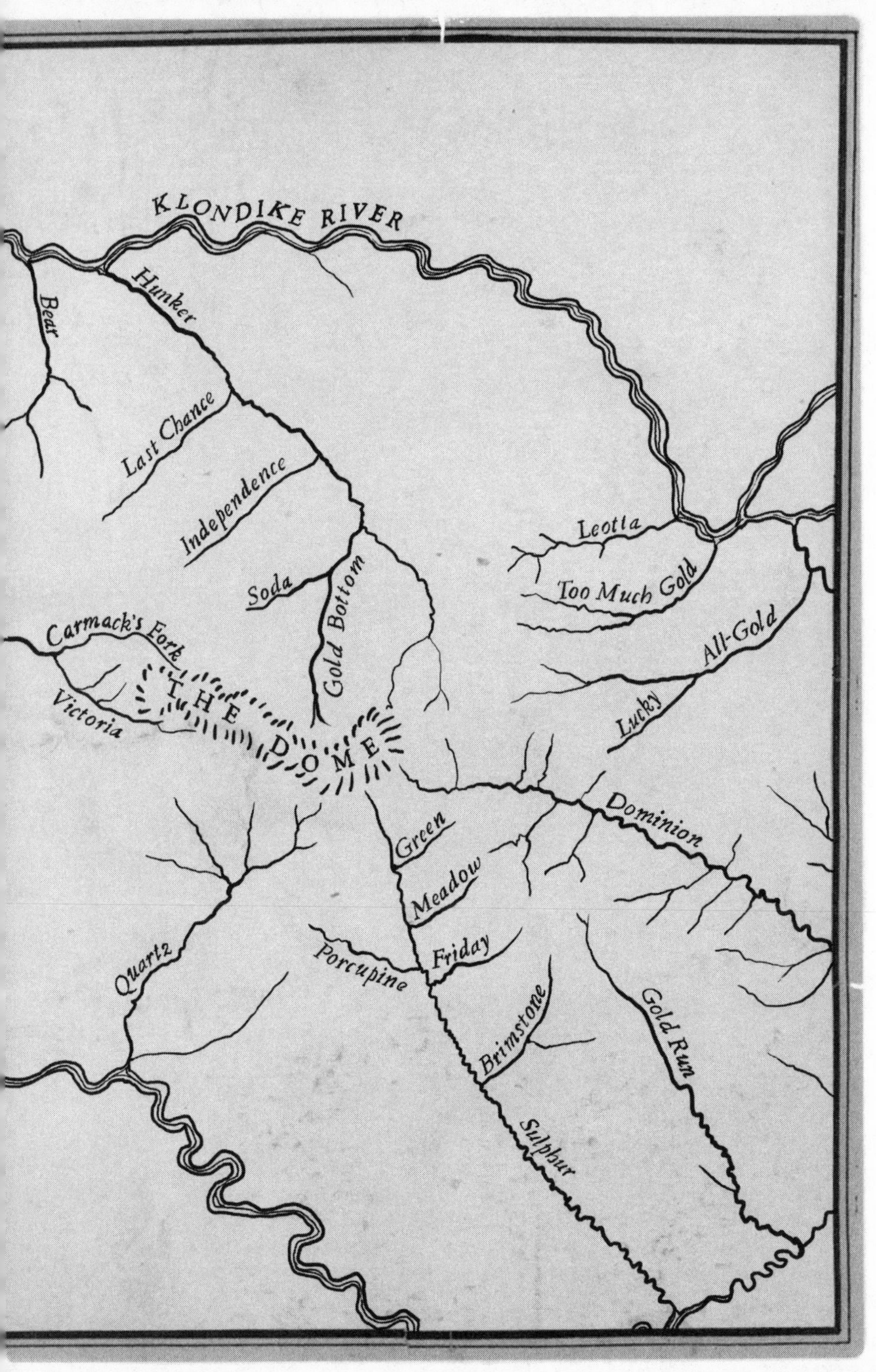

KLONDIKE RIVER
Bear
Hunker
Last Chance
Independence
Soda
Gold Bottom
Carmack's Fork
Victoria
THE DOME
Leotia
Too Much Gold
All-Gold
Lucky
Dominion
Green
Meadow
Friday
Porcupine
Quartz
Brimstone
Gold Run
Sulphur

# Chapter 1

The blanket over my head don't block out the sound, a tapping at the window sharp as hailstones. I roll over and try to get on back to sleep, but the noise gets louder. Then a second sound starts in, this one soft and breathy.

"Jasper," it says.

That ain't a storm I hear.

The room's dark, but a faint light glows outside, enough to see Pa's bed is as jumbled as usual. No telling, though, if he's in there or not.

"Come on, wake up," the voice whispers.

Melvin? My brother's on the porch? I listen close for that funny whistle Mel makes when he sleeps heavy, but don't hear it. Mel ain't in his bed like he should be.

A groan escapes Pa's lumpy blanket as three sharp raps

rattle the windowpane. Don't know how I missed him earlier, blowing in how he does, loud and clumsy as a blind moose. Usually mad as one, too. I grab my glasses, race across them worn floorboards as quick as I can, and crack open the door. There's my brother on the other side. He hoots and grins as he swings a newspaper over his head. The lantern he holds jitters, casting jagged shadows.

"You need to hush!" I slip out onto the porch, shut the door real gentle.

Mel quiets some, but he still dances around. If I didn't know him better, the way he's acting, pure crazy on his face, I'd think he'd got into Pa's liquor. Any second now I expect Pa to fly out of bed, cussing like a kicked cat, and knock some sense into him.

"Where've you been?" I take the lantern from Mel's hand, set it on the top step for safekeeping. "What're you doing out here, anyhow?"

"I was talking with the men at the wool mill and lost track of time." The lantern hardly gives off any light, but even so, Mel's eyes shine unnatural-like. He smiles as though he can't hardly help himself. "Then I had to get to Hansen's for a newspaper before the others beat me to it."

I don't know what Melvin's on about. "But it's the middle of the night."

"Jasper, there's something I've got to tell you that can't wait until morning. That's why I called you out here." Mel glances at the darkened window. "I didn't want to wake Pa."

Mel ain't one to come home late, and he certainly don't run around all hours. My hands feel funny, all hot and cold at once. "What is it?"

"Wait till you see this." Mel smacks that newspaper he's holding. "Mr. Hansen sold me one of the very last copies."

We ain't had a newspaper for years. It's one of them luxuries we can't afford.

"'July 17, 1897,'" I read aloud. "'Latest News from the Klondike. Nine O'Clock Edition.'" It's this morning's *Seattle Post-Intelligencer.* The words run bold across the middle:

**GOLD! GOLD! GOLD! GOLD!**

**SIXTY-EIGHT RICH MEN ON**

**THE STEAMER *PORTLAND.***

**STACKS OF YELLOW METAL!**

"Gold," I say again. The word feels warm and round and strange on my tongue.

Below the story is a map, a spiderweb of wavy lines that lead to a river labeled Klondike. The paper says the whole place is called the Klondike for the river that passes through. It's in some part of Canada far above

Washington, right up against Alaska, about as distant as the moon.

A light breeze ruffles Mel's sandy hair, sets the lantern flame to sputtering. "The paper says the *Portland* pulled into Seattle this morning," he says. "Everyone on board was loaded down with gold."

What I wouldn't give to see some gold up close. Only got to once before, a couple years ago, when Mama showed me Pa's pocket watch. "Think any of them fellows will come out to Kirkland and show us what they found?"

"No one will come to this nothing town." Mel loses his gooney look and puts on the practical face he wears near about all the time, the one where his eyebrows pinch together and his lips flatten into a firm line. "Don't know why I stay sometimes."

"Well, I do," I tell him. "You stick around because you've still got money to earn. You stay because of me."

Mel gives half his pay from the mill to Pa. What Pa don't know is that when he's out carousing, my brother pries back the loose floorboard under his bed and hides the other half in the cigar box Mama once used for recipes. He's saving for the two of us. As soon as he's got enough, we'll leave Kirkland together. Because here's the thing: ever since Mama left, Pa's gone from bad to worse.

Mel shoves his hands deep into his pockets. "I could save every penny I earn and come nowhere near what those men on the *Portland* have. A man in the Klondike makes more money in one week than I'll ever have in my whole life."

There's a prickly feeling at the back of my neck as I think on what Mel said. Gold's worth loads of money, and money's what we need. I don't know one family with enough, but even Cyril's, with them five kids, knows how to make a paycheck last. Once Pa touches the money Mel gives him, it's as good as gone. "There ain't no reason for us to wait," I say. "We could make it on our own right now. In the Klondike." I ain't ever been outside Kirkland, let alone Washington, and here's our chance to go. Not somewhere close by, neither, but to Canada, on the top of the world.

"Listen, Jasper." Mel steps away from me a bit. "About that."

"We could leave next week. Or even tomorrow." I can't slow down what's bubbling up inside. "Sure, I'd miss Cyril and fishing at the lake, and—"

"Jasper," Mel says. "You've got to listen to me."

That's when the front door swings open. Pa stands in the frame, tall and terrible. His eyes are bloodshot slits, his wild hair points in all directions. "Shut your traps," he says, "and put out that god-awful light! What're you boys doing, anyhow? Get inside and go to bed."

There ain't nothing we can do but obey.

My mind don't settle when I cross them floorboards that creak beneath me or when I climb in under my ragged quilt. Mel's whistle says he's drifted off long before that word quits echoing my heartbeat—gold, gold, gold.

Next morning, I'm extra quiet as I make my bed and boil the same coffee grounds I used yesterday. Second-day coffee ain't much different than hot water, but it's what I got to do to make the coffee stretch. There's no sense rattling Pa again, if I can help it. The newspaper Mel carried on about last night is spread across the table. I wrap my hands around my warm tin cup and dig right into the story about the gold. It says that a few days ago, a steamboat arrived in San Francisco, full of men called prospectors and their Klondike treasure. Word got out that another Klondike steamer named the *Portland* was headed to Seattle right behind them. News reporters were so hungry for the story, they rode a tugboat to meet the *Portland* offshore.

The coffee burns as I swallow it down. Men struck it rich last summer, and the rest of the world knew nothing about it until now—a whole *year* later.

The map below the story is called *The Land of Gold* and nearly covers the whole bottom half of the page. I run my finger over its wiggly river lines. There's so many of them. The biggest river, named the Yukon, starts in the mountains of Canada, then heads north and crosses into Alaska, which it cuts clear in half, then snakes west until it meets the sea. From the Yukon on the Canada side flows the Klondike River. The land south of it is where them men on the *Portland* made their fortunes, where me and Melvin are headed as soon as he says go.

Pa stumbles to the table and yanks the paper from me. I reach for my cup but can't steady it in time. Coffee spills everywhere. Pa holds the paper before him like he didn't just snatch it, like he's been reading it all morning. "Don't just sit there," he says. "Clean up that dripping mess."

That's Pa. He makes problems of his own and tells others to fix them. Ain't no way I'd answer back, though sometimes I sorely want to. Arguing with Pa leads to nothing but sorrow. That and the fire of his belt across my legs. Believe me, I don't run my mouth no more. I've learned that lesson good.

I wipe the table, then kneel down to clean the floor.

Pa fans the paper open. "Where'd you get this?"

"Mel brought it home from Hansen's yesterday."

"Mel." He shakes his head. "Throwing away money on a newspaper. And you. Don't know what you two were up to out there on the porch. Loud enough to wake the dead."

Pa's eyes are as dull as they were last night. He's got a stink like that mouse stuck in Miss Stapleton's desk all summer long. But even so, he don't seem too fierce this morning, not as riled as he could be. It's best to keep him that way.

I wring out the rags, set them aside for the laundry I'll have to get to soon.

"Bring me some coffee," Pa says. "And don't you leave a drop for that lazy brother of yours."

Mel stirs in his bed, like he's heard us talking. Ain't no way he couldn't in a house this small.

I hand Pa his cup as he hunches over the newspaper. He mutters to himself. "Klondike gold. Bunch of fools."

Mel shuffles to the stove in his red underdrawers, a union suit that bags around his kneecaps and has worn clean through at the elbows, and reaches for the empty coffepot. He looks a sight. Probably didn't sleep a wink.

Pa lowers the paper. "You read this newspaper yet?"

Mel nods.

"You mark my words," Pa says. "Now that gold's been discovered in Canada, a whole load of idiots will head up there and try to find some for themselves."

I wonder what Pa will say when he learns me and Melvin plan to do exactly that.

Leave here. For good. To get us some gold.

"Them fellows are chumps," I chime in for Pa's sake. "Idiots." The whole time I say it, I make eyes at Mel, try to catch his notice and figure out what he's thinking. But all his attention's on Pa.

"It's the sort of man who ain't worked an honest day in his life that would try something so stupid," Pa says. "The type who wants things easy."

Mel holds the coffeepot like he's forgotten all about it. "What's so easy about leaving everything you know?"

I want to swat my brother with a dishrag, step on his toes and make him holler, anything to draw him back, because this conversation ain't headed nowhere good. Melvin should be quiet after last night's hooting and dancing on the porch.

But he plows ahead. "Familiar is what's easy. It's brave to leave what you know behind."

Pa's lip curls. "You contradicting me, boy?"

I grab the broom, busy myself with the dust that's crept in under the door, get as far as I can from whatever storm Mel's stirring up with Pa. Of course I want to tell Pa exactly what I think, ask him straight out what he remembers about honest work when it's surprising if he gets himself to his job at Hansen's more than a few days a week. But I ain't stupid, either.

Lay low and stay out of the way, that's the rule around here. Melvin taught it to me when Pa lost his job at the mill six months before he got his own there. Mel's always been the one to keep the peace, the one who slows Pa's anger when my mouth runs on its own. So how come all of a sudden Mel's acting like he's forgotten everything?

Mel slams the empty pot on the stove.

"I said"—Pa's words are sharp and loud—"are you contradicting me?"

Mel still don't answer. He stomps straight from the kitchen, pulls out his crate of clothes from underneath his bed, yanks on his trousers, and shoves his arms through his shirtsleeves. The whole time he mumbles but don't look once at Pa.

Oh, my heart thunders to see him act so reckless.

"Don't you talk under your breath," Pa says. "You got something to tell me, Melvin Johnson, you say it outright."

That gets him to stop. Something about Mel looks almost grown, him who's barely sixteen. "Who are you to judge the man who wants a better life?"

"Who am I?" Pa lunges forward. His hand flies out, strikes Melvin square on the cheek. "I'm your pa. Don't you ever forget it."

I duck behind the table, my fists balled up so tight, my fingernails cut through my skin. "Hush, Mel, hush. Just hush," I say.

Mel's face burns red where Pa hit him, but he don't stop. "You want to know what they say about you at the mill, Pa? That you're good-for-nothing. That once Mama died, you took to drinking like it was the only thing you remembered how to do."

"Don't you bring your mama into this!" Pa bellows. He moves in so close, Mel's backed against the wall.

"You could have saved her." Mel's eyes flash. "You could have if you'd wanted to."

I hold my hands against my ears, but it don't keep their voices out.

Pa's like a firecracker set to explode. "What do you mean, if I'd wanted to?"

"You could have taken help the first time it was offered. But you didn't." Mel's jaw is clenched, and his head's pressed hard on the wooden boards behind him. "Want to know what else the men at the mill told me?" He takes a breath and lets it out slow. "They say I'm the one who's the real man around here."

Pa storms across the room, grabs for the empty coffee-pot, and lets it fly. It hits inches from Mel's head. Brown streaks run down the wall. The pot clatters to the floor.

Mel's face is a mix of fear and anger, but anger wins out quick. He jerks the door open and slams it from the other side.

Pa lowers himself into Mama's rocker, still angled near the window the way she always liked it.

I stand on shaky legs. There's too much sadness in this house. More ugliness than I can bear. How I itch to be anywhere else.

Pa looks past the window, unblinking. There ain't no trace of the caring fellow he used to be.

The wool mill hisses and clatters the morning me and Cyril walk past, loud as Mel's been quiet since last month's fight with Pa.

Cyril peers again at the fish in my bucket. "You'll eat fine tonight." Three perch and a smallmouth bass, their sides splotched gray and yellow, flop against the bucket's sides. Cyril grins. His chapped lips don't fit too good around his crooked teeth. "Sure beats my scrawny trout."

"Mel better be home before suppertime if he wants to eat tonight. Pa don't let me keep food out for him no more."

Since that awful morning him and Pa fought, Mel's kept to himself. He leaves early for the mill and gets home long after I'm in bed. Every night I take Mel's newspaper from under my pillow and read through the gold story one more time. I'm set to ask Mel about our Klondike plans—what we'll bring and when we'll leave and how we'll work around Pa—just as soon as I catch him alone.

"Meet you at the lake tomorrow morning?" Cyril asks.

I nod. "See you then."

Cyril swings his bucket as he goes.

The August sun ain't reached its full height, but already it blazes like it means business. My footsteps ring hollow on the porch steps. The house is dark and still. Could be Pa's already left to work at Hansen's.

"Wondered where you were," Pa says as I open the door. He tucks in his ragged shirt and pulls up his suspenders, like he's just made a start to his morning when the day is pushing toward noon.

"I caught four fish for supper." The water slops in the bucket as I lift it to the cupboard.

That's when I see the letter propped against the empty

flour jar. The letter's in Mel's hand. There ain't no reason for him to write a note unless something's wrong.

Pa leans in to study his supper. Quick as that, I push past to grab the letter.

"What was that for?" Pa growls. "You could have knocked over them fish."

"Just checking to see if there's enough flour for biscuits." I reach for the empty jar and give it a shake. "Nope." When Pa ain't looking, I work Mel's note into my pocket.

Pa starts in on how tired he is of perch, how any decent man deserves a bit of variety from time to time when it comes to his supper, but I don't really listen. I'm thinking about that letter.

Pa grips my shoulder, squeezes awful hard. "You hear what I said? I want them fish fried up when I get home. No saving some for Melvin, either. If he wants to eat, he better get back at a regular hour."

"Yes, sir," I say.

The place where Pa's hand pressed aches long after he lets up.

Pa eases himself into a chair to lace his boots. That letter feels like it's burning a hole clean through my trousers. Maybe I could hold it low behind the kitchen counter so Pa don't notice.

I slip it from my pocket, try to smooth it across my leg to work the wrinkles out. *Dear Pa,* it begins, *it's time for me to go.*

I don't read no more. I can't because my head don't make sense of them words. It's like each one's been flipped over and turned around.

*Time to go.* The letter says.

*For me.* Not "me and Jasper."

My name ain't mentioned at all.

"Boy, have you listened to a word I said?" Pa's on his feet again. He motions to my hand. "What's that you got?"

"It ain't nothing." I cram Mel's letter deep in my pocket. "What did you say?"

"I said you'd better see to them fish." Pa chews the inside of his cheek, eyeing me. "Mind yourself, Jasper. I'm low on patience." Pa tugs on his cap, and then he's out the door.

I wait and wait to be sure Pa's truly gone before I try Mel's letter again.

Dear Pa,

It's time for me to go.

Since I brought home that newspaper, all I've thought about is the gold that's been found in Canada. This is my chance, and I'm going to take it.

I know a sixteen-year-old boy's old enough to be on his own. You've said as much a hundred times. But I've stuck around to help out. Mainly I've kept on because of Jasper. He's acted strong since he got over the influenza, but he's eleven, Pa. A kid. Be good to him. That's all I ask. If not for me, then for Mama.

Your son,
Melvin Johnson

An awful feeling squeezes my middle. Melvin's gone. After that talk we had last month, after two years of promises we'd make our way together, he's up and left without me.

What was he thinking to leave me like that?

This is his chance, Mel says. His alone. It don't take long before my blood runs hot. I crumple up that letter, swing my arm hard as I can. The paper ball bounces off the door, rolls under Melvin's bed.

So I'm just some little kid. Oh, that Melvin thinks he's something special, how he holds a job and knows what's happening in the world outside of Kirkland. Miss Stapleton still loves to talk about what a perfect student he was, but that don't mean he knows everything.

I got more sense than ten Mels put together plus a couple more. He thinks he's practically a man, can do what he pleases. But what kind of a man makes promises, then runs off the first chance he gets?

As I reach for Mel's note, the loose floorboard beneath

his bed jiggles. I pry it back, and there's the cigar box, where it's always been. Except it's cleaned out. Empty. The crate of clothes Mel stores under there, that's empty, too. His two books are missing. The knapsack he keeps on a hook is gone.

But there's one real important thing he's left behind.

His extra pair of underdrawers sits right on top of yesterday's clean laundry, the red union suit with the worn-through elbows and the baggy knees. Serves him right to be stuck with only one set of underwear. Old Mel ain't as clever as he thinks he is.

Up there in the Klondike in his one pair of underclothes, how's he gonna get along? With the newspaper map under my pillow, he won't be able to find his way.

And then I remember. Pa's pocket watch.

Mama showed it to me and Mel one winter afternoon while rain streamed down the windows and thunder shivered the walls. It was a few months after Pa lost his job. Mama told us to sell the watch if ever me and Mel found ourselves in a tough spot. We didn't ask how come she could decide about something that belonged to Pa. She knew how hard things were for us. I'm glad she ain't seen how bad it's gotten.

I lift the corner of the quilt on Pa's bed, dig around beneath his straw-tick mattress until my hand closes on a lump of flannel. The gold watch is wrapped inside, all smooth and shiny.

So Mel didn't take it. That was always the plan. When the two of us lit out, we'd take that watch with us in case we ever got in any trouble. We meant to sell it if we were in a pinch and needed money quick.

Mel's heading to Canada on his own. Sure, he's got some money, but he don't got this. I'm the one who can bring it to him. The truth is Melvin needs me. And more than anything, I'm owed an explanation on why he up and left without me.

It don't take long for me to pack. All I've got is a change of clothes, a coat, my green muffler, three pairs of Pa's woolen socks, the fifty-seven cents I won from Cyril on a dare, my school pencil, the front page of the *Seattle Post-Intelligencer*, and the last hunk of bread from me and Mel's secret stash. That red pair of underdrawers Mel's forgotten sits folded up real nice on top of yesterday's laundry. I can't wait to see his face, all grateful and embarrassed, when I hand them over.

But it's not the underdrawers my hand goes for first. It's Mama's washboard. Every time I hold it, I can't help but run my fingers over its middle, which zings with a sound almost like music. This washboard's one of the only things we still own that once belonged to her, and I ain't got the heart to leave it behind. Pa ain't partial to cleanliness. He won't notice it's missing, anyhow.

I drop Pa's watch in my pocket, grab those underdrawers, and strap the washboard to my pack. Mel's got a good head start on me. If I'm gonna catch up to him, I best be going myself. I'm halfway across the porch before I turn around. Pa may be a mess and is as mean as they come, but I took his watch. Sure, I got Mama's blessing, but that don't mean he knows it. The least I can do is tell him what's going on.

The front page of the newspaper's in my pocket folded around my pencil, but I've left the rest on the table. I write a note down one side.

> Pa,
>
> That gold up in Canada. Me and Mel are gone to get some.
>
> Jasper
>
> PS — I got the watch.

Then I hightail it out of there.

# Chapter 2

The dirt road runs long in front of me, soft from yesterday's rain. I turn at Hansen's and hope Pa don't see me through the front window. It ain't Pa who notices, but the tabby with the broken tail. He brushes up against me, twines himself around my legs with a purr that rumbles through his sides.

"Bye, old Tom." I stroke the cat's bony back. "You'll tell Cyril I've left, won't you?" He nudges my trousers with his nose. I take it as a yes. "And don't you listen to him if he invites you to chase them mice that live in the schoolroom wall." Ever since Cyril dared me to let that rooster loose, Miss Stapleton's been uptight about the smallest things.

• • •

It ain't but a mile from here to Lake Washington, where the ferry runs between Kirkland and Seattle. Even if I didn't hear him say so, I know it's where Mel's headed. That's where them Klondike miners docked. That's where a body's gotta start to take a boat up north.

At the shore a crowd already waits to board the ferry, talk of gold a solid hum. Klondike outfits. Sailing down the Yukon River. How long it takes to get to someplace called Dyea. I ain't familiar with the half of what I hear. Me, a near expert on the Klondike after my nightly reading.

"When's the next ferry run?" I ask a man who looks like he should know by the way he checks his watch, a gold one like Pa's but not nearly as fine.

"At one o'clock, about forty minutes from now."

"I must have got here just in time," I say.

The man nods. "Miss this one, and you'll sit here till tomorrow. The ferry makes one trip out and one trip back each day. The ticket booth should open soon."

One boat out means Mel's still here in Kirkland. I don't want him to catch sight of me till at least Seattle. The farther from home we get, the harder it'll be for him to send me back. But it don't look right for a boy my age to travel alone. It's always best to have a plan, and mine is to blend in with other folks.

I make sure Mel ain't anywhere nearby, then wave at a man under a shade tree. "One o'clock's when it leaves, Pa," I shout. "We're right on time."

The man's face scrunches up, confused, but I keep on with my smiling. A body can't just quit when he tries to act ordinary. It's important to follow through.

The window in the ticket booth slides open, and them that haven't lined up yet move in to claim a spot. That's when I spy Mel near the front, his brown coat folded over one arm and his knapsack strapped across his shoulders. I join the end of the line, stick near that man I called to, but not so close he realizes I'm pretending he's my pa.

I'm mighty grateful Cyril's rooster stunt, when he dared me to bring it to class last spring, earned me fifty-seven cents. I couldn't hardly hold on to that ornery bird as he flapped and scratched before he took off squawking around the schoolroom. Sure, Miss Stapleton swatted me with her ruler, but it weren't so bad. Not when the whole school turned silly for the rest of the afternoon. Seeing it costs a half dollar to buy a ferry ticket, that prank was worth every penny.

As many times as I've passed the ferry, I ain't never been on board. I've paddled around Lake Washington before, but that was in a rowboat. I ain't never been on a boat so big as this one. Once I pay for my ticket, it's just three steps across a narrow gangplank, and I'm a genuine passenger. I clomp my heels on the deck, as confident as a sailor. The line to board stretches on behind me. I bet with the gold talk these last few weeks this ferry's been crammed with folks, more than it's ever carried before.

Once, when Mel was a schoolboy and I was a little kid, Mama surprised me with a picnic. She packed some biscuits and preserves in her egg basket and tucked a clean cloth over the top. The two of us walked to Lake Washington and spread a quilt on the shore. As the ferry puttered across the water, we shared them biscuits still warm from the oven and piled high with blackberry jam.

I try to find the spot me and Mama picnicked all them years ago, when we had food aplenty and home was a happy place, but I ain't able. Maybe it's just as well. Them days are long gone.

The engine thrums like the ferry's ready to get going, and sure enough, it lunges forward. Water slaps the boat's sides. The floorboards shift and shiver. It's like trying to stand on the lake itself, but I plant one wobbly foot next to the other and watch for Melvin as the dock gets smaller. The road to Hansen's all but disappears.

"Goodbye, Kirkland," I whisper. "I got somewhere else I need to be."

Two men huddle around a newspaper, fight to hold it open as the wind whips around. Behind them I spot a pair of green socks, ones I've scrubbed a whole bunch of times. Old Melvin sits near the railing on his pack, his long legs folded up, his face gloomy, like he ain't sure where he belongs. Well, if he's lonely, that's his own dern fault.

The ferry lurches, and I grab on to a bench where a beefy gent talks lively with a codger nearby. I slide in next to the gent, near enough on his other side so it seems the two of us belong together. His shoulders block my view of Mel, and I figure if I can't see him, he surely can't see me. The rocking ferry tries to lull me into sleep, but I ain't having that. There's too many things to notice. How the ferry cuts through the water smoother than a farmer's plow. How at the shore it was right calm, but now the breeze is sharp enough I gotta hold on to my cap. The clouds race us overhead, but we're the faster ones.

Just as quick as Kirkland disappeared, Seattle's shoreline comes into view, a city so big it covers every inch of land. We near the dock and the whistle blows. I about jump out of my skin. The beefy gent's eyes grow wide, like he's noticed me for the first time. All around folks gather their things. The bustle gives enough cover for me to watch for Mel unseen and fall in step behind him when he passes.

I almost lose him because the dock's so clogged with folks, but I'm small enough I can weave through the whole lot of them. Keep focused on Melvin, I tell myself, on his sandy head as it bobs through the crowd. My eyes don't quite know how to make sense of so many folks.

Looks like gold talk has brought in ferries from everywhere.

Melvin walks down the middle of the street with short, quick steps like he knows where he's headed. I stick as close as I can. Buildings stretch high above us on either side. Fish and trash stink up the air. Fellows strut about in woolen coats and big fur hats, never mind the summer heat. A cable-car bell clangs and clangs, tells folks to clear off the tracks. No one pays it any mind. Lines and more lines of men snake outside shops with signs so new, the paint shines wet and oily.

Klondike-Approved Apparel! they say.

Pioneer Outfitters!

Genuine Argonaut Ware!

Seattle. This city's huge and full and noisy and fevered up with gold.

Mel picks a line to join. What he's after, I don't know, unless he's realized he's got but one set of underdrawers and has left his map at home.

I stand off to the side, pretend to study an apple cart, but near enough that a fellow, if he tilted his head and squinted a little, might see me as part of the line. It inches forward painfully slow. From the same door folks enter, other men haul out load after load. Fur coats. Sacks of flour and coffee and beans. Boots and blankets. Pickaxes and pans. Enough gear to last a lifetime. Everyone in line acts like it's natural to buy more than a man can carry all at once. Is this what's meant by a proper Klondike outfit? Must be, because when Mel leaves that store an hour later, a clerk helps pile his gear in a wagon parked right behind the apple cart.

"You plan to leave soon?" the clerk asks my brother. He tucks Mel's payment in his canvas apron pocket.

Mel nods as he hugs a little sled to his chest. "On the steamer called *Queen*."

"You'd better get a move on, then. Tickets go fast."

The horse hitched to the delivery wagon shifts on his feet as Mel climbs in. I hustle around to the apple cart's other side, wait for Mel's wagon to roll by. With people everywhere, I can follow behind, hidden right out in the open.

If the city streets are bad, the wharf is worse, a lot more crowded than where the ferry docked clear on the other side of town. The mixed-up jumble of folks feels like parade day plus Christmas plus one of them all-nighters Pa sometimes pulls—the loud kind where things get broken. Seems like everyone in Seattle's marched through the city to end up here. Some are bent on boarding the *Queen*, others on living off the excitement of them leaving their old lives behind.

The ship's a whole lot bigger than that ferry we took from Kirkland. Its bottom half is gray, and its top half is painted white. Bold letters spell out *Queen* along the steamer's side. Thick smoke drifts from a smokestack at its middle. Ropes lash it to the dock, like an animal that ain't yet tame.

Mel stands in line again, this time to pay his fare. He takes a book from his pocket and slowly turns the pages. It's one I ain't seen him read before. I'm down to seven cents, which ain't gonna get me nowhere. I pull out Pa's watch. It rests snug and perfect in my palm. He's never worn it, least not that I remember. Pa sure don't live like he knows the time. And even when he was at the mill, he never could afford something so fancy. Now he's only got money for liquor.

Mel gets his ticket awful quick, faster than I've been able to cook up a plan as to how I'll get my own. My brother lifts the first part of his gear onto that little sled he's held since he bought his Klondike outfit. I think on last winter, when me and Cyril lugged a sled up the ridge behind the wool mill. We called out to Mel, but he brushed us off, too old and important for one quick ride. Now Melvin, so set on being a man, pulls a sled of his own.

My hands get sweaty. Pa's watch is slick in my fist, as trip by trip Mel moves his entire Klondike outfit on board. I wipe the tiny clock clean with the flannel wrap. It sure is fine, with them twirly lines carved into its cover. There are three hands inside, with one that keeps time down to the second. I can't part with it just yet, not until Mel sees, till he knows he left it and I'm the one who remembered, the one who thought to bring it along.

My brother loads the last of his mining outfit on his sled, heads to the *Queen* one final time. I press close to a fellow about to board and hope I might slip past the man collecting tickets. But it don't work. The ticket man's hand shoots out. "Where you think you're going, son?"

"On the *Queen*." I point to the steamer to jog his memory.

The ticket man's cap sits low on his forehead. I can't hardly see his eyes. "Show me your ticket."

That sets my heart to beating fast. I empty out my pockets, pretend to check the ground. "I don't know what happened. It was right here a moment ago."

"No ticket, no ride." He pushes me aside.

"Maybe my brother's got it," I say. "He's already on board. Just paid for passage." And ain't it the truth?

But the ticket man don't care. Already he's helping the next person in line.

"Wait." I elbow my way back in. "I lost my ticket. But there's this." I hold out Pa's watch. It's the last idea I got.

Now I see his eyes, clear as green glass. "You trying to bribe me to get on board? Get outta here, kid."

I wasn't really gonna trade Pa's watch. I just meant for the ticket man to have a little peek. Surely a boy with such a fine timepiece can be trusted when he says his ticket's gone.

But if the ticket man wanted the watch for himself, well, I would have worked with him.

I've gotta get on board. I just gotta.

What I'm gonna do, I don't know, Mel on the *Queen* and me on the dock. I walk through the crowd to the building where Mel bought his ticket, drop my bag, and sit on top. Mama's washboard juts to one side, a reminder of home when I'm so far away. Guess one choice I have is to go on back. I've been quick enough to keep out of Melvin's sights. He'd never know his little brother followed him to Seattle.

But the ferry ain't anywhere nearby. Even if I could find where it's docked, I'd have to persuade the ticket man to let me board. I don't got no money, but maybe he'd let me on the ferry if I promised to pay him later. It might take me a while to earn fifty cents more, but I'd be good for it.

But what if Pa's already found my note? There ain't no way he'd welcome me back after reading that. He don't usually come home in the afternoon, but he also don't hold to any sort of schedule. What was that the man at the ferry said, only one boat to Seattle and back each day? So even if Pa ain't seen my note yet, he'd find it for sure before I made it there.

The more I think of it, the more I'm downright certain there ain't nothing left for me at home. I can't abide that sorry place, not without my brother's company. But it ain't just that. I can't imagine that house without my brother bringing me an apple someone at the mill gave him or pushing me to finish my lessons, much as I hate it. And I won't let go of our plan to escape together, even if Mel's gone and ruined everything.

Someday soon my life won't hang on finding money for a steamer ticket. When me and Mel get some Klondike gold, we'll have just what we need.

The crowd of people at the wharf ain't let up, an ocean of men in blue and gray and brown. But then I catch a bit of brightness fluttering in the crowd. A lady's dress, a yellow one, like Mama used to wear. She walks arm in arm with her husband while seven kids trail behind. Seeing them, it gets me on my feet. If this family has booked passage for the *Queen*, they might be my ticket on board.

Sure enough, the family moves in line. It's easy to hover on the edges, and when they near the ticket man, I shadow the tallest kid. A girl. Her lips get pinched when she eyes me, like she ain't fond of what she sees, but she forgets when one of her brothers pulls her hair.

"Good afternoon," the ticket man says, friendly-like. "Taking the whole family to hunt for gold?" He laughs like he's told a joke.

"We'll stop in Skagway. I'm opening a restaurant," the mister says. "My wife here makes the best pies in Seattle. And we've got plenty of hands to make light work." He waves toward his kids. I duck my head.

The ticket man nods as the missus shoos her brood on board. She pauses for a moment to unwind Miss Prissy Lips's braid from her brother's fist. That's when I shoot on past the rest of them, up the gangplank, and straight onto the deck. I don't stop till I'm at the front of the steamer. I made it. I could reach down beneath the railing and touch them big letters that spell out *Queen*. Even though it's tethered with ropes, the ship still rocks a bit.

But I'm steady on my feet. After that ride on the ferry, I know how boating works.

This has been some day, and I'm right hungry. Thankfully, I still have the hunk of bread I brought from home. It's hard as tree bark and about as tasty, but it fills me up. Wherever Mel is, I ain't seen him on this part of the deck, and I'm grateful for that, since as long as the *Queen*'s still docked, he could use that clever head of his to find a way to send me back.

I stand at the railing, shake the last few bread crumbs overboard, which swirl as they drop. Seagulls scream and snatch them, as pushy as the folks I've spent the day with.

It feels good to settle on top of my bag, lean against the railing, far enough from others that I ain't underfoot. From what I heard on the ferry and here in town, we'll be on the *Queen* almost a week before we reach a place called Skagway, Alaska. The Klondike's north of there. By then, Mel will know I've come along. We'll walk the next leg of the journey—or a fellow could ride something called a Klondike bicycle, if he thought to buy one.

Once we reach some lakes, we'll have to build a boat, then sail beyond them down the Yukon River till we arrive in a place called Dawson City, where the Yukon and Klondike Rivers meet.The newspaper said Dawson's a city that's just one year old, as brand-spanking-new as the gold found last summer, where them miners spend their time when they're not on their claims. Dawson's gonna grow quick, now the whole world's rushing up there, set to try to find some gold.

All around, folks gather in bunches and talk about their plans. If they ain't known each other before, they're right friendly now.

"Just a little camping and some paddling down a river," one man says to another. "It won't be so hard to reach that Klondike town."

"Anybody can get there," his new friend answers, "without much effort at all."

I'm glad to hear that, but truth be told, I'm kind of lonely for old Melvin.

Sometimes in the evening we'd sit on the porch steps and listen to the frogs sing to the early moon. Of course the last few weeks that ain't happened any. Mel's avoided Pa, and he's sure steered clear of me. What's running through his head right now, I'd like to know. Does he regret leaving me behind? Or is Mel so focused on himself, he ain't spared me a single thought?

The sun's finally ready to take its leave as day rolls into night. Those onshore don't budge, just keep up with their shouts, "Hurrah for the Klondike!" They don't need to make plans on where to spend the night, with their homes to return to. But I do.

I squeeze through them that stand near the rooms along the outside deck. Open doors mean space to sleep, I reckon, but the first room I enter, five men are fighting over three beds. In the second I spy the yellow-dressed lady and all them kids that got me on board. Three little ones squabble about a rag doll, and when I back away, Miss Prissy Lips sets her glare on me.

"There's that boy I told you about, Ma." Her finger shakes, like I'm a dangerous sort. "The one that snuck on board!"

Her ma's too distracted with them little ones to pay me any mind. I shut the door behind me, but not before I give Miss Prissy Lips a little bow. Farther down all doors are closed. I take a set of stairs to the level below, where lamps cast ghostly shadows down a hallway. The crowd has thinned considerable, but maybe that's because most doors down here are shut, the beds probably taken. Rooms farther from the stairs stand a better chance of holding empty beds, so I walk to the very last one and knock bold as I can.

The gentleman who answers has got a mustache that fits neat over his upper lip like a little rug. The story comes to me quick. "I'm a poor orphan boy. Had to spend my last penny to get on board." Blinking makes my eyes tear up. I take off my glasses so the gent can get a good look at them. "Any way you could spare some space? I ain't particular."

Behind him, two other fellows bustle about. If they caught my sad tale, they act like they ain't heard a thing.

"Well," the gentleman says. His hands hang strange at

his sides, like he ain't quite sure what to do with them or what to make of me.

"What are you called, sir?" It's something I learned from Miss Stapleton. She got down every kid's name quick as she could. When someone uses your name, you can't help but listen.

"Smalley." He still stands there funny-like.

"Mr. Smalley, I'd be grateful if you'd let me stay." Two tears spill from my eyes right then, which makes the whole act pretty convincing.

Mr. Smalley sure appears to be kindly, but my story don't tug at his heart any. "This room's full. You'll have to find a bunk elsewhere."

I ain't gonna find a bunk elsewhere, not if a family with all them kids has to squeeze in one room. Them men on the dock must have sold more tickets than there are beds. Some folks will have to sleep on the floor or even in those chairs on the deck. But I got another idea. I go down one more set of stairs to the cargo hold, deep in the ship's belly, till I swear I'm as far down as the ocean fish that glide past the *Queen*'s undersides. There's a sign at the bottom of the stairs that says NO PASSENGERS ALLOWED, but I slip inside the door, anyhow. On the left are stacks of lumber and roof shingles. On the right, rows and rows of horses are packed in together. There's gotta be at least a hundred of them. The engine's somewhere toward the back. It stinks to high heaven down here, what with all them creatures, and the air is still and hot. I pick the side with the horses since at least it's got some hay to settle on.

I don't mind saying I'm a little low. This ain't exactly what I imagined when I started out. But it's just one night, I tell myself. Once the *Queen*'s left port, I'll find Melvin. After I put him on the spot, make him answer for the way he up and left, and show him the watch he forgot, he'll invite me to share his bunk. He'll have to.

The horse next to me flicks his tail. I know exactly what he means. This place ain't much, cramped like it is and awful dark, but at least it's secure. It'll have to do for now. I shut my eyes, take a deep breath—thick and hot and a whole lot like a barnyard. The horses keep on with their regular noises, with a couple snorts saved up for special times, like when they're crammed tight in the belly of a steamer. Even so, they'll be easier to sleep near than Pa. Mel, too, come to think of it, with his funny nighttime whistling.

I pull out Pa's watch, unwrap the flannel cover, and though I can't see it, its ticking is familiar. I aim to give the watch the best care I can. I'll wind and polish it, make sure it stays as perfect as it was when Mama first showed it to me.

Mama. My throat clenches tight. It's been a long two years without her, but now that I've left home, missing her has come back extra strong. I wonder what she'd think of her boys heading to the Klondike. "I got Pa's watch," I say into the darkness. "We'll use it if we need to."

The guts of the *Queen* moan something terrible, like the ship's come to life. The walls shudder and the horses complain as the boat roars loud enough to rival them that surely cheer out on the shore.

This is it. The steamer's under way. I can't help but slap that nearby horse like we're old friends. I'm through with Miss Stapleton and her chiding and my temperamental pa. Me and Mel, we're headed for something better in the Klondike.

# Chapter 3

The door crashes open and with it comes a shining light. I burrow in a pile of straw that ain't too stinky yet. "Breakfast," a scratchy voice announces, and I imagine eggs and bacon fixed up nice, not the feed and water that's poured into the troughs. What if the man spots me, the kid-sized lump buried underneath the straw? I shut my eyes and hardly breathe, hope he won't notice, and that he don't stick around to clean. Pa's watch ticks off the minutes that pass, slow as lessons on a sunny afternoon. Finally, the door slides shut. I count out one minute more before I grab my bag and go.

My eyes ache as I pass beneath the lamps brightening the hallway. The *Queen* rolls and pitches, and I bump from one side of the hall to the other. My feet don't behave right, like I learned to walk only yesterday. The rocking grows even stronger as I climb the stairs to the deck above.

I stumble as though I'm wearing skates on a frozen pond, thump against the *Queen*'s railing, and gotta grab on tight. Below, green water foams and breaks and stretches wide in all directions, farther than I ever imagined the ocean could go. Mountains run forever to the east and west.

This ain't nothing like the ferry ride from Kirkland to Seattle. Even though we crossed the middle of Lake Washington, the boat never felt too far from shore.

I fight against the blasting air, the lunging motion of the steamer just to stand up straight. Folks who got their sea legs stroll the deck; men with their hands clamped on their hats, some ladies with their skirts held tight at their sides, and even a couple young ones who laugh and dart about. So Mrs. Yellow Dress ain't the only lady here. There are other kids besides Miss Prissy Lips and her clan. That gets my shoulders to relax some. I won't stick out as much as I feared.

At least a couple hundred people are on this ship, but I ain't seen no sign of my brother anywhere. Mel's here. I know he is. I saw him board the *Queen* with my own two eyes. But knowing it don't bring him any closer. If I could catch a glimpse of him, I'd feel a lot less lonely.

A man walks the deck with a tray before him, and my stomach growls when I catch a whiff of bread. "Ten cents for buttered buns!" he shouts. "Come and get your breakfast!"

Ten cents. That's three more than what I got. There ain't nothing to do but sit on a bench near the railing, imagine the gnawing in my belly ain't hunger but a stomachache from a breakfast so big, I weren't able to finish. I watch the never-ending row of mountains, the waves that race across the ocean, the folks parading past, happy and content to be together.

I feel like the only one who's on this ship alone. For a time I circle the deck and keep in step with them ahead of me just to hear them talk, to pretend I belong. But two fellows eye me suspicious-like, and a lady with a frilly bonnet tells me outright to find somewhere else to go. So I return to that bench and sit there until the sun begins to set and folks turn in.

No food. No Mel. I got nothing but a sunburned face, a starving belly, and a whole lot of lonesomeness as I travel them stairs to them horses in the cargo hold.

On the second morning, no amount of wandering brings me to Melvin, but I do spy that gentleman Mr. Smalley toward the back of the ship. He sits tucked along the *Queen*'s side, out of the sun and wind, a blanket in his lap. He's got a pipe clenched between his mustache and his bottom lip. I touch my head, hope a few scraggly pieces of straw still dangle from my hair, then set myself before him and blink real sorrowful-like.

"Mr. Smalley?"

He studies me, surprised I know his name. "You're that stray," he finally says.

"Yes, sir." I'm glad he remembers my poor orphan state. "I had to stay with them horses in the cargo hold last night"—I try to make my voice wobble a little—"since I don't got a soul in the world."

"Well." He holds his pipe and clears his throat. Mr. Smalley's softening up some, I can see it.

"I ain't hardly had any sleep. Down there the engines hiss and clang, and them horses get real scared, it's a wonder I ain't been kicked. Last night it was so hot, I stripped down to my underdrawers, and now I can't find my socks anywhere."

Mr. Smalley observes my naked ankles. He don't need to know I've got three other pairs.

"I wondered if you might reconsider sparing me some space. Maybe I could take your bunk when you ain't got use for it."

"Well," he says a second time. I'm beginning to wonder if Mr. Smalley knows many words at all.

That's when I notice his shirt's soiled around the collar and dirt's settled in his sleeve cuffs. I can't help but smile, because I've remembered Mama's washboard strapped to my pack. I swing my bag around so he can see it. "If you let me share, I'll wash up your shirt for free."

Mr. Smalley runs his fingers over his grimy sleeve like

he's just seen it for the first time. "Well." There's that word of his again. "No harm in you using my bunk when I'm awake," he says. "Better get a move on, then. I'll leave this shirt with you when I return."

I near about skip down them stairs to Mr. Smalley's room. I don't bother to knock. I've earned my space in there, fair and square. The other two misters stir in their bunks.

"What do you think you're doing? You can't barge in like that," the man in the lower bed growls.

"Hello," I say. "I'm your new bunkmate."

The man in the bed above rubs his eyes. His mouth stretches in a yawn, gapes big as a fish.

"Mr. Smalley says I can use his bed when he's on deck."

The man above swings his skinny legs over the side of his bed. They're so long, it don't take much for him to reach the floor.

I plop my bag at my feet. "I'm Jasper."

"Mr. Horton," the long-legged one with the fish face says. He pumps my hand up and down. "That's Reuben over there."

Mr. Reuben is as short as Mr. Horton is tall. He buttons a checkered vest pulled tight across his middle. His eyelids droop like he don't trust me. "Mind telling me what you're doing here alone, son?"

Best stick with the story I told Mr. Smalley. "I'm an orphan boy. I mean to strike it rich, same as anyone."

"That's the spirit!" Mr. Horton says. I like him already.

I stretch out on Mr. Smalley's bed. It sags a bit, but it's a whole lot better than that pile of straw where I spent the last two nights. I shut my eyes, let out a great big sigh.

"I'm not sure I want to pass the day on the deck again," I hear Mr. Reuben say. "It's about as crowded as Seattle's been."

"Bet that was good for business," Mr. Horton says.

"I can't deny that," Mr. Reuben answers. "Soon as the *Portland* arrived, people flocked to my shop. They were all after Klondike gear."

Maybe Mr. Reuben was the fellow who sold his goods to Melvin. I open one eye to give him a look. He tugs at his checkered vest, but that don't help it cover the bottom half of his belly. Nope. He ain't familiar.

"Sold out of all the tea and beans and bacon I'd thought would take me through December," he says.

"I was on the newspaper boat that met the *Portland*," Mr. Horton says. "Saw those miners and their gold myself."

I sit up, both eyes open now. "You're a newspaperman?" I ain't exactly been invited in on this conversation, but the words slip out anyhow.

"Sure am." Mr. Horton nods. "The *Post-Intelligencer* has sent me to write articles about the journey from Seattle to Dawson. Did you know folks already call us Stampeders?" Mr. Horton's lips quiver like a fish that nibbles a worm. "This is a stampede, all right, straight into parts unknown."

"Stampeders," I say. The name sounds important. And I'm one of them. "Mr. Horton, what's the gold like?"

"It can be fine as sand or the size of a pebble stuck in your shoe. Some miners had nuggets in their pockets as big as a robin's egg. They carried it from the *Portland* in sacks and trunks and jam jars."

Soon I'll be just like them, my pockets fairly busting with gold. "Did you get to touch it?" I shout in my excitement. "Is it heavy? Does it shine?"

Mr. Horton grins. "You've got gold fever, all right."

"I need it bad," I say. Me and Mel both do. With gold we'll be able to eat anytime we're hungry. We won't be separated ever again.

"Well, I wasn't going to stick around when I heard Mayor Wood had up and quit," Mr. Reuben says. "If the mayor of Seattle can get in the gold business, then by golly, I can, too. Put my oldest in charge, kissed the wife, and told her and the kiddies not to expect me to return till next year."

Sounds like Mr. Reuben's got gold fever, too. And even though Mr. Horton says he's going to the Klondike for the stories, I caught that look on his face when he talked of all that gold. The hunt for riches, that's what he's about. Except for Mr. and Mrs. Yellow Dress and their Skagway restaurant, everyone on this boat is here for one reason only. To get rich fast as they can.

"You think you'll get much gold, Mr. Reuben?" I ask.

He waves a hand, dismissing me. "I won't prospect. I'll run some kind of business. Whatever sort is necessary. Those miners will have nothing but gold and time on their hands. I'll find a way to help them ease their loads."

Relieve them of their gold, he means. I know a schemer when I see one, mainly from being one myself. A body can't never be sure what's gonna happen next, so it's always best to be a step ahead of everyone else.

There's no chance I'll fall asleep, not with how my mind whirls with gold talk and my belly rumbles. "Anybody here want their socks freshened?" The room stinks of sour feet. Maybe I could make a bit of money and buy myself some breakfast.

Mr. Reuben, who pulls a comb through his wavy hair, stops quick. "You a washer boy?"

"Yes, sir."

"Think you can take care of this?" He unbuttons his vest and shows me a rusty gravy stain.

"Sure can." There's no reason for them to know Mr. Smalley's laundry is part of my bunk-sharing deal. "Just five cents an item," I say, because my mind's worked on a few things. There ain't many women here, and since Mama taught me to scrub like a regular girl, maybe I can make some money with a laundry service.

Mr. Horton hands over his socks. I grab our slop

bucket, Mama's washboard, and Mr. Reuben's checkered vest, whistling as I climb the stairs to the deck above.

The slop bucket needs to be dumped and rinsed a few times before I can fill it for washing. Though the deck's right full of folks strolling about, there ain't one fellow wearing Mel's brown jacket with the blue elbow patch. I'm able to find a spot to work over near the railing. I sit on my heels, the slop bucket between my knees, and push the clothes beneath the water, till they soak clean through. Then I scrub them over the washboard's bumpy metal middle and dunk them again. I scrub and dunk and dump the dirty water over and over, washing the daylights out of them things.

Even though the water sloshes as the steamer sways, the rhythm's as familiar as the morning Mama first taught me. Mel was in school. It was just the two of us at home. Maybe she got tired of all them questions I asked about what she was doing and how long it would take. She held her soft hands over mine and placed them on the scrub board as she hummed "Through the Long Days," a sappy song about love, but in Mama's voice it was kinda nice. Now anytime I wash up, I feel her near.

On account of me forgetting soap, them clothes smell like a cross between wet sheep and fish guts, but they're passable for now.

The vest drapes nice over the bench I sat on yesterday. The socks, if I let them go, could take flight in a gust of wind and sail off with them seagulls that have been following us since we left port, so I flap them around as long as it takes to shake off their wetness. Once the clothes quit dripping, I take them to the misters, who hang them over the bunk rails. They're so pleased, they pay up quick.

That's how, an hour later, I spread out on that same bench and eat a buttered bun with seven cents to spare. I take the smallest bites I can, chew that bread to nothing, but even so, it don't last long as I'd like.

A bell rings out from near the smokestack. Folks gather around the black chimney that towers overhead as though they're waiting for something, and the crowd only grows bigger when the bell rings again. I walk over to better see what's happening. In the middle of all them people a man in a blue cap pulls a bell rope. He's a member of the crew.

"What's going on?" I ask a lady with a lacy shawl.

"The first mate has news from the captain," she says.

A man looks at his timepiece. "When will you tell us why you've called us here?"

"In a minute," the first mate answers, "once I get the attention of as many people as I can." He rings the bell a third time, then faces the crowd.

All talk stops.

"Earlier today the captain learned we have a stowaway on board." The first mate holds a scrap of flannel and a long gray sock high overhead.

My cheeks burn hot. This ain't news I want to hear.

"The stable hand found these as he mucked out the cargo hold."

I feel for Pa's watch. It's in my pocket where I left it, but sure enough, the flannel wrap is gone. My ankles feel real fresh and airy in the ocean breeze. I don't dare check to see if other folks have noticed I ain't wearing socks. Oh, why didn't I remember to put on another pair? Slowly I back away, scan the crowd for Melvin and Mr. Smalley. Much as I want to see my brother, this would be a rotten time for it to happen, when any second I could be called out as a stowaway. Soon as the mister hears a fellow snuck onto the *Queen* for free, and no one's supposed to be down there with them horses, he'll know I'm the one.

"If any of you have any information, you are to report to the wheelhouse immediately."

What happens to a stowaway, I ain't sure. Maybe he's gotta pay for passage on the spot or mop up after passengers who feel poorly.

Or it could be he's thrown overboard.

Whatever it is, I ain't gonna be caught.

Soon as I can, I pull on another pair of socks, then creep downstairs to hide out in the bunk. I try to rest, but every footstep in the hallway makes me start. What if Mr. Smalley heard what the first mate said, and he's just waiting for me to come here so he can corner me? What if the other misters want a nap themselves and, when they see me, ask a flood of questions about exactly how an orphan boy got money for a ticket? I ain't interested in facing that.

Once I'm sure the hallway's empty, I grab my things and follow the stairs to the cargo hold. What kind of a stowaway would be fool enough to return to where he was found out? But I got nowhere else to go. This time I cross to the side with the lumber and roof shingles. The floor's a whole lot cleaner, but it ain't cushioned with straw. The lumber still smells of sap, but the scent ain't strong enough to cover up the horse stink.

I sit on my knapsack behind a stack of wooden planks. I ain't ever been away from my family like these days on the *Queen*, and I miss Melvin something fierce. Lately we ain't seen each other much, but even so I always fell sleep knowing he'd whisper good night once he got home, and in the morning he'd leave me the last hunk of bread in our secret stash if there weren't any left in the cupboard. I'd put up with his nighttime whistle just to have him near. Oh, Mel. When am I gonna see you again?

It's hunger that wakes me. I ain't sure how much time has passed, though I think I've been in the hold a good long while, as when I check Pa's watch in the hallway it says it's after eight o'clock, but I ain't sure if that means morning or night. Oh, my belly's hollowed out, but seven cents is all I got. I climb the stairs, and it ain't until I reach the deck I see it's morning after all. The bread man stands near my regular bench and calls out his price. I wait till he's distracted by a customer, and swipe a buttered bun. It ain't right, what I done. Even Pa would disapprove. So I set the seven cents on the edge of the bench and hope he sees it.

I circle the deck for an hour, question folks about a skinny sixteen-year-old with sandy hair, but no one remembers Mel. There are eight fellows who kind of look like him but ain't. Maybe Mel's been seasick and ain't left his cabin. Or maybe he changed his mind about the Klondike before we left Seattle and I'm out here all by myself. My heart's as hollow as my belly was.

Smoke from the engines trails overhead, spitting soot and grime so thick, it sets me to coughing. Ash settles on my sleeves and leaves ugly smudges. Everyone's covered in a fine black powder, which makes me think of laundry when I aim to focus on Mel.

The truth is, I ain't thought too much beyond the seeing-Melvin part. Because once Mel knows I'm here, he'll move right into the scolding part of things. My brother likes to remind me how the five years he's got on me makes him right on near about everything. I know he'll think following him is the wrongest thing I've ever done.

I ain't the only one with clothes covered in ash.

Looking around, it seems a whole bunch of folks could use some freshening up, and I could use some money. So maybe I should forget Mel for now and do some laundry.

A gentleman whose room opens to the deck lets me use his slop bucket in exchange for some washing. I kneel down near the front of the *Queen* and get to work. By the time I've finished with his trousers, a crowd has formed.

"What do you charge?" a fellow asks.

I think fast.

"Nine cents a piece." The new price is steep, but with the soot and grime, so's the need. I hope my voice sounds sure and strong. Even so, I tug my cap. Could be someone saw me sneak on the ship. I don't want no one to recognize me as the stowaway.

"You got it." He hands over his jacket.

A lady offers me some soap if I scrub her handkerchief, and suddenly, it's all I can do to keep up with demand. And my, how the dirt collects in the slop bucket. Folks wait for me to wash and rinse, then hold their wet laundry. Talk turns to the gold we all hope to find once we reach the Klondike.

"What've you heard?" one fellow asks another.

"Gold up there, it grows on trees."

I stop my work, sit back on my heels. "On trees?" I never would have thought it.

"Sure does. Must be a special variety."

"I heard it sprouts wild in fields," another man says. "Ain't that what we're heading for? Goldfields? I bet it grows as bounteous as corn or wheat."

"You don't have to work none to get it, either. Just grab as much as you can carry, whenever you like."

"I heard the nuggets are so plentiful, you could stub your toes on 'em," a fellow adds. "You can sit down in the middle of the road and shove 'em into your pockets is what my bunkmates told me."

"And the best thing is we'll find gold the day after tomorrow," the first man says, his thumbs hooked on his suspenders.

"The day after tomorrow?" That's when we'll get to Skagway, not them goldfields. "We're still months from the Klondike."

"Months?" He pulls his thumbs loose and his suspenders snap. "That ain't what they told me in Seattle! Just get on a steamer to Skagway, they said, and you'll see gold straightaway."

"There ain't gold in Skagway," I tell him.

"That's right." The man who says it is thick and round as a pickle barrel. "We've got to go on to Dawson for that."

Oh, that man with the suspenders ain't happy. He storms off saying words that would have made Miss Stapleton want to swat him with a ruler if he weren't a grown man.

Mr. Horton joins the circle of folks, a pair of trousers

folded over his arm. "You can't believe all you hear," he says, "but I've learned some things that are the honest truth." He hands me some washing, and I can't hardly look him in the eye.

What if he reckons I'm the stowaway?

"When the *Portland* docked, I learned the first gold found last summer came from a creek called Bonanza. It was a nugget big around as a man's thumb. I met a miner named Berry who'd worked a claim with his wife. Together they struck it rich. Mrs. Berry left the *Portland* with a hundred thousand dollars' worth of gold wrapped in her bedroll."

I don't remember how many zeros a body's got to write to reach a hundred thousand dollars, and this Mrs. Berry had that much gold stashed in her blanket alone. What about her husband? Surely he carried some, too.

"There may be large amounts of gold up there, but you just can't take any you see," says a fellow in a fine gray suit who holds a walking stick. It ain't like he's old and needs it, either. "First you have to stake a claim. The old-timers say if gold's nearby, the willow trees will lean a certain way. The river valley you stake can't be too wide. It can't be too far upriver."

That Mr. Horton, he says not to believe everything, but he sure is listening careful-like.

The man with the cane keeps talking. "The sourdoughs—that's what folks call the old-time prospectors—they say the rivers with gold even have an unusual taste."

Special trees. Narrow valleys. Old-time sourdoughs who find gold by wetting their whistles. True or not, I hang on to every word I hear because here's the thing: the more I learn, the better chance me and Mel got to find some gold.

When I shake out Mr. Horton's sopping drawers, the legs are even longer than they were before. "Nine cents," I say, though last time he paid me five.

Mr. Horton don't hesitate. He offers me a shiny dime. "Keep the penny. A few months from now we'll all be rich."

I knew it. It ain't only stories Mr. Horton's after. He's been hooked like a fish dangling from a line. Mr. Horton wants gold bad as anyone.

"It's easy to be tricked by fool's gold, you know," says a man with a stovepipe hat. "One's smooth to the touch and the other's gritty. 'Course, I can't remember which is which."

That man in the fine gray suit thumps the deck with his cane. "There's so much gold talk flying about, it's hard to separate truth from rumor."

"Well, I heard some information of an important sort." The pickle barrel fellow holds up a finger. Just like that, he's got everyone's attention. "There's a Klondike claim worth millions, free for the taking. The old prospector who worked it says he's through. He's got no need for more riches."

"Are you talking about the crazy old coot who's given up his claim?" a fellow asks.

Pickle Barrel waves his finger through the air. "One and the same. The claim is free, but a fellow has to find it first."

The man with the walking stick leans in. "And how does someone do that?"

"The coot—One-Eyed Riley is his name—he made a fancy five-line riddle that leads a soul straight to it. Only the lines—clues, really—you have to search for them. They ain't easy to find, even harder to figure how they fit together."

"Where do you get these clues?" I ask.

"That part ain't exactly clear," Pickle Barrel says. "Some say Riley told one to each sourdough he passed when he left his claim that final time. Folks who'd always called him crazy didn't think to listen. You bet they wish they had now. Others say he wrote the clues down and sailed them on the Yukon as he left Dawson City. If that's so, they could be scattered the whole length of the river. A few men swear he whispered them into the wind, that if you listen careful on a summer evening, you might hear them. Whatever he did, word is them sourdoughs have searched for his mine near about eleven months now."

A breath of wind ripples through the crowd, sets everyone to murmuring. I shiver. It ain't from the cool ocean air, but the promise of a mine guaranteed to make its owner rich.

"Clues sailed down the Yukon and whispered into the wind." The man in the gray suit shakes his head. "That sounds a little ridiculous, don't you think?"

"Not any more ridiculous than some other things we've heard," Mr. Horton says.

It sure sounds like Mr. Horton's open to Riley's story being true.

"If there are five clues," a lady asks, "how do you know which one comes first and which is last?"

Pickle Barrel shrugs. "I've told you everything I know. Except this." He clears his throat. "I've got it on good authority *nine below's the way to go.*"

"What's that?" Mr. Horton tilts his head.

I wonder the same.

"I said." Pickle Barrel punches up the words a bit. "*Nine BELOW'S the way to GO.*"

"What's that supposed to mean?" a fellow asks.

"It's one of them Riley clues." The whole crowd turns to me, a mass of curious faces. "At least that's what I reckon."

"The boy's right," Pickle Barrel says. "But what's it mean?"

Could be Riley's gold is buried in a hole nine feet

deep. Or maybe nine below's a temperature. It might even be the name of a far-off place. Everybody's talking about ideas, but no one knows what's true.

Over near the railing, someone catches my eye. Sandy hair, dark coat, like so many others. But there's a bright blue patch sewn crooked over his elbow, and his feet move so fast, he'll soon be out of sight. Melvin.

"Mel!" I don't think about what might happen next, I just call out. "Melvin! Over here."

"That's the boy, Ma, that's him!" A flash of yellow moves through the crowd. Miss Prissy Lips pushes through, drags her mother behind. "He's the one who snuck on board." Her finger points right at me. "He's the stowaway!"

Mr. Horton's nostrils flare. "Stowaway?"

The crowd shifts and closes in. Their faces ain't friendly no more.

Mel turns at the ruckus.

I shove the bucket hard as I can. Sudsy water flows everywhere. Them folks step aside, and I race past Prissy Lips and her ma. I've almost made it to the stairs when someone grabs my arm.

"Oh no, you don't." Mr. Horton's got ahold of me. "It's the captain you'll be seeing."

He walks with quick and measured steps and bangs on the wheelhouse door. "I've got the stowaway."

The first mate opens up, nods curtly at Mr. Horton. "Thank you, that will do." He grabs my collar, yanks me across the deck, and dumps me in a tiny room no bigger than a closet. I slump against the wall.

Caught as a stowaway two days out from Skagway, thanks to that prissy girl. My bag and washboard are still on deck. The only light I got comes from beneath the door. For the first time since I boarded the *Queen*, my stomach turns. What's gonna happen to me?

I don't got no company here but my own thoughts. What did Cyril do when I didn't show up to fish a couple days ago? How's Pa faring with the whole house to himself, without them suppers I served up every night? Did Mel hear when I called to him on the deck? I pull off my cap, wipe my sweaty forehead with my wrist. The thought of him watching Mr. Horton march me to the wheelhouse twists my belly even more. He'd be shocked, that's for certain, and real disappointed I'd done something as reckless as run away from home. "I'm here for us, Mel," I say like he can hear me. "I've kept your promise."

But maybe if I'd shouted his name one last time, Mel would have looked past all that. He's my brother. It's his job to take up for me.

Oh, what was I thinking not to call for him again?

The *Queen*'s engines hiss and clatter from somewhere below, and I hear the horses fret.

This room's so hot I ain't hardly able to breathe. A couple times loud voices from the hallway boom through the walls, and my spirits rise, like this could be my chance to escape. I pound my side of the door, but the voices fade. I'm as stuck and forgotten as I was before.

Sometime much later, when I fall into a restless sleep, the door swings open and just as quickly slams shut. A piece of bread's been left on the floor. I tear right in. The sour taste means it's moldy, but what my eyes can't see my belly don't need to know. The sea grows rough and the bread in my belly ain't too happy there. So I focus on them things Pickle Barrel said. An old coot with a rich claim up for grabs, free to the first person who finds it. I ain't ever heard of anything so grand.

# Chapter 4

The closet door thumps against the wall, startling me awake. Outside stands the first mate, his uniform as neat and clean as if it's freshly pressed. "Let's go," he says, and grabs my shoulder. He pushes me ahead of him, through the deck where folks are gathering. The air crackles with excitement as the *Queen* creeps toward the muddy shore. The steamer shudders, belches out its last smoky breath. "Hurrah!" Voices rise from all around. "Hurrah for the Klondike!"

Oh, how my feet itch to get on dry land.

If only the first mate would let me go. Where's he taking me?

Until a minute ago, I weren't sure the first mate would

let me out of that closet where I've spent the last couple days. I'd near convinced myself he'd keep me there until the *Queen* docked again in Seattle. So I'm right surprised to be out here near the railing, with them who wait to go ashore.

The first mate releases me from his grip. He's got a patch of whiskers near his jaw where his razor didn't reach. Somehow them whiskers give me hope. Under the captain, he's the most important member of this crew, but he's also a fellow who don't always shave just right. Maybe he'll be kind to me.

"Normally I hand stowaways over to the authorities, but Skagway is a mess. Crooks and no-goods run this town." The first mate shoves my shoulder hard. "Get on with you. And keep out of trouble."

A smile stretches across my face. He ain't gonna send me home. I don't got my knapsack or Mama's washboard, but I'm free.

In the distance, snowcapped mountains grow wild. There's a circus in the water and onshore. Canoes and freighters and cargo boats fight to get as close as they can in them shallows. Sheep bawl mournfully as a man drives them from another ship right on through the water. A wooden box lifts over the *Queen*'s side and opens from the bottom. The horse inside crashes into the bay. It flops around, finds its feet, and falls in line with the sheep.

On board, folks surge forward, set to be the first to leave. My bag and washboard could be anywhere, but I don't got time to search. I've gotta find my brother now.

The gangplank don't connect to any land, but runs straight into the bay. Men start down and have to trudge through water clear to their knees. Others who've paid an extra fee ride to shore in flat-bottomed scows filled with mining outfits. The gold-crazy bustle in Seattle, that was only a taste of the commotion here in Skagway.

I fight hard to keep my place next to the railing, but get pushed by folks who jostle to be the next in line. Mr. Reuben passes by, bits of dried food decorating his checkered vest, and the lady whose handkerchief I washed.

Then I see him.

"Mel!" I shout.

He still hugs that little sled of his, his knapsack slung over one shoulder.

"Melvin Johnson!"

He mustn't hear me, for he don't look or turn around.

I'm stuck behind a broad fellow who won't budge, who watches a canvas bundle as it sails through the air and crashes into the shallows. A mining outfit, same as all them others.

In just a few steps, Mel's on that gangplank lickety-split.

If this big fellow ain't gonna move, if he aims to stand here and watch the gear go overboard, then I'll have to work around him. I get on my knees, crawl right between his feet.

He stumbles back. "Hey, kid!"

But I'm already down the gangplank, gone. My shoes plunge into water cold as Christmas. I lift my knees and walk on through.

Onshore, mud runs in all directions. Men scale a mountain of crates and ropes and trunks. Even more piles of gear are dumped onto the mess. It'll take hours to unload, even longer for each Stampeder to find which outfit is his own.

Mel lifts flaps of canvas and shifts some crates around. He must not see anything that's his yet, because he glances at the *Queen* and all the gear still coming, then joins the other passengers who cross the mudflats, past a collection of mismatched tents set up in a cottonwood grove, toward mountains, layers of them, as pointy as teeth on a metal saw. Mel heads straight toward Skagway.

I follow behind a whole bunch of folks, close enough to call for Mel, but all of a sudden, my belly cramps like I've swallowed spoiled milk. What exactly will Melvin say when he learns I trailed him these past five days? Maybe it would be best to let things play out natural-like. Once Mel's found some breakfast, once his gear is accounted for, maybe I can walk over and greet him like I might back home.

A few steps ahead, a line of kids weaves behind the lady in the yellow dress. My eyes dart to Miss Prissy Lips in the rear, the one whose shouting got me locked up in the dark. Oh, I'd love to knock her over, see her frilly skirt spoiled in the mud. I push in close to tell her what I think and see she's got ahold of something. Her bony arm is wrapped around my mama's washboard!

I grab on tight and yank hard as I can.

She yelps in surprise, but her eyes squinch when she sees it's me.

"Give it," I say. "That washboard's mine."

"I know that." She wears a twisty little smile. "That's why I took it from the deck this morning. I'm looking for the perfect place to dump this junk."

Oh, she gets me steamed. This girl's worse than a weeklong rash. I pull and pull on the washboard. It don't bother me that she hollers, because what she's got is mine. When she lets go, I take real satisfaction that she falls on her bottom. Right in the mud.

I leave her howling there for someone else to worry about.

The mudflats stretch from the shore to the mountains beyond. They don't really end, just turn into the road that leads to town, if this place can be called that. A couple buildings and a whole load of grungy tents are scattered on either side of a slick, cramped street. I'm nearly knocked over by a pack of stray dogs rushing past.

The strays dodge men and horses, just missing the tree stumps left in the middle of the road, and cluster around a busted barrel of salt pork that must have fallen from a wagon. A couple men lay the first few planks of a wooden sidewalk, but that's as nice as Skagway gets.

Some town this is.

I step over a puddle and move to the side of the road, where the ground ain't so sloppy. "Outta the way!" a pointy-chinned man shouts as he stumbles from a tent, and its canvas door flaps in a puff of wind. Inside music tinkles from a sorry old piano. I gotta lean against the tent to keep from getting stepped on. The canvas wall sags under my weight. Above me hangs a placard: BONANZA SALOON. Bonanza's that creek Mr. Horton talked about, where the first Klondike gold was found. Even though the saloon don't look like nothing I've ever seen before, I know this kind of place real well. It's the sort where Pa don't think twice about drinking up the money meant for supper.

Ahead, Mel trudges through the filthy street, past a wooden building called RELIABLE PACKERS and a tent with a painted board that reads PAINLESS TOOTH EXTRACTION. The road swerves right and narrows so much, a wagon passing through would run into some trouble.

Mel stops in front of an old pair of trousers that hang from a string, MEALS painted across the seat, an advertisement for the open-air restaurant nearby. I'm close enough he'd see me if he turned around, and boy, am I hungry. Last time I ate was yesterday, when the first mate gave me that awful moldy bread. Maybe this would be a good time to let Mel know I'm here and—

That pointy-chinned man slams into Mel, sends him sprawling in the mud. His cap, his trousers, his patched-up coat, everything is splattered.

Another fellow holds out his hand and pulls Mel off the ground. He's a broomstick of a man, like a twig that wears clothes.

Mel uses his heel to scrape off the mud glopped around his knees.

Broomstick points to the restaurant and Melvin nods. The two of them walk in together, like they're the best of friends.

My belly rumbles, but somehow it don't feel right to jump in now. Mel and Broomstick sit at an empty table near the road, right next to a store with a broad canvas shelter. I move under the shelter and crouch between some crates stacked outside the store. Both Mel and Broomstick have their backs to me, but I'm close enough I can hear what they're saying.

"Don't want you to think we're all as rude as that man who knocked you down," Broomstick says. "Let me buy you some breakfast."

Broomstick signals to a lady who carries trays from the cook tent, and she places two bowls before them. The peppery scent of stew tickles my nose. My belly growls again. I don't remember when it's ever been this empty.

The store behind me is really a tent that brims with mining gear, but I also spy a barrel of apples near the counter. Bet I got enough money for a couple. I dig through my pocket for the coins I earned on the *Queen*, step inside, and pay for the biggest two I can find. They're withered and kind of wormy, but do they ever taste fine.

I eat my breakfast behind them crates as Mel works on his at the table. Mama would have hated how he shovels stew into his mouth with that dirty cap of his on, that knapsack still across his back. He puts the whole bowl of stew away before I start my second apple, like he never learned no manners.

"You want another?" Broomstick asks.

"That would be awfully kind," Mel says slowly. His forehead wrinkles like he's got a couple questions he'd like to ask but ain't quite found the words for yet.

"It's the least I can do. I'd hate for you to get the wrong feel for Skagway, is all."

Old Broomstick, he sure is friendly, but why lay it on so thick? What's it to him if some boy new to town gets knocked into the mud?

"It's a good thing you met me," Broomstick says. "Because fine as Skagway is, there's some here who ain't the decent sort."

The wind picks up. The man with the stew pot runs

to secure the MEALS trousers as their legs kick higher with each gust. A couple diners point at the sky and make to leave. Wind snaps the canvas shelter overhead, and I crane my neck to get a look at what's going on. Black clouds boil over the mountains, all set to burst with rain. Next to me, the store clerk tugs the tent flaps closed.

Broomstick shifts a little closer to my brother. "So many folks are new to town, and most don't know the rules on how to keep safe. Have you ever heard of the likes of Jefferson 'Soapy' Smith?"

"No, sir," Mel says, his brown eyes careful.

Broomstick spoons up his last bit of stew, wipes his face on his shirtsleeve. "Soapy runs this town. He figured those who want to mine for gold have only a few ways to get to Canada, Skagway being one. Came up from Denver with five of his con men. They run games that poor, unsuspecting greenhorns like you—beg your pardon—fall for. Some lose all their money before they even set foot in Canada."

The tent door rustles beside me, and out steps a man who looks mighty familiar. He's got one shoulder hitched up higher than the other and his chin juts out just so. And then I remember where I seen him. He's the one who rushed from the Bonanza Saloon and knocked Mel into the mud. He stays beneath the canvas shelter, watching the storm clouds that tower even higher than before, but he's also real interested in Broomstick and Mel. He steps out into the open, one hand in his pocket, the other limp at his side. Then quick he flings that limp hand out and plunges it into Mel's knapsack. Mel whips around, but he's too late.

That man filched from my brother!

The fellow takes off running, and I fly out from behind the crates. I ain't gonna let him out of my sight.

"He's got my wallet!" Mel shouts from behind.

I run so fast, I barrel into the thief, hold on to his legs as strong as I can.

"Get offa me, you little rowdy!" He kicks me hard in the chest. My glasses fall. There's an awful crunching sound as he rushes off.

Another set of footsteps pounds past me through the slippery muck.

I can't see a dern thing without them glasses, the ones Mama saved her egg money for so faithfully. And now they're broken. Busted up and in the mud. Bent into a brand-new shape with one lens smashed. I polish what's left and put them on. It's like seeing half the world through a smudged-up window.

I gotta shut one eye to see right. It must have been Mel I heard race by. He's far down the road when he slows to a walk, leans forward with his hands on his knees.

That man got away with Mel's wallet. Two years of savings gone.

"Mel!" I shout.

Mel comes toward me, still breathing hard. "Jasper?" He says it barbed and pointy.

I'm kind of glad I can't see his face too clearly.

"What are you doing here?"

The truth's all I got to offer. "Following you to the Klondike."

"Of all the stupid things." Mel grabs his cap and throws it to the ground. He stomps around before he grabs it. The cap's real dirty now.

I remember what the first mate said, that Skagway's full of cheats, how that first fellow was nicer to Mel than he needed to be. "Them two worked together. The friendly one distracted you so the other could swipe your money."

"I must have looked like easy pickings." The muscle in Mel's jaw twitches. "He got all my money."

There's still some hope. "Not your gear, he don't got that."

Mel shakes his head as if to clear it. "Why'd you come after me?"

I push my crooked glasses back in place. "We were supposed to come here together, remember?"

Mel's eyes dart away from me. "What'd Pa say when you left?" he asks.

That's when things get stirred up inside. "Do you mean what did he say when he found your note? Because he didn't. I did. So how about you ask how I felt?"

Mel lowers his eyes.

"You promised I could come with you," I say.

"That's not what happened." Mel speaks so soft I ain't sure I'm meant to hear. "I never promised anything."

Now I get it. All them days and nights Mel stayed away last month, he was probably earning his last dollars for his steamer ticket. But he also was avoiding me. Anger presses hard against my chest. "So you let me think I was invited."

"Listen, Jasper." Mel said them exact same words the night he brought home the newspaper, the night he let me think I was included in his Klondike plans. "I came here for the two of us."

"That's a lie, and you know it!"

The wind kicks up even harder now, and with it, sheets of rain. In moments the muddy street has turned into a river.

"Come on. We'll talk later." Mel pulls me with him into the tent store. The tiny space is even darker than them black-bellied clouds outside. Above, the canvas drips as the rain pours down. Mel signals to the clerk who sold me the apples. He wears a stiff canvas apron that reaches past his knees. "I could use some help," Mel says. "My money's been stolen."

"Well, now, I'm sorry to hear that," he says, not sorry in the least.

"Know of any packers who might carry my gear and let me pay them later? I'm going to the Klondike."

The clerk tucks a pencil behind his ear. "Ain't you all."

"I've got this"—Mel pats the sled he cradles in his arms—"my pack, and, of course, my mining outfit. The steamer I came in on is still unloading gear. There's no way I'll be able to carry everything alone."

"If you were paying, I'd send you to Reliable Packers down the street." The clerk opens the tent flap, points in the direction we came from. "They carry gear up the White Pass Trail and into Canada and never overcharge. But since you got no money, well, that's not an option."

"What else can I do?" Mel says.

"You can haul your outfit by yourself. A whole lot of fellows do. They break their gear into smaller loads, carry it to a certain point, then stash it on the trail. Folks swear no one touches another man's cache. But it takes months of travel. If I was you, I'd head home, and fast."

I scrunch my eyes and wink at the world outside, try to figure out how to see regular now that my glasses are smashed. Down the street, a man who's skin and bones talks with a fellow whose chin pokes straight out in front.

I know them two. The thieves. One knocked Mel down on purpose, and when he couldn't steal Mel's money while he was flat on the ground, he got it another way.

Oh, what a fine time they're having. Them two celebrate like they've hit it big.

Pointy Chin slaps Broomstick on the back.

"Mel, look. Right over there!"

I rush from the tent and don't even check to see if Melvin follows. Mud holds tight to my shoes with each step, but at least the rain has let up some.

"Hey!" I push in between them. "You took my brother's cash. You better give it back."

Pointy Chin shrugs. If he's surprised to see me, he covers it up good. "Don't know what you're on about."

Now Mel's next to me. He stares Broomstick down. "You bought me breakfast so your friend could take my money."

"Son"—Broomstick puts an arm around Mel's shoulder—"your mind's addled. I can assure you we haven't touched your things. If you're missing money, though, you could take it up with Soapy Smith."

"Soapy Smith?" Mel shrugs off Broomstick's arm. "You told me Soapy cons unsuspecting greenhorns."

Broomstick grins. "I said he runs this town. You've got a problem, take it up with him."

"Give it over, you no-good crooks!"

"Jasper, watch your tongue."

Pointy Chin tips his hat, like he's done us a favor. An oily smile slides across Broomstick's face as the two of them walk on.

I try to run after them, but Mel spins me around. "You can't talk like that, especially to men who aren't above stealing."

"They took your money!"

"I know. But there's nothing we can do."

We cross Skagway, which takes no more than a minute, and trudge to the shore. "So you were the stowaway," Mel says. "What were you thinking?"

So Mel didn't see Mr. Horton drag me to the wheelhouse. At least there's that. "You know exactly what I was thinking. That you'd abandoned me."

"Now wait," Melvin says. "It wasn't like that at all."

"Tell me what it's like." Since the rain pushed through and we ran into the tent store, I've waited for Mel's story on why he left me behind.

"I need to get my gear first." Mel drops his bag at my feet. "You wait here."

The pile of goods on the mudflats is as cluttered as before. Plenty of men dig around to separate their belongings.

Mel's little sled makes a real good seat. I watch seagulls waddle across the shore and poke their beaks into the lapping water. They burst into flight as a short man sturdy about the middle draws near.

Pickle Barrel. The fellow on the *Queen* who talked about that old coot who wants to give away his mine. "You're awfully young to be out here alone," he says.

"I ain't alone. I'm here with my brother. He's fetching our things."

"Well, I'm waiting for Reliable Packers to load my

outfit for White Pass. That's how to travel, with someone else to do the heavy lifting."

Me and Mel ain't got much choice. "Folks like us gotta rely on our own sturdy backs."

Pickle Barrel tilts his head toward the pile of goods. "Is that your brother coming this way?"

Mel walks toward us, but something ain't right with him. His shoulders are hunched up near his ears, and he stares at the ground. Mel drags a weathered piece of canvas behind him.

"It's gone," Mel says.

"Gone?" My belly feels like it's loaded down with stones.

He shuts his eyes. "My tent. My gear, all my food."

"Sure you didn't overlook it?" Pickle Barrel asks. "Took me almost an hour to find my outfit."

Mel shakes his head. "I tied my handkerchief to this canvas cover, so that when I searched for it, I'd know which one was mine." He holds up the handkerchief that hangs from one corner. "This is all I found."

"What are we gonna do?" Mel has to have the answer, because right this minute, I can't think of how to make things better. Since we've come to Skagway, it's gone from bad to worse.

"You could start fresh in Dyea. I heard it's one town over. But I don't know what you'd do there without any gear." Pickle Barrel taps a finger on his lips, considering. "Or you could go on home."

"Home. Guess we got no other choice," Mel says.

He wants to go back? "Mel, there ain't no way I'll do that."

"You weren't ever supposed to be here, remember?" Mel swings his fist through the air, punches at something no one can see. "And now we're stuck. In Alaska. The middle of nowhere."

It's Skagway that's the problem, where Melvin lost his money and his gear. What we need is a fresh start. "Where's Dyea?" I ask Pickle Barrel.

"I think it's over that direction." He points west, down a lonely mudflat that tapers down to nothing but a mountain at the edge of the ocean. At least that's what it looks like. With my busted glasses, I can't see too far in front of me.

Pickle Barrel studies me real careful. "Say, do I know you?"

I shake my head. Ain't about to tell him he saw Mr. Horton hand me over to the *Queen*'s first mate.

His face lights up, and I know he's figured it out. "I do recognize you. The washer boy," he says, right proud of himself. "You're the one who stowed away on the *Queen*."

"That's him, all right." Mel shakes out that sorry canvas, wads it up like it's to blame for his worries, and shoves it into his pack. "This isn't the time for talk. What we need is a plan."

Mel said "we," like he sees us as a team. I need him to think we're exactly that. If I can get the *Queen* out of his sight, maybe he won't try to turn around.

"Let's walk to Dyea," I tell him. "We've worn out our welcome in Skagway." I talk like Mel means to let me stay, like he won't somehow try to send me back to Kirkland. The more I show him I've got some good ideas, the better chance I got to stick around.

My brother shrugs, picks up his sled.

Mel don't have any ideas of his own. He don't even answer, him who knows everything and usually don't let me forget it. With his gear and money gone, Mel's lost his fight. It worries me.

"So long, boys," Pickle Barrel says, like we don't got a chance in the world.

We set out on the empty mudflats as storm clouds billow overhead.

"I wonder how Pa's doing on his own," Mel says.

"How Pa's doing?" Here I've been concerned about old Mel with what happened in Skagway, but that bit of kindness toward him burns up in a flash. "What about me? For two years you promised we'd get out on our own together. Then you up and left."

Lightning cuts the sky. The rain starts up again, like before was practice. "I can explain," Mel says.

"So do it." I stop in front of Mel so fast, he almost trips.

"Right here on this muddy beach." Water courses down my neck and soaks my shirt beneath my jacket. It streaks the one good lens I still got in my glasses.

Mel wipes a handkerchief across his forehead, but that don't stop the rain from dripping. "I know Pa's hard to live with."

"Ain't that the truth." When he ain't drunk or angry, sadness hangs over him, the kind that lasts for days. I stomp hard, just to slosh some mud on Mel. It splatters both his legs.

"I promised I'd take care of you," Mel says. "Why'd you think I came here, anyway? The gold I find, it'll be worth more than I could ever earn at home. I was going to come back for you."

"That's a sorry excuse. How'd you ever think it would be better to leave me with Pa?"

"Jasper," Mel tries again. "It wouldn't have been forever."

But I don't listen. I turn up my collar to block the rain, to shut out Melvin, too.

"You've learned how to deal with him. You would have been okay."

Lay low and stay out of the way. Mel's rules for living with Pa. Guess Mel thinks he's taught me so good, he don't have to concern himself no more.

"I ain't interested in okay. Don't you get it? We were supposed to leave together. It was a promise you made me. And you broke it."

It's just like when Mama left. I thought she'd be with us for always. Then she wasn't anymore.

"Jasper?"

I blink real quick. My feet get moving on their own.

"Where are you going?" Mel says from behind me.

I walk so fast, I gotta break into a run.

"Come back!"

The mud slops beneath me as the distance between us stretches. And when this beach runs out and I have to climb up into them foothills, I ain't gonna wait for my brother.

I've had my fill of Melvin Johnson for one day.

# CHAPTER 5

An hour later, I reach the mounds of mining gear scattered along Dyea's waterfront. Last time I saw Mel, he'd made it over the foothills. It suits me fine he's still back there by himself.

Tents and a few wooden buildings bunch together a little farther from the shore. I wander the muddy main street, following the smell of baked apples. It's been a week since I had a hot meal, and my stomach's talking.

The sweet aroma leads me to a meal tent. Outside, its tables glisten in the passing rain. Though it's late afternoon, the tables are right full of folks, and it ain't baked apples they eat, but thick pieces of pie. Oh, I'm glad I got a little money still left over from the *Queen*.

I buy a heaping slice and pick the only open bench I

find. A man with enormous sideburns already sits at the table. Them whiskers of his resemble pork chops cooked up nice. My stomach growls. I gotta get some food in me.

The man nods in greeting. "You here all by yourself?"

I ain't sure how to answer that. "For now," is what I tell him. I tuck into my pie, all warmth and sugar-spice. I ain't had a better meal since Mama was with us.

"Good thing we ain't in Skagway," he says.

My fingers feel for my knapsack before I remember I don't got it anymore. By now it's probably been tossed out by a crewman on the *Queen*. Is this man a crook like them that stole from Mel, a fellow who talks nice just to nab things from a person all alone? Well, if he's angling for something to grab, he better not try Mama's washboard. Miss Prissy Lips can tell him about that.

The man looks across the mudflats where I last saw Mel. "That new trail over in Skagway, the White Pass, I hear it's slow going on account of all this rain. If parts wash out, White Pass could close till winter."

"That's one of them trails we gotta hike into Canada?"

The fellow nods so firm, his sideburns waggle.

"The Chilkoot Trail out of Dyea, though, is shorter. Twenty-six miles to White Pass's thirty-seven. Sure it's steeper, but the Chilkoot's always open. A fellow like me, who hauls his gear alone, it takes a good two weeks to get his outfit the eight miles from here to Canyon City, and that's just the first camp on the trail. I've been at it twelve days now. I sleep here and move my gear farther along the trail for most of the day. Sometimes on a trip back for more I'll stop in for a slice of pie. If the Chilkoot closed down, like could happen to the White Pass, I wouldn't get all my gear to Canada till next spring."

If only Mel could hear this fellow. The Chilkoot Trail ain't as long, and it don't ever close. Here's another reason it was smart to clear out of Skagway, why we should keep on to the Klondike.

"You said White Pass is the new trail. Ain't both of them new?" I ask. "Word about the Klondike gold only got out last month."

He scrapes his fork across his plate, licks off every last crumb. "Folks have always hoped there might be gold north of here. Fifteen years ago prospectors started traveling the Chilkoot Trail, my brother one of them. Back then the trail was a Tlingit Indian trade route. Most folks ended up in Fortymile and Circle City, mining towns not far from the Klondike. 'Course, after last summer's discovery, those towns emptied fast. Them prospectors left their claims to stake new ones along Bonanza and other nearby creeks. My brother Bill got himself a Bonanza claim. That's where I'm headed now."

My mind's cluttered up with names of places, a couple I heard before and others that are new to me. But what stands out is them sourdoughs who left the claims they had to find even better ones. I imagine them old-time miners surrounded by their riches and all that other good stuff gold must surely bring.

That old coot, One-Eyed Riley, I wonder if his mine is on Bonanza or somewhere else close by.

That's when I see Mel tramp into town. At least that's who I think it is, far as I can see. He hardly bends his knees. The mud on his trousers must have dried pretty stiff.

"You okay?" the man asks me. "Did you get a mosquito in your eye?"

Must be I'm squinting bad. "I ain't able to see too good on account of my broken glasses, but I think my brother just made it to Dyea." I point to the fellow I think is Mel.

"The boy in the brown coat?"

"That's right. Has he got a blue patch on one elbow?"

He leans in to get a better look. "Sure does."

"That's Melvin, then."

Mel stands in the middle of the main street near a wagon a few tents down, watches the folks who pass him, lost and pitiful. I chew my last few bites of pie slow as I please. Maybe he's fretting about where I've gone off to. It would do him a world of good to worry some, since he thought it no big deal to leave me with Pa.

But I can't stay mad at Mel forever. "Thanks for sharing your table, mister . . ."

"The name's Shaw." He holds out a calloused hand.

"Mr. Shaw. I best catch up with Mel."

Mr. Shaw's eyes linger on my brother. I know exactly what he's thinking. Mel's a real sad sight.

I hitch my washboard on my shoulder and head toward the road. Around him, people bustle, but my brother is right still. "Hey," I say, like bumping into him on a muddy Alaskan street happens all the time.

"There you are." Mel wraps his arm around my shoulder. "Please don't run off like that again. You had me worried."

An hour ago I would have asked what did he care. I would have bellyached. But now I lean hard into him. "If you're worried, why are you just standing here?"

"I figured you'd cool off soon, that all I had to do was wait somewhere near the front of town." Mel turns my shoulders so I face him. His cap is dirty. His hair's all over the place. "Know what I should have told you earlier? That I'm glad to see you. I've missed you since I've been gone."

We got no money to speak of, no tent, no blankets. Could be the pie in my belly, but in this moment here with Melvin, things don't seem so bad. There's gotta be a way for us to figure out a plan that gets us both to the Klondike.

"First thing we'll do is find out when the next steamer leaves for Seattle," Mel says.

Like that, Mel's smashed my hope to pieces. So he still wants to send me home. Or maybe he aims to go back, too. I don't want nothing to do with it, but I ain't gonna fight right now.

"We've got no money for our fare." I ain't gonna show him Pa's watch. That's for when we're desperate, and we ain't there quite yet. Anyhow, Mel don't need to know that we could get some cash to make it home, because home's not where we're headed.

"It's not our fare we need"—Mel don't blink at all—"only yours."

I pull away, almost bump into some folks who cross the street. "You just said you were happy to see me."

"That's right. And I'd be happier if I knew you were safe."

"With Pa," I say. I don't want him for a minute to forget that home ain't a safe place. Sure, I've learned to watch my words and avoid Pa when he's fired up, but where's the ease in that? "I ain't going anywhere without you, and I mean it. I'd rather risk whatever's ahead than turn around."

"I don't have money," Mel says, "or gear."

I see them men who wander Dyea's streets, carrying tents and crates of food, set with everything they'll ever need. "I know. I ain't pretending it won't be hard, but the gold's gonna make life right for us. We ain't never gonna have another chance like this."

"I don't want to put you in danger, Jasper, don't you

understand?" Mel's forehead puckers. "You've had more heartache than a boy should ever see."

Mama left us. And then there's Pa. There ain't one word that speaks of all the ways he's changed these last two years, from a man who was dependable to one who sometimes don't even get out of bed.

"Do you have to decide about the steamer this afternoon? Can't it wait?" I pat Mama's washboard strapped to my back. Mel needs to see I can earn some money. "A laundry would buy us supper, and you could use some freshening up."

How I wish I still had that red union suit I packed, the underdrawers that were Mel's very own. I'd love to hand them over and see his face. What better sort of partner could Mel take to the Klondike than a brother who helps him in his time of need?

Mel's filthy, that's for sure, but he ain't the only one who could use a laundry service. Dyea's a week out of Seattle, for those of us who came by steamer. When you're in a new place and tired from your travels, there ain't nothing better than a fresh pair of trousers. Ten cents for a spiffed-up pair, well, I'd say that's a steal.

"All right," Mel finally agrees. "No more steamer talk until tomorrow. I'll try to find someone who might let us bunk with him tonight."

Oh, that suits me fine.

We split up at the nearest camp. Folks have spread

their tents on every open piece of ground, which ain't nothing more than sloppy mud. I ask around for a bucket I can borrow to start my work, but don't find one. I keep at it until I see a fellow who sits outside his tent, picking his teeth with a pocketknife, an overturned bucket his stool.

"Can I use that pail of yours?"

"Using it myself," he says.

He don't exactly say no. Could be I have a chance. I spy his mining outfit stacked against his tent and covered with a faded piece of canvas. An idea comes to me. "Those your things?"

He nods.

I drop my voice to a whisper. "Because I seen some fellows mighty interested in what's under there."

That makes him move. As soon as he's turned the corner, that bucket's in my hands.

"I don't see no one," he says when he comes back, "and furthermore—hey, what are you doing?"

I've got both arms wrapped around his bucket. "Can't I use it for some laundry?"

"Give it over." His eyes say he ain't kidding, so does the pocketknife he's tucked in the waistband of his trousers.

I swallow hard. "If you let me borrow it, I'll wash up your shirt."

"My shirt?" he says. "If you don't want trouble, you'll wash all my clothes."

I can work with that. Since I lost my piece of soap on

the *Queen*, I tell the fellow I'll wash his blanket, too, if he lets me borrow some. I do a right fine job of it. The trousers lose their caked-on mud, the shirt is almost white again, and the blanket, well, at least it smells better than before. Though I talk up my laundry to every fellow who walks past, the rain comes and goes in waves. I guess no one wants to hang clean laundry out to dry just to have it soaked again. There ain't no one besides the man with the bucket who's gonna use my services today.

Before I give the fellow his clothes, I snap off a piece of soap and stash it in my pocket. Not a lot, just the bit I would have used if I'd had other customers. I ain't one cent richer, but at least there's that.

I got nothing else to do but wait for Mel at the camp where we split.

By the time he finds me, it's almost nine o'clock. Only a trail of sunlight lingers in the sky. Mel's slicked his hair and dressed in the clothes he brought from home. Oh, it makes me itch in my wet and dirty things. "Did you make some money?" he asks.

"Nope. Did you find a place for us to stay the night?"

I hate how Mel shakes his head, like my future's certain, and it's in Kirkland.

Then I remember Mr. Shaw. "I met a man at the meal tent earlier. Maybe he'd let us bunk with him." Mr. Shaw told me this town's best to leave from. Maybe he can talk to Mel, help him understand that going on from Dyea's a good thing.

It ain't too easy to see on account of twilight and the rain that's started up again, but I can just make out a lantern that hangs from the meal tent's entryway. Mr. Shaw ain't at the table where I left him, but when I say his name and describe them pork chop sideburns, the cook knows exactly who I mean.

"Shaw stops in when he comes to town to gather more of his gear," the cook tells me. "You'll find him a few tents down."

Me and Mel go from tent to tent. We call out his name. At last a tent flap opens. "I see you found your brother," he says.

I nod. "It's wet out here. Could we come in?"

Mr. Shaw spits a wad of chewing tobacco near my feet. "Don't you got your own tent?"

Me and Mel look at each other. How exactly do we explain all that's happened today?

Mr. Shaw sighs. "Get on in here." Oh, are we relieved. Apart from a single candle set on a leather trunk, it's real dark inside. The whole tent's almost filled up when we stand together. "So where's your gear?"

"It went missing in Skagway," Mel says.

"What's that?"

Mel ain't making himself clear. "It was stolen."

"Stolen?" Mr. Shaw strokes his naked chin. "You boys are in a heap of trouble, then. A ton of gear per person. A year's supply of food. That's the standard. Best turn around while you still got the chance."

Mr. Shaw don't tell Mel directly, but I hear it all the same. Only a fool would continue. It's the word most folks use for Pa and is near about the worst name you could call my brother.

This ain't what I wanted him to say. Mr. Shaw was supposed to persuade Mel to keep on going, not turn around.

The rain patters on the canvas above, and I can't help but shiver.

"I've heard rumors that the North West Mounted Police will set up camp at the border between here and Canada, that once they do, they won't let anyone in unless they've got the proper gear. Know why?" Mr. Shaw grins, his teeth brown and slimy. "Because they don't want to have to mess with your dead body a few months from now."

My ears burn, though my rain-damp clothes have chilled me pretty good. If Melvin goes on alone, I won't know if he's safe.

"Some folks think travel from here to the Klondike will be easy," he says. "I even seen a man who thinks he'll bicycle there. It's almost six hundred miles from Dyea to Dawson City, where the Klondike and Yukon Rivers meet. You seen those mountains behind us?" He points to the tent's darkened wall, but I can picture them on the other side. Big and mighty. Reaching for the clouds, like Mount Rainier back home. "It's straight over you'll go and down the other side until you reach Lake Lindeman. Then you'll sail across a couple lakes and down the Yukon River through dangerous rapids and on to Dawson in a boat you build by yourself. Ever built a boat before?"

Mel shakes his head. His cheeks are chapped and sunburned. Grit fans out like bird's wings from the corners of each eye. That's exactly what he's like, his head tilted to one side. A bird, studying his situation.

"Mel." I got to talk before Mr. Shaw convinces him it's best to leave, and oh, I hope he'll listen. "Home ain't a real home anymore, not for either of us. We don't got a future there. This journey's been our dream since you started saving, and sure it's gonna be harder than anything we've ever done, but that ain't no reason to quit, not when we're finally on our own." I scoot a little closer. "There's gold in the Klondike just waiting for us. Can't you feel it?"

From my pocket I take Pa's watch and let it swing from its chain. The gold winks in the candlelight. My heart's thumping in my chest. I ain't sure what Mel's gonna say or do. "Here's the other reason I came. You left this behind."

Mel blinks in surprise. He reaches for the watch, rubs his thumb over its shiny lid. "I left this for you."

"I'd never sell Pa's watch on my own. Mama said it was for the two of us."

"That watch is nice," Mr. Shaw says. "But it won't buy you much of anything."

"Jasper, you came all this way to bring me this?"

I nod because it's true, but also to spur Mel on. So maybe Pa's watch won't bring us loads of money, like Mr. Shaw says, but it's shown Mel I'm devoted, that I'll stay by him no matter what. Something's changing in my brother, I can feel it. He's letting himself see I belong with him, which I most surely do.

"If we go, it will be dangerous."

If we go, Mel says, like he's considering it. All those lonely nights on the *Queen*, I waited for this moment.

Mr. Shaw shakes his head. "More dangerous than you know."

"So we'll have to travel those six hundred miles quick as we can."

"That's for sure," Mr. Shaw says. "Winter can hit Canada in September."

"And we'd have to partner up, find someone who would let us share his tent and eat his food until we could pay him back."

"In gold," I say.

Mel nods.

Mr. Shaw lifts his face to the dripping canvas. "Ain't no one who will go for that."

"We have to promise to stick together," Melvin says.

I can't help but break into a grin. "I promise."

Mel reaches for my hand and gives it a firm shake, the watch pressed between our palms.

"You think you can do it?" he asks.

"I know I can." I think over everything Mr. Shaw's told us. He ain't painted a pretty picture with his words. "Not because it won't be hard, but because you'll be with me."

Mel turns to Mr. Shaw. "Guess my brother and I will have to make it into Canada before those Mounties settle in."

Mr. Shaw opens the tent flap and spits tobacco onto the rain-soaked road. "You boys are dern fools."

He thinks we're crazy. We got nothing to our names but Mel's bag and sled and Mama's washboard. What Mr. Shaw don't know is that this decision is the smartest the two of us have ever made, trusting in ourselves rather than relying on Pa. But even so, what Mr. Shaw said about them Mounties not wanting to mess with them who don't got proper gear, it weighs heavy on me.

"I'm set to turn in." Mr. Shaw still holds the tent flap open. "You two better go now."

"But . . ." I can't get out them other words, the ones that ask to let us stay. Because it's right clear Mr. Shaw wants none of that.

The rain comes down in waves. It's too dark to see.

Mel pulls the canvas from his knapsack and drapes it across our shoulders. I wrap it in one hand and hold on to him with the other as we race through the darkness. Mud and water fill my shoes. My shirt soaks through fast.

I ain't sure where we're headed, but I know Mel's looking out for us. Ahead, the lantern at the meal tent shines. We run until we reach it, then slip past to the tables around back. Mel crawls under the first table we come to, pulling me with him. "This is the driest place we're going to find."

The slanting rain pounds and splatters. It's awful hard to rest. My mind spins dreams about the Klondike though I'm still awake, dreams a whole lot better than sleep. We can make it. I know we can. Haven't we already come this far?

Darkness starts to fade not too long after five, Pa's watch says, but we're up even earlier, shivering in the awful muck and wet that's soaked through the canvas cover. Once the cook sees we've spent the night on his lot, he shoos us off, and we ask some fellows along the road if they could point us to the Chilkoot Trail. Their faces don't hide what they think of two boys with a whole bunch of nothing, but even so they tell us to follow the Taiya River.

The trail begins at the riverside, cuts through waving grasses and patches of flowering weeds. It crosses the ice-cold Taiya over and over again and slowly winds higher up the base of a mountain. Mr. Shaw said the Chilkoot Trail leads into Canada and ends twenty-some miles on the other side of these sharp and jagged mountains, at a lake called Lindeman.

My wet clothes chafe against my skin, but at least them raw spots distract me from my hollow belly. Me and Mel are the only ones not bent double with extra-heavy packs. Guess that's one thing going for us, without any gear. We're traveling faster than them other fellows.

We climb through groves of spruce and cottonwood. The sun sometimes drifts from behind them storm clouds, but mostly the rain keeps on steady. Mel insists I wrap the canvas around me like a slicker, but I hand it back when my clothes turn hot and clammy.

We move ahead of them others with outfits loaded on their shoulders. It don't take long to see folks dump stuff they don't want no more. A sewing machine. A pile of cook pots. Even a piano. How a body carried something that big, I don't know. They ain't in tidy bundles like the ones stashed here and there, the gear a body means to store for now and move later down the trail. These things are tossed aside. They ain't worth holding on to anymore.

I dodge a stove that's been left right in the middle of the path. "First thing I'm gonna do up in the Klondike is pick gold from them bushes."

Mel laughs. "That's ridiculous."

"Is not. I heard about it on the *Queen*. There's so many nuggets scattered on the ground, you have to make sure you don't trip."

"If all that's true, why haven't I read about it in that mining book I picked up in Seattle?"

"Bet the fellow who wrote it ain't seen them bushes yet."

"Then why didn't those miners on the *Portland* bring back shrubs to plant?"

"Maybe they don't grow so well outside the Klondike," I say. What's Mel know, anyhow? Farthest he's ever been from home before now is Seattle. "Have you thought about what you're gonna do when you get some gold?"

Mel shrugs. "Oh, I don't know. Buy an umbrella, maybe."

On a day like this, an umbrella would be right nice to have.

"You know what I really want?" he says. "I'd like a whole shelf full of books. Ones I haven't read before."

When Mel left school to work the mill, it weren't his choice. He had his mind set on college someday. Miss Stapleton sent him home with two books of her very own, for him to keep his learning.

"Well, I'm gonna build us a house," I tell him. "It'll have four windows and yellow shutters, like Mama always wanted before"—there's a funny feeling in my belly—"before she left."

Mel slows. "Hey, Jasper," he says, his voice kind of strange. "You know Mama didn't leave us. You remember what really happened, don't you?"

Mel's broken the rule, the one that comes straight after lay low and stay out of the way. Except this one ain't about Pa. It's a rule we ain't ever mentioned, but it's as true and certain as the other.

"I don't want to talk about that." Before Mel can say any more, I push past until I'm the one in the lead.

I reach the gorge ahead with Mel a few steps behind. Here giant cedars stand tall enough to hold off the rain, their roots thick around as a man's leg. Boulders litter the trail, stones bigger than a barn. We struggle to climb over them, but if we want to keep on, it's what we gotta do, and I'm happy I can't think on what Mel said.

This whole world's existed long before we ever came here, will keep on long after we pass. "It's beautiful out here, isn't it?" Mel says.

"I ain't never seen anything like it." But pretty don't make the going easy. The climb gets tougher, and oh, my legs throb. My clothes are soaked clean through.

The sun moves out from behind the clouds, and with it comes the heat. Around the next bend in the river is a little canyon with a mishmash of rocks, shiny and black and sorely out of place. I wait till Melvin catches up. "I need a rest." We ain't stopped since we left Dyea around six o'clock. Now it's almost three. I'm also curious about them shiny rocks.

Mel finds a shady spot and sits on his sled. "Ten minutes," he says, "and then we're moving on."

"I'll be right back." I leave the trail and walk a stretch along the riverside. Them rocks I saw ain't rocks at all, but a mound of rubber boots dumped by someone who don't want them no more. I grab two pairs and turn around.

My pair fits fine over my river-soaked shoes. Mel sticks his in his pack. "I'm gonna get a couple more sets."

Mel's mouth quirks up on one side. "What for?"

"Maybe I could sell them. You never know when they'll come in handy."

This time through the canyon's quick. I dig in that pile of boots to find two matching sets.

Voices echo off the steep rock walls, a tangled mix of sounds that's faint but grows louder.

I peek from behind the mound. On the other side of the river comes a man who drags another by the arm. Though it's August, the first man wears a long fur coat clear down to his shoes. He's as big and hairy as a grizzly bear. A horseshoe mustache dangles past his chin. His face is flush and shines with sweat.

"You'll pay up, all right, taking my supplies like that," he says to the man he pulls along.

The smaller man stumbles like he can't keep up, like if Grizzly let go, he'd fall over. He holds his derby to his head. "I gave back the bacon I took. I'll do anything you want. Just don't bring in the law."

Grizzly jerks the man in the derby off the ground, holds him so close, the fellow has to lift his chin to meet Grizzly's eyes. That derby hat of his slips off, and underneath he's got a shiny bald head. He's maybe a little older than Mel, but he don't got any hair at all.

"What's in it for me if I don't turn you in, you no-good thief?"

Baldy scrambles to get loose, but Grizzly's got a mighty grip. "I said, why shouldn't I turn you in?"

"I know. A couple things. That could be. Useful," Baldy chokes out. He twists his neck to catch his breath.

I drop to the ground so he don't see me, but I ain't quick enough.

"Who's that kid over there?" Baldy says.

Grizzly's face takes on a thunderous look. "What do you think you're doing, kid?" He drops Baldy fast and strides through the water, straight toward me. My heart pounds with everything it's got. I ain't gonna let him scoop me up like he's done to Baldy. I snake my arm out till I reach them boots, push off the ground, and run faster than I ever have before.

"You'd better watch it if you know what's good for you!" Them last words of Grizzly's ring through the canyon. I only stop once I find Mel.

Mel eyes me curiously. "Why'd you run over here like that?"

"There was a big grizzly and—"

Mel's on his feet. "A grizzly bear?"

"Well, no, not a bear." I breathe deep to settle my racing heart. "A man in a long fur coat and just as big as one. He had another fellow by the arm. He hollered when he saw me, would have nabbed me, too, if I didn't take off running."

Mel's eyebrows pinch together, same as they did back home when Pa would shout. "Maybe I shouldn't have brought you here."

I lash them boots to Mama's scrub board and swing it over my shoulder. "I got here all by myself, remember?"

"There's all sorts of men going to the Klondike. A lot of fine ones, sure, but there's got to be others that aren't up to any good."

Oh, I'm certain of that.

"If ever you see that man again, promise you'll be careful. And, Jasper?"

I meet Mel's eyes, which go serious.

"Promise me you'll watch what you say."

Old Mel still thinks I can't control my tongue? Well, I've gotten good at that. I open my mouth to fuss at him, then close it right on back. Maybe that ain't the best choice right now.

So I nod my head.

"Good," Mel says. "Let's go."

We've walked all morning and most of the afternoon. The trail twists away from the river, climbs ever higher, then dips low through a valley, and then we're here, at Canyon City, a camp eight miles from Dyea, where Mr. Shaw, with his whole outfit, will arrive a few days from now. It's got a fancy name, but Canyon City is just a clearing where folks set up tents beneath the trees. I'd love to get these boots off, rinse out my gritty socks.

While Mel asks questions of a couple men as they set up a tent, I spy that Grizzly fellow and a crowd of Tlingit packers carrying all his gear. He ain't loaded down with one thing except that enormous coat he wears. Must be some way to travel. He talks with big gestures and a booming voice, like everyone's real interested in what he's got to say.

I move behind a clump of trees. There ain't no way I want to catch Grizzly's eye.

"The next stop's Sheep Camp," Mel says when he finds me. "It's five miles farther on. Think you can make it?"

It's so good to sit here in the shade. "Can you?" I ask.

He nods. "If we push hard, maybe tomorrow we'll reach the Chilkoot Pass."

Mel means the part of the trail that goes right up the mountain, the one with snow on top, where folks who carry gear, according to Mr. Shaw, sometimes take four months to cross over into Canada.

How will we manage without food and proper shelter? The truth is I ain't sure. I think of them Mounties Mr. Shaw talked about, how they don't want to deal with the bodies of men who don't got enough gear. We gotta be quick, otherwise we could end up just like that.

"Let's keep moving, then," I say, "so tomorrow we can climb the pass."

• • •

Though it's almost nine o'clock when we reach the waterfall right outside of Sheep Camp, a little sunlight lingers. Tents in the camp are packed so tight, there ain't no space between, and in the only open spot, folks gather around a rickety foldout table where someone sells whiskey.

"Climbing's thirsty work. Hit me up again," one man shouts.

"Arizona Charlie Meadows," another slurs, "you got the best whiskey in all of Alaska."

Without a word, me and Melvin move away. We know that sort of talk. It starts off light, but it don't take long to turn mean and ugly.

Besides the tents, Sheep Camp has a hotel called Palmer House, which ain't nothing but a squatty, rough-board building. It sure ain't much to look at, but it's the only thing here made of wood or stone, the best option we got.

"We're gonna stay at the Palmer." I gotta get these boots off and my wet shoes underneath.

"And how will we manage that?"

"I'll use my last few coins," I say, "and if that ain't enough, I'll offer to do some laundry."

Mel don't argue, he just takes a seat in front of the Palmer House. Guess he's as tired as I am.

I stick my head inside. The Palmer don't got any windows. A curtain makes an extra wall so the Palmer family can have some privacy. Tobacco smoke hangs thick over the dinner table. The room buzzes with conversation. And, boy, a crowd's still eating at this hour.

"Excuse me." I step inside and wave to a woman who rushes about. "I'm looking for Mr. Palmer."

She uses the edge of her apron to wipe her hands. "What do you want with my husband?"

The missus. Even better. "Mrs. Palmer, how about I wash your bed and table linens?"

She smiles at me. "What's it you're after, young man?"

"Some supper. A place for me and my brother to stay the night. I got a little money. I'd pay for the rest by washing up."

At the table behind us, two fellows begin to argue.

Mrs. Palmer dips forward so I can hear. "We don't have table or bed linens. Or even beds, for that matter. Folks sleep on the floor. This place holds forty if they squeeze in close enough." She wipes her hands again. That apron of hers ain't got a clean spot anywhere.

"How about I wash your apron and the dishrags in the kitchen, then?"

"Now, that I'd be grateful for." Mrs. Palmer don't resemble Mama, but even so, I find I think on her, how she'd stay calm no matter what kind of fuss was kicked up, how her smile could soften even Pa.

Mrs. Palmer lends me a washtub, which after the buckets I've used is a treat. I carry it outside and fill the tub with water from the stream. Melvin sits on a stump to keep me company. My sleeves are pushed up high, and still the suds climb to the cuffs of my shirt. There ain't much light to work by, but I trust them rags are cleaner than they was before. With Mel's help, I string them up to dry.

The missus is real pleased. "You boys come get some supper," she says when I return her washtub and hand over them last coins in my pocket. She leads us straight to the table. The crowd has cleared out some, but a couple folks still eat. I take the empty seat near a lawyer in a dark suit who plans to live in Dawson City. Mel sits between a farmer from South Dakota with a head of hair bright as a pumpkin and an English nobleman called Lord Avonmore. The lord's brought a whole pile of servants to haul champagne clear to Dawson. Seventy-five cases of it.

"The lord also has one hundred pounds of toilet paper, whatever that is," the farmer tells me.

Lord Avonmore's got tiny, close-set eyes and a long sloping nose. He looks down that nose of his and sniffs. "It's certainly not a topic to discuss at table."

That's how he says it: "at table." Wonder what Miss Stapleton would say if she could hear him, this fancy fellow who skips words like that. Maybe he don't know it ain't a proper way to talk.

"I bet them servants and all that gear must have cost a pretty penny," the farmer whispers. It ain't easy to catch all his words in this noisy place. But the lawyer don't miss a thing he's said.

"You mean a pretty sovereign." He breaks apart the piece of bread Mrs. Palmer hands him. "Isn't that what they call money in your country, Avonmore?"

Lord Avonmore sniffs again. I guess money ain't a topic to discuss at table, neither.

The curtain behind us shivers as someone bumps it from the Palmer family's side. Forty people crammed in this part of the building, with just a sheet to separate us from the Palmers' home. It's gotta be a tricky way to live. That Klondike gold sure has made folks do some crazy things.

Mel don't talk, just shovels food into his mouth while it's still hot. I gulp my tea, try to wash down a fatty piece of bacon. Oh, it tastes fine.

"What gold stories have you heard so far?" the lawyer asks.

The table heats up with answers.

"I heard them prospectors that arrived in San Francisco had flour sacks crammed with nuggets," the farmer says. "Was the same in Seattle."

Lord Avonmore parts his skinny lips. Now he's set on talking. "Some had suitcases that weighed hundreds of pounds, overflowing with gold."

The lawyer fills his pipe with tobacco and strikes a match. Wisps of smoke join the hazy cloud above. With no windows in this place, I reckon that cloud's been hovering overhead since supper first was served.

"Anybody heard about a secret mine worth millions, whose owner is ready to hand it over to the first person who finds it?" Mel's the one who says it. He ain't never mentioned the old coot's mine before. If he sat closer, I'd thump him under the table. Sure, I want to learn all I can about Riley, but that don't mean I plan to give up what I know.

The lawyer shakes his head. Smoke swirls around him. "That's a bunch of malarkey."

"Well, I've heard about it, and I think it's true," the farmer says. "One-Eyed Riley's his name. Claims he's got more than enough gold. Now all he wants is to live a life of solitude."

I can't help but join in. "I heard Riley ain't been seen these last eleven months." Them fellows at the table set their eyes on me, including Melvin. I shrug a little. "I learned it on the *Queen*."

"What's the story on his claim?" Lord Avonmore says.

"There are many." The lawyer flicks a bread crumb from the table. "It's hard to believe any hold a thread of truth."

"What I've heard is Riley's happy to give it up, but first he wants a little fun," the farmer says. "The claim goes to the first person who can find it, but that's the hard part. There's some tricks, see? Riley's left some clues. All riddles."

"They're nothing but nonsense," the lawyer says. "One's about the temperature come sunrise."

So that clue Pickle Barrel spoke of really is about the temperature. *Nine below's the way to go.* Must get right cold on a Klondike morning.

The farmer cuts a hunk of bacon and wipes his knife on his sleeve. "Give us another clue. We'll decide if it's nonsense or not."

"*Gold on the bottom of the creek.* That's one. What sort of clue is that? Of course that's where the gold is. At the bottom of creeks. That's why we've got mining pans, to separate the gold from dirt and water."

I almost tell the lawyer what I heard, that nuggets also grow on trees and bushes. Mel sure don't believe it, Mr. Horton neither, but those fellows on the *Queen* knew all about it, so it must be true. But the thought of saying so makes my ears grow hot. It does sound strange that gold could be picked easy as apples. Maybe it's best to keep it to myself.

"Oh, and a final one," the lawyer says. "*Friday's the last chance to be lucky,* whatever that's supposed to mean."

"Where did you all learn this?" Lord Avonmore asks.

The lawyer shrugs. "Word gets around. They say the clues fit together in a certain order, a step-by-step guide to finding the claim."

The farmer whispers them riddles to himself again and again, like he wants to hold them in his memory.

Maybe me and Mel don't need to stake our own claim. If we could just find Riley's mine, we'd be set. Of course, we'd have to beat a whole bunch of other folks who hope to reach it first.

Lord Avonmore scoots back his chair. Mel stands when Mrs. Palmer approaches, and helps her stack the plates. I've been so caught up in the news on Riley, I got to gulp my last few bites. "Thank you," she says to Mel. "Could you also help me move the table?" She and Mel scoot it right against the curtain. Already men take off their shoes and settle on the floor.

"You ready for bed?" Melvin says.

Boy, am I ever. Twelve miles of walking, it's about done me in. We spread out best we can on the wooden boards, under rafters strung with muddy boots and socks that smell worse than a dirty dog. My own clothes have dried stiff as leather and got their own special scent. I can't get comfortable. Even though I'm tired, my mind's too busy to sleep.

Mel's got his nose deep in his mining book.

"I gotta find the outhouse," I whisper.

"You keep to yourself out there." Mel must still be thinking about that Grizzly fellow.

"I will. I promise."

I slip outside, and to keep my words honest, I find the outhouse first, then sit down on an old stump. The crickets sing, and the rain's let up long enough for the moon to show, just like at home. Except this place, it ain't nothing like I've ever seen before. In Kirkland, the wilderness has been pushed back. The woods that run along the mill hint at it, so does Mount Rainier in the distance, but mainly Kirkland's orderly. Alaska, though, it's overrun with untamed mountains and giant trees. They don't follow rules. They do as they please.

I ain't too fond of rules myself. This wild place fits me better than Kirkland ever did.

I've gotta get down everything I've learned about One-Eyed Riley and that claim of his, see it laid out plain. The moonlight's bright enough to work by, and I write on the edge of my newspaper page all I know:

1. Riley's an old coot. He's through with gold and ain't been seen for the last eleven months.
2. His claim is worth millions.
3. It's free to the person who finds it first. Oh, I hope no one's got it yet.
4. Pickle Barrel said Riley left five riddles to help a body along. Maybe he told them to others. Maybe he wrote them down or set them loose on the Yukon River or whispered them into the wind. The details ain't too

clear. But how's a fellow to know what's true and what ain't? Is five the right number of clues, anyhow?

5. That clue "nine below's the way to go" is about the temperature.
6. There's two more I've heard: "gold on the bottom of the creek" and "Friday's the last chance to be lucky."
7. Somehow the clues will fit together and lead a body, step by step, to One-Eyed Riley's claim.

Mrs. Palmer's laundry billows in a burst of wind that's downright chilly for the end of August. It brings me back to where I am. A camp partway up a mountain in Alaska, surrounded by folks eager for gold. I listen hard for words the gust might carry, secrets somehow left for me to find. But there ain't nothing.

I read them clues once more. A temperature. Gold in a creek bottom, where the lawyer says all gold's found. A lucky day of the week. What's so special about Friday? Maybe it's gotta reach nine below zero before a body can find Riley's claim. I need to learn as many clues as I can between here and Dawson City, so that once we arrive, I can jump in and find that mine.

On the other side of this darkness is the Chilkoot Pass, the highest point Mel says we'll have to go. Three steep miles from here in Sheep Camp, at a place called the Scales, is where the climb gets serious. From there it's another two and a half miles straight to the top. As hard as today's been, it's simple compared with what's ahead.

There ain't much room left on my paper, though there's one more thing I gotta get down. It's the truest thing I've ever known.

8. Me and Mel need Riley's mine more than anyone.

Who else out here's got no supplies, no money, and no home? I gotta find all them clues. I gotta convince Mel that Riley's mine is our best chance to make it on our own.

# Chapter 6

"*Jasper.*" Mel touches my shoulder. "It's time to leave if we want to beat the snow."

Did Mel say snow? Maybe I'm still dreaming, because when I went to sleep, it was summer outside.

The floorboards rattle underneath me and voices boom above, like near about everyone hopes to make an early start.

"When you sit up, go as slowly as you can."

I raise myself up on one elbow. It's more than I can take. "Feels like a wagon rolled over me and shattered all my bones."

Mel don't look like he's slept a wink. "Once we're moving, it won't be so bad. At least that's what I hope."

I sit outside the Palmer House as Melvin gathers up

his things. The farmer said Sheep Camp's the last place we'll see any trees on this side of the mountain, that from here on out it's too high for them to grow. For a moment, the fog clears off the peaks, where men tiny as ants trail through the snow.

That'll be me and Mel later today. We don't got any provisions, and aside from Melvin's piece of canvas, nothing to protect us when night falls.

Mel signals it's time to go, and we fall in with them who leave Sheep Camp. Twelve miles scaling the foothills of a mountain and a night on a wooden floor have left me sore all over. It takes a good mile before my legs loosen up enough that not every step is awful. At first the air is sweet, and here and there purple flowers hang on tight to the mountain's rocky side. But that's as welcoming as it gets. What we walked yesterday ain't nothing compared with this steep climb. Snow ain't falling yet, but patches of white already dust the ground. We get a little higher, and it ain't long before everything is blanketed in a smooth, clean layer. It's hard to know where to step. Yesterday, when the rain let up, I was downright hot. Today the fog's so thick, water droplets cling to my hair. It's cold enough that my teeth chatter.

"Here's the plan." Mel's words come short and choppy as he fights to catch his breath. "We'll reach the summit. Spirits will be high. Surely someone will want to partner with us."

His voice holds the kind of hope Mama's offered when I first got the influenza, when she hummed a lullaby and promised the aches would pass. Later, I called and called for her, but she weren't the one who answered. Someone unfamiliar with a cool, damp cloth tended to me instead.

The memory hits so fast, I gotta shake my head to knock it loose. It ain't something I want to dwell on. I gotta focus on what's here in front of me.

It's near impossible to see through fog when my glasses are fixed up normal, but with this broken lens, things are double hard. I stay close enough to Melvin I can grab his coattails when I start to slip. The men ahead of us weave in and out of my vision, like shadowy forms. It's the crunch of their boots on the snow that reminds me they're here, that we ain't alone.

"Everybody on the *Queen* was so excited to leave Seattle," I say, my breathing jagged. "I wonder what they think now."

"Bet they're glad they didn't know how hard it would be," Mel answers. "Otherwise they never would have gotten on that steamer."

That talk last night about One-Eyed Riley, it's still got me pepped up. "How come you didn't tell me you'd heard about Riley's mine, Mel?"

"I didn't see a reason. It's a good story, but that's it."

"We should search for it. It's got what we need."

Mel holds out his hand to help me over a tree that's

fallen on the path. "I'd rather stake my own claim than chase after some dream."

I stop once I'm on the other side, determined Mel will hear me out. "We don't got a tent. If Riley had such a wealthy mine, don't you think he'd have a cabin all set up from his years there? And if he's through mining, don't you figure he'd leave his gear behind?"

Hard work and luck. Mr. Horton and Melvin say that's what it takes to make it in the Klondike. Don't sound no different from what's needed to find a mine already stocked, one guaranteed to have plenty of gold.

"I don't want to rely on someone else," Mel says. "I've had enough of that."

Well, I ain't gonna give up on Riley just because Mel ain't with me yet. We got a long trip ahead of us with plenty of time to think. I'll do my part to make him come around.

The snow's been falling for an hour by the time we get to the Scales, where everything a body hauls is weighed before going on. Those who've used packers to carry their gear this far ain't gonna bail out now, and the packers, they're smart about it. Their rates go up to a dollar a pound. The place swarms with mules and horses turning back because they can't climb any higher. Outfits crowd up every space. The wind blows so hard, the snow blasts sideways. A fellow's gotta work just to keep his balance.

Has Mr. Shaw even made it to that first camp, Canyon City, with all his gear? Once he carries his whole outfit here, he'll have to break it up again, carry it bit by bit to the top of this mountain. Up there he'll have to find a place to stack his cache, then slide back down through the snow and mud. Over and over. Could take him months before he's through.

But he can afford to travel slow. He's got everything he needs.

We move past them who weigh their outfits and join in the snaking line of people that heads to the Chilkoot Pass. There ain't nothing gentle about this part of the mountain. It ain't just steep. From where we stand, it looks as straight as a wall.

How are we ever gonna get to the top? We should have taken that White Pass Trail, the one that's longer but don't climb as high.

The man in front of Melvin scoops up his dog, and even with it crying and wiggling around, he's able to carry it over his shoulders as he climbs. Guess even dogs can tell this journey is a load of trouble. The snow comes down fast, a swirling curtain of white, which cuts across my sunburned cheeks.

A slab of rock's embedded in the mountain's side, so flat and smooth beneath my feet, I can hardly keep from slipping. A few folks bend forward under the weight of their packs to hold their balance. Some take to crawling.

We're all so close, if one man was to stumble, he could knock the rest of us clear off this mountain.

"Mel!" I grasp his coat as my feet slip from under me.

Before I fall, Mel's got his hand wrapped around my wrist. "Let's get down on our knees," he says.

Rocks cut deep into my palms. Through my trousers and my union suit beneath, stones tear up my skin enough to turn it slick and bloody. After a time, I ain't able to tell what's blood, what's sweat, what's melted snow.

That dog ahead of Melvin whimpers. His owner stops to shift him on his shoulders and stroke his head, and like that we pass the both of them. The man's lost his place. He's left alone while the line of men moves on.

"Someone let me in!" I hear him shout. No one pays him any mind because manners and decency ain't part of climbing up a mountainside as steep and slick as this. He'll have to go down and start again.

I wish I knew how long ago we left the Scales to start this climb. The sky's so thick with clouds, the sun won't give me any clues, and I don't dare reach for Pa's watch when I've got need of both my hands.

It feels like all I've ever done is crawl up this mountain, dig in my toes to keep the wind from knocking me over. I shut my eye behind the broken lens to help me focus on Mel's shoes right in front of me, but one good eye ain't no match for all this blowing snow.

Finally, I stumble the last few steps to the summit. My

feet sink deep in snowdrifts up to my knees. Somehow the wind up here is even fiercer than it was below.

This mountain ain't no friend of mine.

"You okay?" Mel has to shout for me to hear him.

"I ain't going any farther, if that's what you're asking." I gonna rest right where I am, no matter that folks gotta step around me and ain't too happy about it. I won't take one step more.

"We can't stay here," Mel says. "There's no camp on the pass."

"I said I ain't going any farther. I gotta rest."

Mel points toward a pile of mining outfits heaped together. "Settle over there for now, out of the wind. I'll see how far the next camp is." He disappears into the crowd.

Bandannas and ratty socks whip around the ends of wooden poles, the only way to tell one cache from another. I slump against a pile, worn out worse than my holey socks. Pa's watch says it's nearly five o'clock, almost six hours since we left the Scales below, almost eleven since we left Palmer House in Sheep Camp.

A fellow in the crowd who's just made it to the pass stands out, a giant wrapped in furs that thrash his heels with every gust.

Grizzly.

He swings around, shouts directions at them Tlingits who carry his gear, and motions them over to the pile of outfits, which stacked as they are form a solid wall, a shelter from the storm.

Grizzly nearly steps on me with them enormous feet of his. I scoot over, pull my cap down enough to hide my face, but it don't work.

He knows exactly who I am.

"It's that eavesdropping brat. Should have figured you'd be somewhere underfoot." His dark eyes glare, the ends of his mustache blow across his face.

Grizzly points to my hand. "Where'd you get that fancy watch?"

I squeeze my fist shut. I don't want to answer, but what else can I do? "My mama gave it to me." I bite my lips to keep them from trembling.

He laughs and shakes his head. "You expect me to believe that? This Chilkoot Trail is full of crooks."

"You think I stole it?" Like that bald man he nabbed yesterday, like them thieves that work for Soapy Smith. My mind flies to him charging across the river back in the canyon, when he knew I'd heard him threatening Baldy. What would Grizzly have done to me if I hadn't taken off?

Grizzly sneers. "That's exactly what I think. You're a thief."

His words hit sharp. Because easy as that, they could be taken as truth.

Ain't no one gonna listen to a kid like me.

"It ain't stolen!" I can't help how fast I say it. A few of

them Tlingit packers who rest nearby look over. "It ain't," I say again, this time more quiet.

Grizzly's face says he don't believe me. "That's enough of a break," he tells his men.

The whole crowd follows his command. They file past, with Grizzly in the lead. Not until they're swallowed by the snow do I realize how hard I'm breathing, like I dodged some kind of threat.

I tuck in between the mining gear, as far from sight as I can get from folks like Grizzly. Farther off, the Mounties in their bright red coats swarm about, but they ain't come over to where I am. The vicious wind wails between the piles of gear and seeps clear down to my bones. I wrap my green muffler around my face so only my glasses peek out, turn up my collar to hold back the storm. My eyelids grow right heavy. It's been so long since I've had a decent sleep. The next thing I know, Mel's shaking me.

"Jasper, you awake?"

My eyes don't want to open. I hear a rustling sound, then feel Mel spread something heavy across my body and tuck it at my sides. His canvas wrap. "Lake Lindeman is eight more miles from here."

Mel's voice ain't hopeful like before, it's empty.

I force my eyes open.

"Not one person I've talked to is interested in a partner. All anybody wants is to help himself." Mel swallows, his gaze set far away on nothing. The wind has turned his cheeks red as radishes. "I can't force you to keep on, not without food and you so tired out. We'll stay here until morning."

"What about the Mounties, Mel?"

"We're still on the American side of the pass. Even if they did come by, all they'd see is a lumpy canvas stashed between these outfits."

We got no other option, since I'm too tired to go on. Me and Mel squeeze in together, best as we can.

Come sunrise, the storm has blown itself out. The sky's so clear, I finally see where we are. The Chilkoot Pass is the littlest dent of land cupped between two mountain peaks, a place that with the storm now gone has fallen silent. A couple clouds drift by, neighbors to the snowy mountains.

It's just a short stretch of land between here and Canada.

Me and Mel gather our things and begin through the pass. I want to remember every ridge and stone, compare them with what's on the other side, because surely things look different in another country.

We walk as far as a Seattle city block, and we're in Canada. Of course the mountain is as huge here as it was in Alaska. It's the same one we've been on since yesterday. But somehow in a few short minutes, we've crossed into somewhere entirely new. The snow beneath my boots don't feel any different, but oh, I'm right proud of what we've done, how far we've come.

Before Pa lost his job at the mill, sometimes he'd tell stories about when he was a boy, how he loved the mountains, how Mount Rainier felt like a friend. Whether sun glistened on its snowbanks or clouds hid it from view, he took comfort in the mountain being near. Sometimes he'd wonder what it would be like to stand on the highest peak.

Pa would love it here.

On this side of the Chilkoot, the steady stream of men is down to just a trickle. Mel drops his pack onto his little sled and I jump on behind. "Catch you down below!" I shout. The sled flies through the snow, and I wish Cyril could see me, up here on the top of this mountain clear over in Canada.

It ain't too long before we've left the snow behind. The trees return, and the trail winds down past lakes and endless slabs of stone pressed firm into the mountain. By afternoon we near Lake Lindeman, a tent camp set up on its shore. This here's where we'll stay for a week or two to build a boat, where surely we'll find a partner to sail with down the Yukon.

Me and Mel, we sit on his sled on the edge of camp. It's good to rest awhile.

Twenty-six miles we've hiked the past three days. Melvin says them folks on the *Queen,* if they make it over the White Pass Trail, will end up at Lake Bennett, seven miles farther on.

Lake Lindeman's in a valley with mountains all around. Tents set up on the scrubby shoreline ring the big blue lake. Everywhere there's pines. Men bustle about, cutting down trees and sawing logs. I wonder if there's one fellow here who's ever built a boat before.

"So," Mel says, standing up, "it's time I find us a partner."

My brother's got two scrawny arms and a narrow back. Sure, he worked at the wool mill two years, but he never used his hands. His book learning's so good, he was hired to keep numbers in a ledger. With no tools of our own, there ain't no way we'll get to Dawson and the goldfields just beyond without someone else's help.

"You gonna offer to pay him later?" I ask.

Mel's mouth is set in a determined line. "I'll offer what we've got. Hard work, and gold, once we get some. And your laundry."

I'll do all sorts of wash if it means we'll get shelter and a boat ride down the Yukon. "Well, I aim for us to eat tonight. I'm gonna start a laundry by the lake. How about you meet me there once you find that partner?"

Mel nods. "Let's hope I find him quick."

I weave between the tents and set up near the lake, where the ground is covered in sticks and brambles. It takes a while to clear a spot. "Want some wash done?" I ask anyone who passes by. Most ignore me. Some laugh. Out loud.

One man stoops to fill a bucket. "I got one shirt to my name. Not about to leave it with you," he says.

I sit back on my heels, keep at my question. "Need some washing?" But no one listens. A whole hour passes. Then another. I don't mind saying I'm discouraged. Men who surely need some laundry have ignored me. What I wouldn't give to have some fresh clothes of my own. But with my knapsack long gone, all I've got are the dirty things I wear.

Wait a minute. Maybe folks ain't interested in my laundering because I ain't too clean myself.

There's only one way to solve that problem. It ain't gonna be a pretty sight, but if I want supper, I gotta swallow my pride. I strip down to my underdrawers, a gray union suit that's gone pink around the knees from crawling up the Chilkoot. I dip my clothes in Lake Lindeman and scrub them good on Mama's washboard. Oh, it's fine to see them rinse so nice and clean.

I'm setting my clothes on a sun-warmed rock when an old man happens by. His shoulders are stooped and his silver hair's so greasy, I bet he ain't washed it since the days it was its natural-born color.

I sit up straight, try to act dignified, despite what I wear. "Jasper Johnson's Laundry Service. One item for ten cents or three for a quarter dollar. See how fine I've washed my shirt and trousers?" I point to where they dry. "I could do the same for you."

"I don't got any coins. Will you take gold instead?"

This man's got gold? "Oh, I'd be right fine with that." I hope my voice ain't gone squeaky like some silly girl's.

"Well, then," the old man says, "how about you wash these socks of mine." He unties his boots and pulls off his socks right there on the spot.

They're crusted with dirt and sweat and too much wear. Even when I dunk them into the water, they keep their stiffened shape. "Can I ask where you're from?" It's polite to talk to customers, but I'm also itching to know where this fellow's found his gold.

"Virginia, though I ain't been there for twenty years," he says. "I've mined since I left, first in Dakota's Black Hills, then in Colorado's Cripple Creek. Four years ago I traveled north to mine along them streams folks now call the Klondike goldfields."

My fingers prickle, and it ain't just from the cold lake water. "Your name ain't Riley, is it?" He's old, all right, but this sourdough's got two eyes, not one.

He looks me over, careful-like. "That story's made it down here?"

I can't hardly believe this. Here's an old-timer who knows of Riley, who's come straight from them goldfields where he mined. "I heard about One-Eyed Riley on a steamer from Seattle." I dunk them socks still shaped like feet into the lake and crush them against the washboard.

"Seattle. That's where you should have stayed," he says.

"What's that?" I stop my work. Surely I ain't heard him right.

He pulls a knotted handkerchief from his pocket and holds it in his palm. Inside the hankie is a bundle as big as a scoop of flour or a handful of dirt. "I gave my life to mining. This is all I got to show for it."

A huge shadow passes over me from behind. "Well, look who's here."

My heart jumps because I know that voice.

The sourdough nods curtly. "Frank Hazard. It's been a while."

I look from the sourdough to Grizzly. These two know each other?

"Old Joe. Last time I saw you was in them Colorado mines. So you're heading to the Klondike, too," Grizzly says.

But he ain't Grizzly, he's Frank Hazard. That name suits him better than fine.

"Oh no," Old Joe answers. "I'm leaving. I'm done with prospecting." He touches my shoulder with his gnarled hand. "Well, son, I'll be back in a little while to get them socks." Old Joe stomps his bare feet into his boots.

"If you're leaving your things with this boy, don't expect him to return them," Grizzly says.

"Now, why's that?" Old Joe asks.

"The boy's a thief. That's why."

"I ain't!" I bite down on my tongue to keep a flood of words from pouring out.

Old Joe runs a hand through his silver hair. "There ain't no reason for him to take my only pair of socks."

Frank Hazard watches after Old Joe as he shuffles off, then sets his eyes on me. "I don't know what you think you saw in that canyon on the Chilkoot Trail, but you're going to forget it."

I nod to show I'll disremember him dragging around a bald fellow who shouted he'd pay up for the food he stole.

Only what's so important that I need to forget?

"Did he pay you back?" I want my words to sound brave, but they hang in the air, crooked and wrong.

Frank crosses his arms over his chest. Them meaty things bulge like ham hocks. "He returned the side of bacon."

That ain't what I mean. "The man said he knew some things that might interest you." I regret them nosy words soon as they're out of my mouth.

Frank grabs me about the neck and swings at me. Fast. His fist slams into my arm, hard as a hammer driving a nail.

His eyes stare straight into mine. I can't hardly breathe. I shake bad as a wet dog.

"What he told me ain't your business. Don't you ever forget that."

"I won't." I can't barely speak, Frank holds me so tight. When he lets me go, I crumble to the ground.

Even after he's long gone, I feel his big hand at my throat, the throbbing place he punched me. My fingers shake as I push up the sleeve of my underdrawers. There's a knot, red and angry. Memories spark of how awful the last two years have been, recollections I thought I left in Kirkland.

"Excuse me," someone behind me says.

I near about jump out of my skin.

"How much for laundry?" The man's face is covered in mosquito bites, and where they haven't gotten him, the sun has baked him red.

I pull myself together best as I can. "Twenty-five cents an item," I say, because a few months from now we'll all be rich. What's a few more pennies to a man who'll soon be swimming in gold?

He don't question my price, just hands me some socks and shirts. "Bet my partner has some things he'd like washed up, too. You're the only person with a scrub board I've seen for weeks." He steps a little closer and peers at my arm. "Say, what happened to you?"

It's swollen good. "Nothing," I mumble.

I soak his things and tell him to come back in an hour. Finally, I got a moment to myself. I can put on my trousers, still damp but clean and fresh.

• • •

"Frank Hazard did that to you, didn't he?"

The question startles me. I nearly drop the clean shirt I'm setting out to dry. I thought I was alone. I glance over my shoulder to see who's there.

Old Joe. He's so light on his feet without them crusty socks, I don't hear him till he's right next to me. I roll down my sleeve right quick. There's no reason to tell him what happened. I don't need any more trouble from the likes of Frank.

"Frank's a nasty fellow. I'd stay clear of him, if I was you."

Oh, he can count on that.

"In Cripple Creek, Frank felt cheated by any man who found more gold than he did."

"It's kind of strange you ran into him out here in Alaska."

"Not strange at all," Old Joe says. "When news of a gold strike hits, a lot of prospectors leave their claims in search of a better opportunity. I've known men every place I've mined."

I hand him his socks, real pleased with how they've softened. When Old Joe gave them to me, I thought they were brown, but they're closer to the color of fresh cream.

"You've done a good job." Old Joe unties the corners of his hankie and dips his fingers into a fine gold powder. I ain't never seen anything so amazing. "Is there something you can put this in?"

All I got is my newspaper. I tear off a corner and hold it out. Old Joe sprinkles a pinch of gold right in, and I twist that bit of paper tight. It looks a lot like Old Joe's knotted hankie.

"Why are you leaving the Klondike?" I can't help but ask.

"Mining's hard and I'm older now. Like most men, I never found much."

"That can't be right," I blurt out. "What about all them prospectors on the *Portland* fairly weighed down with gold?"

"It most surely is, son. Those men on the *Portland* were the lucky ones." His blue eyes keep with mine. "It's best you know that going in."

I watch Old Joe as he walks away, hoping he might turn and say he got things mixed around, that almost every fellow finds more gold than he needs. I wait till he ain't nothing but a tiny speck, his back the last part of him I see.

The sun reaches far across Lake Lindeman before I'm through with all my work.

It's been a long while since I've seen Mel, and the more time passes, the lower I feel. He ain't found someone to partner with, otherwise he'd have come and told me. I can't shake them words of Old Joe, neither, that it ain't usual to find a lot of gold. That makes Riley's mine all the more important. Oh, why didn't I ask him if he'd heard any clues?

I strap on my washboard and leave the shore, walk from tent to tent to see if someone might sell some supper for a couple coins or a pair of rubber boots. But no one's home. Not one cook pot's boiling, because them fire pits are cold ash. Though it's gotten late, the sun's still up, and that means everyone's still working on their boats.

I leave the tents, head to the woods where folks cut down trees and assemble boats. It don't take long to spot Mel wandering from one crew to the next. He says something, and they listen respectfully, but when he's finished, they shake their heads.

I don't got the heart to hear just yet that Mel's found no one to take us in. So I search for a place that ain't too damp under an enormous pine and clear branches from this spot where we'll spread the canvas for another night alone.

# Chapter 7

Smoke rests low in the valley and morning sunlight stretches through the pines as Mel folds the piece of canvas. The smoke drifts from nearby cook fires, carrying with it the smell of frying bacon. Our last meal was supper at the Palmer House two days ago.

"I'll buy us breakfast," I say, and trust that Mel follows me through the tents packed tight together in messy rows.

My laundry money gets us two biscuits stuffed with bacon from a fellow who's right friendly, but as soon as Mel brings up partnering, he shakes his head. "Everyone in Lindeman City has found someone to team with or has hired on some help, far as I can tell. But seeing as you're desperate, you could try the Therouxs." He points down the crooked path between the tents.

Mel's eyes brighten in a way I ain't seen for days. "How will we know who the Therouxs are?"

"You can't miss them. I promise you that."

We pass folks who've just woken up and others who've gathered around fires set to have a meal. All's hush and quiet.

Then there's an awful clang and solid thunk. A cook pot rolls in front of us, bumps against Mel's shoe. Brown water thick as mud clings to its rim.

"Boy, didn't your ma teach you anything?" someone shouts. "That ain't how you boil coffee."

A man leaves a campsite set back between the trees. He's got a graying beard, the out-of-control kind that's kissing cousins to the hairs that sprout from his ears. His belly sits right on top of his trousers. Suspenders bend around it on their way to his shoulders. Though he's an old codger, he snatches up the cook pot like a spry young man. "What are you boys staring at?" he says with a scowl.

"Mr. Theroux?" Mel asks.

"I'm Theroux. What of it?"

Here's our chance! "We really need to partner up." Them words of mine leap out before I even know I've said them.

"What my brother means," Mel says, "is if you'd consider partnering with us, I'd help you build your boat. I'll pay you for your trouble once we stake our claim. And Jasper here could cook and do some laundry."

"We don't got gear to weigh your boat down, neither," I say.

"Jasper." Melvin squeezes my wrist. "Let me handle this."

But it's me Mr. Theroux inspects like a farmer after a brand-new cow. "Them's some strange glasses you got there."

I push the frames back up my nose. "They broke in Skagway."

"You know how to boil coffee?"

That's something Mama taught me years ago. "Yes, sir. I'm right good at it."

Mr. Theroux moves on to Mel. "You ever worked in a saw pit before?"

"Well, no," Mel says, "but I'll learn quick."

I ain't sure what a saw pit is, unless it's them platforms set up all over camp meant to hold a log off the ground. One fellow stands on the platform above and one below, and both grip the ends of a long whipsaw between them. They push and tug the whipsaw through that log with all their might. It ain't easy. Sharp words fly thick as sawdust between them who work the pits.

"Hmm," Mr. Theroux says. Around his neck is the filthiest kerchief I've ever seen, stained with tobacco juice and who knows what else. Probably been there since he left home, keeping that scraggly beard of his company. "Follow me." He heads beneath them pines. "Stanley!" he calls. "You'd better come out."

We skirt around the coffee splattered on the ground. Mel wears a goofy smile, and I bet I look the same. Finally, someone's willing to take us on. Oh, we're fit to burst.

A boy with a jumbly set of arms and legs stands at the entrance of their tent. His cheeks are covered with them pimples some fellows get. He's a couple years younger than Mel. "Who are these two, Uncle?" he says, real wary.

I best speak up, since Mr. Theroux don't even know our names. "I'm Jasper, and that's my brother, Mel."

"These boys want to pair up with us." He puts a hand on his hip, which makes that belly of his poke out as round as the cook pot he still clutches. "Listen here," Mr. Theroux says. "If Stanley and I like what you got to offer, we might let you stay around till Dawson City."

That don't sound promising. Do them Therouxs plan to let us start the journey down the Yukon River only to leave us on the bank whenever it strikes their fancy?

I glance at Mel, but he's still grinning. "We thank you kindly," is all he says. Could be he's so happy we've finally got a partner, he ain't focused on the fact it's on a trial basis. Or maybe he's been hypnotized by that strange beard on the mister's face.

"You're in charge of coffee now." Mr. Theroux thrusts the cook pot at me. "Get some boiling. We'll want it soon."

He throws his arms around Mel's and Stanley's shoulders. "Well, boys, we best get to the pit."

The three of them disappear beneath them stately trees. Mr. Theroux tries to whistle "Oh My Darling Clementine." He don't get one note right.

I stroll toward the big blue lake, the cook pot under my arm. For once, things are looking up. Me and Mel, we got full bellies and a couple brand-new partners. Tonight we even get to sleep in a tent.

The air's spiced with pine needles, and the clear sky's spread wide over Lake Lindeman. I ain't ever seen a more perfect morning. Surely Mel and the Therouxs won't need coffee straightaway. They're just getting started in the saw pit. So I got some time to explore and get back to them Riley clues.

The thing is, I've got an idea. Write down what I learn. Think and think what it might mean that Riley whispered clues into the wind and sailed them on the Yukon River. Because here's something that's a fact: stories can get knotted up like thread, but if you're patient, you can pick them apart, unravel them until you find the truth inside.

How did Riley sail them clues? Did he write them out and drop them in the currents? Paper ain't nothing but a soggy mess once it touches water. Maybe Riley sealed his riddles in jars or bottles before he set them free. The guidebook Mel's been reading says the Yukon flows north.

So there ain't no way those clues could be down here, south of Dawson.

Unless.

Maybe One-Eyed Riley traveled upstream when he left town. Maybe he waited till he was far from Dawson and released his clues along the way. Didn't Pickle Barrel say something like that when we were on the *Queen*? Riley could be like them kids in that fairy story Miss Stapleton told us who left a bread-crumb trail. Could be he dropped his very last clue right here, in Lake Lindeman, before he hiked over the Chilkoot and on to Dyea.

On my hands and knees, I search for an object that might have washed up onshore. A glass jar's what my mind's set on, but I'll take anything that feels out of place.

Them Riley clues run through my head as I push aside the branches of them thorny bushes near the lake. *Nine below's the way to go. Gold on the bottom of the creek. Friday's the last chance to be lucky.*

They don't make any sense. What I gotta do is think of patterns in them clues, let my mind work over them as my eyes are busy exploring.

Nine below. Gold on the bottom. Below and bottom are words that are almost the same, but them two clues don't fit together. One's about a temperature and one's about a creek.

Something's stuck under a piece of wood that don't look like it belongs. I dig it out, but it's just a dirt-caked spool with the thread long gone. It could float, all right, but there ain't no message on it, no way to prove that it was once Riley's.

I search the bank while I go over them clues. *Nine below's the way to go.* That one's got the number nine. *Friday's the last chance to be lucky.* That one ain't about numbers, but if I look at it different, flipped over and turned inside out, I could count from Sunday until I landed on Friday. The sixth day.

Below. Bottom. Nine. Six. Do them patterns mean something?

I'm so wrapped up in what I'm doing, I don't notice how far I am from camp. I check Pa's watch and see over half an hour's passed. Besides that spool I ain't found nothing other than a broken button.

The coffee should be boiling, and I ain't even gotten water yet. My first task for the Therouxs, and already I'm behind.

I run to where I first reached the lake and fill the cook pot to its brim. Once I'm at the Therouxs' tent, I set it over the coals and dig through their supplies in search of coffee. Oh, they've got a fine stash of food. Bacon, flour, cornmeal, rice. Oatmeal, butter in a can, and even dried-up fruit. There's also something called compressed soup, which I set aside. That's gonna be the first thing I'll make come dinnertime.

Soon the pot of coffee's boiling, its rich, warm smell right homey. I carry the Therouxs' cups in one hand, the cook pot in the other. Their saw pit's set back a ways, and I pass a fair number of men who tug their sharp-toothed saws through sturdy logs, thirsty fellows who call out for a taste of coffee.

"I'd give you a dime for just one swallow," says a fellow with his sleeves rolled up, his forearms damp with sweat and coated in layers of sawdust.

It's awful hard to shake my head. "It ain't mine to sell. It's for the Therouxs."

"Pull harder!" A shout rings out, as mean as poison. "I can't saw this log alone." The words are loud enough to set a flock of geese to flying high above the treetops.

"You'd better hurry, then," says the fellow with the rolled-up sleeves. "The Therouxs have been howling like that all morning."

It ain't easy moving fast with a sloshing pot of coffee, but I hustle best as I can. Them voices grow louder. The Therouxs' saw pit's in a clearing with no one nearby, no one but Mel, who's down below, watching, near a pile of wood that's been hacked to pieces. I think them things are meant to be planks, but they look more fit for a campfire. The elder Theroux stands on the raised platform, high as if he balanced on another man's shoulders. He's got a log between his feet. A whipsaw hangs from one hand, and he points with the other at the younger Theroux beneath him. "It ain't acceptable to force an old man to do all the work. And me with my rheumatism."

Stanley grips the saw's other end. "Are you saying I don't do my share?" He jerks it hard enough that the saw flies from Mr. Theroux's hand and clatters to the ground. "You sure wouldn't get much done if I weren't here."

Oh, what is Stanley Theroux doing? He ain't much younger than Mel, so why's he talk to his uncle like that? Even I'd never dare be so ornery with Pa.

In all my days, I ain't never seen a family like this one.

Stanley strides off, his long arms swinging. Mr. Theroux shouts for him to come back, but it ain't until Mel calls out that he turns around. Them two talk together for a moment, and Mel says something to calm him down. Keeping the peace. Mel's had lots of time to practice that at home with Pa.

Mel sees me coming. "Coffee's here!" he calls. Them Therouxs dip their cups into the cook pot. Sawdust falls from their arms and floats across the coffee's surface, which don't bother them at all.

Mel waits to take a drink. He don't talk with his mouth, but his eyes speak plenty. No wonder nobody in this whole camp wants to work with the Therouxs, they say. Them two are awful to each other. 'Course Mel would use his fancy words, ones Miss Stapleton would approve of.

Stanley climbs the stand, set to take his uncle's place

and yank the whipsaw upward. Mr. Theroux fills in below. Mel stays near them pitiful boards piled on the ground. He looks like he ain't sure what to do. They push and pull that saw maybe four times more before the crowing starts again, this time in reverse.

"You got sawdust in my eyes!" Mr. Theroux yells.

"Put some muscle in it," Stanley throws back.

"It's been like this all morning," Melvin whispers. "No wonder nobody else set up saw pits near them. I don't know how they did anything before I came along. It's only when I took up the saw earlier that any real work was done."

Two weeks to build a boat is what Mel says it takes, a couple more to sail from Lindeman downriver to Dawson City, if them Therouxs let us stay on. That's a lot of bickering between now and then, a lot of soothing ruffled feathers for Mel.

"Soup and biscuits will be ready in a couple hours," I call out.

I'll do all I can for them to keep us on from here till Dawson City.

Each morning over the next two weeks the sun arrives a little later and sets earlier than before. While daylight lasts, men labor in the saw pits. Come sunrise, some gather at the shore to sail off in fresh-made boats. And every day, more men trail down from the Chilkoot Pass, add to the numbers camped along the lakeside.

When I ain't doing chores, I walk as far around Lake Lindeman as I can. I search the ground for anything that feels out of place, that could have once been Riley's.

The only things I've found have been a rusty razor and an empty flour sack.

Mel's done his best to hold them Therouxs together, and if all goes well, today they'll finish the raft, the only type of boat they've been able to make. It took three tries and a lot of Melvin's coaxing to get them this far along. Mr. Theroux has rested these last few days while Mel and Stanley cut and carried and lashed them logs together. It's real interesting how his rheumatism kicks in just when heavy labor's needed.

The Mounties here in Lindeman City urge everyone to build their boats long and strong and sturdy, and the sorry raft ain't that, but it's all we got.

Tomorrow, we'll be the ones leaving for the Klondike.

It's rained off and on all morning. Still I'm right occupied with laundry. After two weeks sleeping in the Therouxs' fouled-up tent, I finally persuaded the mister to let me wash that slimy kerchief he keeps wrapped around his neck, and oh, I'm looking forward to a night without my nose tucked in the crook of my arm. Mel and Stanley, their clothes ain't too much fresher, from all their boat work, and I take pride in how everything washes so clean. Once them things are strung up to dry, they serve as good advertising. It ain't long before other folks, including a couple ladies and even a Mountie, ask for my services.

Frank drags his boat to the shore nearby, a fine-looking scow. Word is he paid a couple of his Tlingit packers to stay on a little longer and help him build it. He's still wrapped in that fur coat. Sure, it's cooler than when we got here, but not enough to stay dressed up like a bear. I ain't seen him in a while, and I've been better than fine with that.

"I see you paired with them fool Therouxs," he says when he notices me. "No one else in camp can abide being near them."

It ain't just their fighting nobody likes. It's the way Mr. Theroux treats the other Stampeders, like he's an expert and they don't know a dern thing. But I don't want to talk with Frank Hazard, not now, not ever.

The Mountie whose wash I've done hurries over. "I've called a meeting everyone must attend. The whole camp's to report to the shore five minutes from now." When he rushes off, he don't even remember to take his laundry with him.

Soon dozens of men cram in close, where a few moments ago it was only me and Frank. Where's he gone? Being so tall and thick it's usually hard to miss him, but I don't spy him anywhere.

Mel and them Therouxs stand on the outer edge. I can't quite tell with my ruined glasses, but it seems like Melvin's searching for me. When our eyes meet, he gives a little nod.

The Mountie hoists himself on a fallen log so all might see him. "I'll get right to it. We've had a theft reported in camp. This gentleman here is missing gold." He helps an old man step up, his gray hair slick and shiny. It's the sourdough who quit the goldfields to go home to Virginia. Old Joe.

Fellows shift on their feet and glance at their neighbors, the ones they work alongside every day and camp by at night, because the truth is anybody could have taken Old Joe's gold.

I crane my neck. Where is Frank Hazard?

The Mountie says if he has to, he'll search every tent in camp.

I ain't seen that bald fellow in the derby since Frank pulled him through the canyon, but I know he's a thief, a hungry one, if he stole a side of bacon. Maybe he's lurking at Lake Lindeman, waiting for the chance to get his hands on other people's things.

After the meeting ends, the Mountie keeps his word. He goes from tent to tent, starting near the shore and moving farther back. It's almost dark when he reaches ours, but he's prepared for that. The Mountie's got a lantern to rely on as he combs through all the gear and makes us empty our pockets. Mr. Theroux pulls out a couple nails and some chewing tobacco. Stanley holds a broken twig and a hankie. Mel's pockets don't got nothing.

I didn't steal Old Joe's gold, but I've got a pinch of it. Will the Mountie believe me? I hold the twist of paper in my cupped hand and hope he'll hear my words as true. "I got this from Old Joe himself when I washed his socks. He paid for his laundry in gold dust."

The Mountie nods. "What else is in your pockets?"

I show him the soap, the newspaper and pencil, and Pa's watch. If it weren't for Melvin vouching for me, I ain't sure the Mountie would believe the timepiece is my rightful property.

Mr. Theroux's eyes flash with surprise and something else when he sees what I got. Soon as I can, I shove everything deep into my pockets. Here we are, two boys who said we don't got much, with an extra-fine timepiece and a pinch of gold. I ain't comfortable with our partner knowing we could pay him for his troubles now.

But Mr. Theroux don't ask about it. "Come, boys," is all he says. "We best turn in. We've got a big day ahead of us tomorrow."

I ain't sure if that gold is ever found. But I do know this. When we cast off in the morning, the boat that belongs to Frank is already gone. I ain't saying Frank Hazard stole Old Joe's gold, at least not outright. But it's real strange how quick he was to disappear yesterday, when the Mountie called that meeting. And now his boat ain't here at the shore.

Melvin and Stanley start the first shift of rowing. The Therouxs shout farewell and wave to them that labor back at camp in a way that's downright friendly. If I didn't know better, I'd think them old chums with everyone at Lindeman. Mr. Theroux must be so excited to get going, he ain't as prickly as normal. And Stanley, well, he's relaxed. He don't cringe like he's waiting for a scolding. He's got no reason to talk back. It's a peek at what he'd be like if Mr. Theroux were a different kind of man.

Our raft skids past a fellow who floats in a mess of nailed-together packing crates, and them Therouxs don't crack a joke about how long the thing's gonna last (not even the seven miles to Lake Bennett, we find out soon enough). They don't even snicker about them ladies who've rigged up petticoats as a sail. There ain't many women Stampeders, and most of them have husbands. But these two are out here on their own. Even with their laundry dangling from their mast, their boat glides as grand as the *Queen* compared with our sorry raft.

My mind keeps drifting to Frank Hazard and how he lit out like he did. Maybe he didn't steal that gold. He could have forced Baldy to steal it for him and the two took off together. Baldy sure acted like he'd do anything for Frank as long as he didn't turn him in. But that don't make a lot of sense. With that fancy coat and string of Tlingit packers, Frank ain't hurting when it comes to money, far as I can tell.

But Old Joe did say that Frank couldn't stand it when a fellow found more gold than him. What if seeing Old Joe and his hankie full of gold was enough to set Frank off? He could have swiped it out of spite and left Lindeman quick as that.

I spread out as much as I can on the crowded raft, tuck my arms behind my head, study them slender trees along the shore with leaves that flame yellow and the endless parade of folks who stream through the Chilkoot Pass. We're lucky to be leaving in the middle of September, a week or two before winter creeps in. With a couple weeks to build a boat, how many people only now reaching Lindeman will make it out before ice forms on the lakes and rivers?

Mel whistles as he pulls the oars. Stanley tries to follow, but he don't hold a pucker right. Them two ain't exactly friends, but they get along together fine, almost as good as Mel did with some of them fellows at the mill.

Stanley ain't the quickest boy. Mel said it sometimes took a few tries for him to understand how to build the raft, but there ain't no harm in that. I'd take a heap of Stanleys any old day over his uncle Theroux.

We ain't had much sun for days, just spitting rain and misty clouds, and this bit of sunshine is a treat. I wonder what Cyril's up to back at home. Surely he's at school.

Miss Stapleton's probably got him practicing elocution, say-ing-ev-ery-syl-la-ble while she taps along with her ruler for them words with extra-long parts. That work Miss Stapleton had us do, it never meant nothing to me but words and nonsense, stuff that don't matter in the least. Adding turnips, saying isn't instead of ain't, finding Belgium on a map, none of that did me a lick of good. I'm finished with schooling, and that's a fact.

Oh, I wish Cyril could see this place. We'd bring in loads of fish from Lake Lindeman if we ever had the chance. Out here in the open is a hundred times better than some stuffy old schoolhouse. The rain these past few days has given the air a crispness like the whole world's been washed clean. I ain't tied down. I get to decide what's important and what's not, and it sure ain't Miss Stapleton's silly lessons or tiptoeing around Pa.

No one's ever gonna be the boss of me again. Riley's gold will see to that.

"When I get some gold," Stanley says, "the first thing I'm gonna do is pay someone to draw me a nice, hot bath."

That sounds real fine. The closest any of us have come to washing up these last two weeks is a bowlful of water from Lake Lindeman.

"And then I'll order me a sandwich and a plateful of eggs. That's what I miss most about home, a good plateful of eggs cooked up over easy." Stanley's eyes go dreamy, like them eggs are set before him now.

"When me and Mel get rich, I'm gonna celebrate by taking the whole day off. Imagine an entire day without a bit of work."

"What about you, Mr. Theroux?" Mel asks. "What do you want to do with your gold?"

"My old partner, he always said, 'Don't count your gold before you got it, Theroux,' so I try not to think like that."

"Where was it you mined?" I ask. "Was it in Colorado, at that place called Cripple Creek?" I'm proud I remember where Old Joe and Frank met. For once Mel ain't the only Johnson boy who knows a little something about the mining life.

He strokes his grizzled beard. "In Fortymile, I partnered with Salt Water Jack. You boys ever heard of him?"

Melvin shakes his head. "You were in Canada before?"

"Of course," he says.

I wonder why Mr. Theroux's never told us that.

"Where's Fortymile, Mel?"

"It's a mining town not far from Dawson City. Remember Mr. Shaw back in Dyea? He said hardly anybody stuck around in Fortymile once gold was discovered on Bonanza Creek."

Bonanza, that creek where the first nugget was found, the place that stirred up everything.

Mr. Theroux's got a wistful look in his eye. "Yessiree, that Salt Water's one of the best Fortymile's ever seen. Me and Salt Water mined alongside Buckskin Miller and Pete the Pig. The four of us was right close. I trusted them boys with my life."

I gotta bite my tongue to keep from laughing. Mr. Theroux worked with some critter from a barnyard?

"Last summer when the word got out about that Klondike gold, Buckskin, Salt Water, and Pete rushed over to stake a claim. They promised me a share of whatever they got. On account of my rheumatism, I went home to Omaha to fetch this one." Mr. Theroux pokes a dirty thumb straight into Stanley's chest. "My second set of hands. We left Omaha a few days after them steamers arrived in San Francisco and Seattle with the gold. Once we make Dawson, the five of us will work that claim together."

"Good thing you're out here now," Mel says. "I'd hate to be caught on the shores of Lindeman during freeze-up."

"Freeze-up?" Mr. Theroux sounds confused. "What's that?"

"You know, when winter starts in."

"Could happen in the next few weeks," I say.

"Oh, that." Mr. Theroux nods. "Freeze-up ain't so bad."

What can he mean? Word is them at Lake Lindeman and Lake Bennett better finish their boats quick if they want to reach Dawson before next spring.

Mel pulls the oars, with his eyes on Mr. Theroux. "I've read in my guidebook about Fortymile's early days," he says. "How an empty cabin was available to anyone, as long as a person passing through remembered to chop wood for the next fellow. And when new gold was discovered, it was never kept secret. Folks talked about it openly. Everyone kept an eye out for each other and helped when they could. The Miner's Code, they called it."

Mel's learned a whole bunch these last few weeks. I can't help but feel a bit of pride in my Klondike partner.

"So I was wondering," Mel says, "has the Miner's Code changed any with the big discovery in the Klondike?"

Mr. Theroux scratches his gut where the bottom button of his shirt is missing. He stares at Melvin hard, like he ain't real fond of those facts Mel's learned. "Here's the thing, boys. Mining's easier when you've got a team."

That ain't exactly what Mel asked, but I understand Mr. Theroux's meaning. Like Mama used to say, any task is sweeter with another pair of hands.

"See," he continues, "when you got more than one set of eyes on a claim, it's easier to get the gold. Take me and Salt Water Jack. While he picked the nuggets off the bushes, I could focus on the trees."

Oh, I knew it. "I told you, Mel! It's true about them nuggets."

Mel's oar goes sort of wonky. He lifts it from the water, so for a moment, Stanley's the only one who rows. My brother leans in close as he can to Mr. Theroux, like he's waiting for something important. "Say, what are those winters like in Fortymile?"

"Tell them, Uncle, how it ain't as cold up north as some claim and how the sun stays out all night. Most of those harsh winter stories are told to keep new folks away."

"Sounds like you told them for me," he says.

Back home in Kirkland, the sun's pretty scarce in winter. Most days are cold enough to keep me hoping for the spring. How is it Fortymile stays so mild if Lake Lindeman and the Yukon start to freeze around the end of September?

Mel don't say nothing more. Instead he plunges his oar into the water and focuses on rowing. I don't know what he makes of Mr. Theroux's stories, but his face says he's thinking about what he's heard.

As for me, I ain't sure what to believe.

I've got my own question for Mr. Theroux. "Did you meet a fellow named One-Eyed Riley when you were here before?" If Fortymile's so close to the Klondike, it could be their paths crossed sometime.

"Riley?" Mr. Theroux says. "I ain't ever heard that name before, nor seen a man with one eye, neither. And I ain't one to ever forget a face." Mr. Theroux glares. "What's with all the questions, anyhow?"

"I heard of him," Stanley says. "He's the one who left the Klondike and said a lot of funny things. A man at Lindeman told me about him."

I'm real interested in that. "What did he say?"

"For one, Riley sure liked creeks."

*Gold on the bottom of the creek.* That clue fits with Stanley's words. I nod, hope he'll keep on.

"And he was fond of the end of the week. He thought Friday was lucky."

I nod again. That clue's familiar, too.

"For some reason, Riley fancied things low to the ground."

"Well, ain't that something," I say, because I noticed the same.

"He said hunker down but not too much."

I sit up straight. I ain't heard this clue before.

"Riley said those words?"

"He sure did. I remember because I wondered what that means. How much hunkering down would be too much?"

"If anyone should hunker down, it's you," Mr. Theroux says, just as cranky as can be. "The more you talk, the slower you row."

Stanley dips his oar and works to hold the same pace as Mel.

Mel, he ain't said much, but that's probably because he ain't too fond of Riley.

When it's my turn at the oar, the sun reflects off the water in patches so bright, I have to squint to see where we're headed. No matter how hard I pull, no matter how far the raft glides forward, it feels like we're getting nowhere. Me and Mr. Theroux row till we can't make it any farther, then Mel and Stanley take over. I'm pretty sure this is the longest day since the world began.

"How about we stop there, Uncle?" Nobody's talked for hours, and Stanley's words sound strange in this great big empty wilderness. He points ahead where the mountains slope gently to the shore. The trees are colored in reds and yellows and greens, like a bundle of paintbrushes that ain't been rinsed.

"That'd be fine," Mr. Theroux says.

Mel and Stanley work them oars, and soon the raft thumps over the shallows. Mel wades out, and with a rope he guides us to the bank.

I'm ready to settle in and let my body rest, but Melvin won't have none of that. "Jasper and I will fetch some firewood," Mel calls to the Therouxs, "while you two set up camp."

On second thought, collecting wood's a great idea. Could be I'll get the chance to see if a Riley clue has washed ashore.

But Mel ain't interested in staying near the river. He heads toward the forest to gather twigs and broken branches. Soon we're deep in the woods. Trees blot out the setting sun. It's grown dark awful quick. We can't see camp no more.

"I'm not sure if you've noticed," Mel says, "but Mr. Theroux sure loves to talk."

"I've been on the same raft as you, Mel. Caught every single word."

"What I mean is he doesn't always make a whole lot of sense. Don't be quick to believe everything you hear."

"What he said about wintertime, it don't quite sound right. And also," I say, though I hate to do it, "that story about gold nuggets on the trees."

"That's it exactly," Mel says. "Just be aware."

Mel picks up branches scattered near his feet. "Get as many as you can," he says. "No sense in coming out again tonight if we don't have to."

My load's so big, I can't barely see around it, so I rely on Melvin's footsteps to lead me back. The wood clatters as I dump it near them Therouxs, who are bickering again. It seems they don't remember how to set up the tent. That buys me a little time to search for Riley clues once we get to camp.

"I'll just be a minute." I take my chance to race off to the shore. Oh, it's good to stretch my legs and be on my own, if only for a little while. The last rays of sunlight sparkle on the water, and pink clouds stream overhead, the same shade as a bonnet Mama once wore.

Mama. An ache rises in my throat.

I've gotta find Riley's mine. It's what's gonna make

things right. Mama wanted the two of us to be taken care of, and his mine will do just that.

Though I turn over stones and kick aside some broken limbs, I don't find nothing out of place.

"Jasper!" Mel calls. "The fire's ready. You need to get supper on."

So I return to camp. I ain't found nothing yet, but my list of clues has grown to four. Less than three weeks from now, when we reach Dawson City, we'll be a short walk from the Klondike goldfields and One-Eyed Riley's mine.

That sunny morning five days back when we pushed off from Lake Lindeman was our one bright spot between stretches of steady rain. We ain't seen a day like it since. Every night when we set up camp, Mel builds a blazing fire for a head start on the nighttime's chill, and this just three weeks into September.

We're one day out from Miles Canyon, the first set of river rapids on the Yukon, when that drizzle turns to snow. It comes heavy and quick, weighs down the evergreens along the riverbank and soaks through our clothes.

"Looks like my mining book was right about September snow," Mel says, real pleased with himself as he and Stanley row.

"Enough about that mining book," Mr. Theroux says.

Mel presses his lips together. I bet he won't say another word.

"I'm about fed up with this river." Mr. Theroux scowls at the three of us.

We got two more weeks of travel. A few days less, if we're lucky. They're gonna be real pleasant if Mr. Theroux keeps up like this. But he mellows when he sees something on the shore.

"Would you look at that fine specimen." He points to an enormous critter that lumbers through soggy drifts, its shaggy coat made for winter weather. "The cows here sure are big. Never have I had better meat or sweeter milk than from those cows in Fortymile."

The animal's antlers are wide as a wagon seat. Its muzzle reminds me of a horse. I cover my eye behind the broken lens, point my other toward the shore to make sure I see what I think I do. That ain't no cow. It's a moose, like the one that crashed past me and Cyril in the woods last fall.

Mel glances at the creature. Surely he'll tell Mr. Theroux he's wrong, but he don't say a word. Each day he's gotten more quiet till he don't hardly talk at all.

"That's a moose," I say for him.

"What's a moose?" Stanley asks.

"A wild animal that's cousin to the deer."

"I tell you, that's a cow." Mr. Theroux licks his lips. "What I wouldn't give for a fried-up steak."

I ain't ever been in Canada, but even I wouldn't mix up a moose with a cow.

"What I wouldn't give if you rowed some more," Stanley mumbles.

"Pardon me?" Mr. Theroux says.

"That rheumatism of yours." Stanley stops his oar, makes his voice bold and loud. "Never bothers you except when your turn comes around."

Mr. Theroux jumps up fast as a man who don't got any aches. The raft wobbles beneath us, and I hold on tight. "Ungrateful, that's what you are. And me, going all that way to fetch you back in Omaha. I brought you here to help me out. You ain't hardly done a lick of work."

The little raft pitches and bobs in the Yukon's mighty current. There's no room to stretch without bumping into someone, and there's no space to be alone. Like the sun that disappeared after our first day on the water, the Therouxs' good spirits dried up in a snap.

Oh, I'm ready to be somewhere else, without these two nearby.

When we stop for the evening, we all get to our chores. The Therouxs clear snow to lay out the tent. It took a few nights of fumbling, but they finally remembered how it works. Mel unloads the pots and pans. "Ready to fetch some wood?" I ask Mel long before he's finished.

I practically run between the trees and riverbank, I'm so eager to talk. Once we don't see them Therouxs no more, I'm certain they can't hear. "A cow! Mr. Theroux called that moose a cow!" I can't hardly hold my laughter in. "He ain't been here before, has he?"

"Nope," Mel says.

"So why would he pretend he has?"

Mel tucks a few pieces of dry wood under his arm. "He's up to something, though what I couldn't say. Best we play along."

I nod. "No sense in encouraging him to dump us on the riverbank."

The fading light leaves the woods in shadow. Between a slab of rock and the stump of a long-departed tree, something catches my eye.

"Wait a second, Mel."

I dust a bit of snow from the object. It's a glass bottle tinted with a hint of blue. Dirt clogs the bottle's neck and something's wedged inside! I tip and shake till it tumbles loose.

"What is it?" Mel asks.

"I ain't sure, but I sure hope it once belonged to Riley."

"Riley?" Mel says. "Why would he have left a bottle here?"

My cold hands fumble to grab the thing that's caked in dirt and not much bigger than my finger. "It's . . ." My heart beats strong. I shut my eye behind the broken lens to get a better look and use the corner of my shirt to wipe it clean. And just like that my heart slows with a thud. "It's the broken end of a spoon." I toss it over my shoulder as we move on.

"Why did you think that bottle could be Riley's?"

"Because of them clues. Riley sailed them down the Yukon. Maybe he wrote them on bits of paper and sealed them up in bottles. Could be he left clues from Dawson City to Lake Lindeman."

"Jasper," Mel says, but I cut him off.

"So that bottle ain't what I wanted it to be, but even so, I got four clues. *Nine below's the way to go. Gold on the bottom of the creek. Friday's the last chance to be lucky. Hunker down but not too much.* I ain't sure what they mean yet, and I don't know if they're real or fakes, but Riley left five clues behind, and I almost got them all."

"Jasper," Melvin says again, his face set with that practical look he's so good at.

"What?"

"Just don't get your hopes up." Mel speaks slowly, like I might not want to hear. "Our best bet is our own claim, not poking around for some old man's forgotten mine."

Mel's words don't hold any faith, like there ain't room for nothing in this world but proven facts.

"Don't see why we can't do both."

I focus on my rubber boots, how the snow under them gives gently with every step. "You wait until I find all them clues, Mel. It'll come together."

"You know what this reminds me of? When Mama died—"

I shove Mel so hard, he stumbles. The wood he holds clatters to the ground. "This is not like that."

Mel grabs my hand, forces me to stop. "Jasper, she died. She didn't leave us. Tell me you remember."

"You ain't supposed to talk about it. You ain't." I pound him with my fist.

Mel don't speak. He wraps his arm around me, rests his cheek on my head.

When I was sick, Mama cared for me, all day and through the night. But then she got the influenza, too. She died, Pa said.

How could I believe him when the quilt, the broom, the coffeepot stayed right where she had left them, as though she'd be home any minute? When her rocker was still angled how she liked it, set to catch the sunlight that raced across the wooden floor? When I never attended a funeral and Pa didn't cry for the longest time?

I whisper into Melvin's chest. "If Mama really died, wouldn't Pa have acted different?"

"Sadness doesn't always look the same," Mel says. "Remember what Mama told us when Cyril's mother lost her baby? 'Sometimes heartache cuts so deep, it tears a soul apart.'"

I take in the towering trees, the smell of pine sap sharp in the air, how steady Mel is right beside me.

"Mama would never have left. She loved us too much. Don't you ever forget that," he says.

"Mel and Jasper!"

The eerie call hangs in the night's empty spaces, echoes through the trees.

"Where are you?" Stanley calls.

We collect our branches and walk toward camp. Stanley happens on us, near the river's edge. "I thought you two had gotten lost," he says. The older boys talk together, but I don't listen. I'm remembering what Mel said. Mama would never have left. She loved us too much.

"Get over here now," a gruff voice shouts.

The three of us pick up the pace.

# Chapter 8

I hear them river rapids thunder like a thousand horses before I see the canyon. The Yukon's green waters hurry us toward walls of massive rocks alongside the riverbanks. Last night I tried to picture Miles Canyon, but my head couldn't imagine these sheer cliffs and the sound of rapids pounding so loud, it thrums in my chest.

Before they reach the canyon, the boats ahead of us gather along the Yukon's bank and men unload their outfits. They don't only unload them, they carry their gear up and over a snowy path, like they did on the Chilkoot Trail. Folks travel back and forth, saddled with belongings or retracing their steps to fetch some more. Mounties wave their broad-brimmed hats to show the new folks where to go.

"Greenhorns." Mr. Theroux shakes his head as though he feels sorry for them who walk the trail high above the currents carrying their gear. "Only men without experience on the Yukon choose to portage."

"Portage?" Stanley asks.

"Carry a boat to get around rough waters," Melvin says.

Mr. Theroux lifts his scraggly chin. "I'm real tired of them facts from your mining book. I could have explained just fine myself."

Mel stays quiet, his brown eyes on them rock walls growing bigger up ahead.

Stanley's voice wavers. "You mean we ain't gonna carry our raft and walk around them rapids like those men over there?"

The wind and currents are so strong, we don't need to row. The raft picks up speed, and we fly so fast, it feels like them enormous cliffs ahead have grabbed ahold and yanked us closer. Oh, my belly's knotted up.

"I don't want to stay on the river." Stanley's cheeks have lost their color.

"Well, you don't got that choice now, do you? We ain't going to portage; we're going to ride," Mr. Theroux says. "It will take them fellows at least a day to travel over Miles Canyon when it could easily take five minutes. A little bumpy on the rapids, sure, but not too bad."

"Let me off," Stanley pleads, and I'm right there with him. I don't want to stay on this raft a minute more.

Mr. Theroux acts like he don't hear a thing.

We're stuck on this flimsy raft, forced to ride through dangerous waters just because Mr. Theroux wants to act like he's sailed down the Yukon before.

The canyon walls grow steeper the nearer we get. How easily the racing Yukon could slam us into them! It ain't just the roar of water I hear. I can see white waves churn and thrash.

I grab Mel's wrist and don't let go.

If we keep on, we'll be bashed and broken, sucked under and destroyed.

A boat slips past us, then another, and at first I think they mean to brave the rapids. But both turn off to join the others on the shore.

"Mr. Theroux," Mel begins. "I'm not so sure this is a good—"

The mister points straight at my brother. "You, Melvin Johnson, got no respect for my experience."

My fingernails dig deep into Melvin's flesh.

"I ain't gonna drown!" Stanley stands, and the raft sways wildly beneath him. "I'll swim right back to Omaha if you don't let me off this raft."

"Greenhorns," Mr. Theroux says, but just before we slip past them boats on the riverbank, in the last moment before the cliffs swallow us whole, he dips an oar and turns. In a few swift strokes we push through the current and reach the shore. I ain't never been so happy to feel the bank bump beneath us. "Get out if you're afraid of a couple rocks and some rough water. I'm tired of the lot of you."

Me and Mel and Stanley grab our things and scramble out. Once Mr. Theroux pushes off, the raft shoots forward, bounces between boulders before a wave crashes overhead. After that, I don't see nothing. Did the wave pull the raft under or snap it clean in half?

Did Mr. Theroux wash overboard?

Stanley stares at the river. He don't move at all, like his toes have sprouted and put down roots. Mel has to pull him from the riverbank. "Come on," he says. "Let's go see what happened."

The three of us rush up the snowy path past men who've just arrived at the canyon. Some carry outfits and even empty boats. Others who've hauled their loaded boats from the river push them over sets of logs, which roll like wheels along the portage trail, and is it ever slow. As the boat inches forward, the last log must be carried to the boat's front end, so it can keep on with its rolling. We gotta dodge all of them. It's hard to match the older boys' pace and even tougher to see with only one good lens which bobbing jackets belong to Mel and Stanley.

I think I've lost the two of them. Mel and Stanley probably ain't noticed I'm not behind them anymore.

A man not far ahead strikes me as familiar. He pushes back his derby and scratches where his hair's supposed to be. Then he walks with hurried steps straight off the trail and disappears into the woods.

Baldy. The thief who might have taken Old Joe's gold.

Old Joe labored all them years just to have the last of his gold snatched away. It ain't right. My feet move on their own, not down the trail but after Baldy.

Sunlight filters through giant pines so big they block out the sky. The ground is steep and slick from dampened needles and patches of snow. I keep track of Baldy best I can, my eyes fixed on his hat, my feet quiet as a rabbit's. Has he robbed someone else and come out here to examine the loot?

Then a rough hand covers my mouth.

Jerks me back.

I land against someone solid as a tree trunk.

An awful feeling spreads through my chest.

"Here he is again, the kid who can't keep to himself, minding everybody's business but his own."

Frank Hazard's got ahold of me. Mel and Stanley don't know where I am. Oh, I'm in a heap of trouble.

I gotta keep my head.

"Come on out, Albert. Looks like we've got ourselves a visitor."

Baldy leaves the cover of a broad-limbed spruce. His eyes get jumpy when he sees me. "The boy from the Chilkoot? What's he doing here?"

"That I'd like to know," Frank says. He uncovers my mouth and turns me around. Both men wait for me to speak.

What am I supposed to say? "I thought the woods might be a shortcut." It's steep and icy off the trail, not exactly easy going. My story don't sound likely, even to me.

"I don't buy that so long as you're here." Frank pulls the green muffler from my neck and wraps it around my wrists. "I want to know exactly where you are and what you're doing." He finishes with a solid knot.

My fingers grow real cold and clammy.

"Now tell me why you really came."

"I saw Bal—" I swallow and start again. Frank called this fellow Albert. "I saw Albert walk into the woods and thought I'd follow. Because—" I glance at him real quick. He ain't tough or mean like I reckon a criminal should look. "Because I thought maybe he'd taken something that wasn't his."

Albert goes white. "Did you call the Mounties on me?"

"Well, what do you know?" Frank's lip curls. "One crook keeping an eye on the other."

Frank means Pa's timepiece, which he accused me of stealing at the Chilkoot Pass. I ain't gonna take the bait. I don't know what he's got planned, my wrists tied up like this, but I sure ain't gonna give him a reason to do nothing more.

Frank pushes hard on my shoulder. "Take a seat."

I plop right down on them damp pine needles.

He unwinds part of the muffler from my wrists and wraps it around a tree trunk. "Get comfortable," Frank says. "You ain't going nowhere."

"Why'd you tell me to meet you here?" Albert asks.

"We've got to talk," Frank says. "I got some questions about what you told me. You'll answer, too, unless you want them Mounties on your tail."

"No Mounties. Please. I'll tell you anything you want to know." Albert eyes me nervously. "What about the kid?"

"Don't worry about him. We'll talk over there." Frank points to a cluster of bare trees, a few yellow leaves still clinging to their lower branches.

The wet pine needles below cover the sound of their footsteps as they walk across the forest. The farther they go, the more silent this empty place is. Are they gonna leave me here, tied up like this forever? Frank stops near them trees he pointed to, far enough away I can only catch a word or two of what they're saying.

If Albert really did steal Old Joe's gold for Frank, this is when he'd hand it over.

I squint to get the best look I can. Frank talks, then Albert starts in, but he don't give Frank that knotted hankie. He shakes his head and moves his hands in front of him, like Miss Stapleton used to do when she'd had enough.

No. Stop. Enough. That's what Albert's telling Frank with his body.

Maybe he means he won't do Frank's dirty work, that if he wants to steal an old-timer's gold, he's got to do it on his own. I'm so wrapped up in the story I'm spinning, I almost miss the words.

"All staked." It's Albert who says it.

Frank holds up empty hands, and Albert nods.

Staked? That word's used when a mine's been claimed. What's Albert know about that? Frank's the fellow who's mined before.

Frank's feet are set wide. His fists are planted on his hips. He's two heads taller than Albert, and Albert's no shorty.

Whatever Frank says to him, it makes Albert wither, like a plucked leaf in the sun.

Frank grabs him around the arm and gives Albert a shake.

Albert hangs his head. Then he does a real interesting thing. He slips his hand in his pocket and offers what he's got to Frank. It ain't Old Joe's knotted hankie. It's a piece of wood about the size of a book. Albert touches the wood, then points in the direction of the Yukon.

Frank runs his fingers over it and holds it to his face.

A spark ignites in my belly and tingles down my arms. That's a Riley clue. I know it! Albert's telling Frank he found it in the river. Something's on that piece of wood, I can tell from the way Frank studies it so closely. Riley must have dropped pieces in the Yukon with his clues carved on one side.

Frank shoves the clue in the pocket of his long fur coat. He makes a fist with his other hand, his thumb pointing up on top. Then he motions over his shoulder with it. What he's saying's clear as day. Frank wants Albert to go.

Albert takes off running, and Frank lets out a belly laugh, real deep and ugly.

He starts to leave the same way Albert went, but then he turns around. Frank Hazard's heading toward me.

I drop my head. He don't need to see I watched everything that happened with him and Albert. My heart pounds faster the closer he gets. What's he mean to do with me?

Frank squats in front of me, so we're face-to-face.

"No wonder you've always got one eye screwed up so tight." He pokes a finger straight through the spot where my missing lens should be.

"You got yourself a Riley clue." I don't realize I've said them words out loud until Frank's eyes go cold as stone. I duck, afraid his fist is gonna swing.

He smirks, like he's thought of his own private joke. "You didn't see nothing here, you understand?"

Before I know what's happened, Frank's wrenched my glasses off my face. I just make out his arm as he tosses them over his shoulder. "Best of luck finding the trail again."

The blur that's Frank Hazard disappears.

Every part of me shakes. I can't see two feet in front of me, but at least I ain't hurt.

The muffler's snug around my wrists. I yank and pull my hands apart until the knot loosens, then tug with my teeth till the muffler falls. One tug releases it from the tree trunk, then it's back around my neck. I run my hands over the ground, feeling for my glasses. Snow soaks through my trousers, and pine needles prick my palms. Where did Frank throw them? How far? They made a soft sound when they landed, so they didn't hit a rock. Oh, I gotta find them. There's no way I'll make it out of these woods without them.

On my hands and knees I scramble around. I gotta be careful not to crush the other lens. I know Mel's gotta be worried by now, but I ain't leaving here without them. Where can they be?

I inch forward, my hands pat every space around me. Just up ahead sunlight trickles through tree branches. There's a patch of gleaming light. My glasses? I squint hard as I can, but I ain't sure what I see. I crawl a little closer until I reach the sunny spot. And then I feel them. I wrap my hand around them glasses and hold them near my face. Oh, thank goodness. They ain't any more bent out of shape than they was before.

Swift as I can, I race to the trail high above the canyon

walls. The whole time I run the path, I try to make sense of what happened back there.

Albert shook his head no and said all staked. Then Frank grabbed that piece of wood. He didn't say it was a Riley clue, but he didn't deny it, either.

*All staked.* All taken's what that means. Is Albert saying there ain't any mines left in the Klondike? How would he know that? Then I remember what Albert said on the Chilkoot, that he knew something that might be useful to Frank.

My feet pound the trail as I dodge them fellows who roll their boats and haul their gear. A sharpness twinges in my middle with every breath, but I won't slow down.

So Frank's got a piece of wood I'm sure is a Riley clue. But he ain't gonna find One-Eyed Riley's claim and neither is Albert. That's for me and Mel to do.

I make it clear to the other side of the canyon, where men reload their boats before traveling on. Mel and Stanley watch at the end of the trail.

"Where've you been?" Mel rushes to me. He ain't mad, only relieved. "What happened?"

"Sorry. I got turned around and had to run to catch you." It's sort of true. "Is Mr. Theroux all right?"

The color in Stanley's cheeks has come back. "See for yourself." He points to a heap of gear scattered on the shore. There's a whole lot less than what the raft carried earlier. "Most washed overboard. Uncle's drying what's left."

We should have portaged. The three of us know it, but me and Mel, we ain't free to say so.

"Help me load, why don't you?" Mr. Theroux says when we get near. Beyond the tent, there's a wooden crate and two soaked sacks of flour. Nothing else is left. "I sure saved us a lot of time riding through the canyon. Bet we'll beat them that portaged by at least a day."

Almost everything is gone, and what ain't is nearly ruined. Forget that coffee Mr. Theroux likes so much, that's a treat compared with eating regular, which ain't gonna happen now that so many things are gone. How are them two gonna sleep without their blankets or work a mine without gear? Don't Mr. Theroux think he made a mistake?

No one says anything. Oh, my head's crammed full of words I want to tell him. I can't hardly peek at Mel for worrying I'll let something slip, words that will cost us our trip to Dawson City.

Me and Mel load one of them flour sacks, which is near about worthless now. "Why are you boys so quiet?" Mr. Theroux asks.

Stanley answers. "I'll tell you why."

"I ain't interested in you. It's him I want to hear from." Mr. Theroux steps in front of Mel, that kerchief around his neck as stained with tobacco juice as it was at Lindeman. "What was it you wanted to tell me back before the canyon?"

"Nothing." Melvin hangs his head.

"What's that?"

He lifts his gaze to Mr. Theroux, looks him straight in the eye. "It was nothing."

Your plan to ride the rapids was plain stupid, I holler in my head.

Mr. Theroux crosses his arms and rests them on his bulging belly. "I've watched and listened since we took you on, and you know what? You got an air about you I ain't fond of, Melvin Johnson."

Mel presses his lips together.

"Here you are, new to everything, but not once have you asked for my advice. Not when we built the raft. Not about mining. Nothing."

Still Mel don't say a word.

Mr. Theroux could have never made that raft without Melvin. He and Stanley did most of the work while the mister moaned about his achy joints.

"You go on and on about that mining book of yours. 'I heard this' and 'I heard that.' Well, you know what I heard? It's an impolite boy who don't ask direction from his elders. But what did I expect? A pa who lets his young'uns run off to Canada without him surely didn't learn them any manners."

"My brother's better than a whole pile of you any day

of the week!" The words jump out before I can stop them, but you know what? I don't care. What's Mr. Theroux know about manners, anyhow?

"Jasper," Melvin whispers, "careful now."

"Why should I bother? He said you don't have any manners when Mama taught us good and—"

"Jasper," Mel says, "hush!"

"Well, now, knock me over with a feather. I had no idea you two had a mama. Sure don't act like boys raised by any sort of woman I know. She's got a thing or two to learn about mothering if you boys are evidence of her skills."

Splotchy red patches burn on Melvin's neck. His eyes get fierce. "How dare you talk about our mama like that."

Mr. Theroux's grin is smug. "I can say what I please. I'm in charge, if you recall."

Mel draws his arm back and lets loose a solid punch, socks Mr. Theroux right in the face!

He clutches his cheek and howls like a lonely dog.

Stanley don't know what to do.

"That's it." Mr. Theroux's voice is muffled, since he talks through his fingers. "I won't take you two any farther."

"We wouldn't go another mile with you if you were the only man on the Yukon," Mel says.

Mr. Theroux moves his hand from his cheek. Already it's puffed up red. "It's time for you boys to pay up for your ride."

"Pay up?" Mel says. "For half a trip? You got more than enough work from us. I say we're even."

Them eyes of the mister's have gone shiny. Now I recognize what I saw in his face when he spied Pa's watch and that gold dust at Lake Lindeman.

It was greed.

I hold them firm in my pocket.

"I recall Jasper here has a mighty fine watch and a bit of gold. A couple weeks of food and shelter, another sailing down the river. Sounds like a fair deal to me."

"I earned that gold fair and square."

"That watch is our pa's," Mel says.

Mr. Theroux's eyes near about sparkle. "And I'm sure he knows you've taken it."

Oh, he thinks he's clever. Well, he ain't the only one quick on his feet. I cook up a story on the spot. "We took it with our mama's blessing. She told us to take it to our pa. See"—I get bolder as the story builds—"he's already in the Klondike. We didn't run off without him. We plan to meet him there."

A smile tugs at the corner of Mel's mouth.

"Our pa's got an awful temper. If he knew you'd taken it from us he'd . . . he'd turn you in to the Mounties." The threat don't have much bite, but it's all I can think of. Somehow it gets the mister moving.

"Come on, Stanley. Load what's left." Mr. Theroux grabs

the only crate that made it through the rapids and tosses it on the raft. His cheek has swollen enough to puff out his scraggly beard to one side.

Stanley glances at us with eyes big and sorrowful. Slowly he lifts the other sack of useless flour. Mr. Theroux unties the raft from where it's tethered and pulls Stanley on board.

Since Lindeman City, them Therouxs have been our only chance. We ain't gonna find another.

They pole out into the middle of the Yukon. "Good luck finding your way to Dawson City," Mr. Theroux shouts as the raft disappears around a bend.

# Chapter 9

"So," Mel says.

"So," I answer. "Just the two of us again." We don't have to deal with them Therouxs no more, but now we're all alone with no means to get to Dawson.

Mel's shoulders are hunched, his hands sunk deep in his pockets. "That punch. It wasn't the smartest thing I've ever done."

"Mr. Theroux deserved it, if you ask me." No one talks about Mama like that. Though she wouldn't have approved, I'm right proud of my brother. "That's the last we'll ever see of them."

"It better be."

Beside us, the Yukon swirls, slower now that it's past them rapids. Men who portaged shove in to ride. Them with boats are a couple weeks out of Dawson. And here we are with nothing but our own two feet. What are we gonna do?

Where before there was sunshine, fat clouds drape the sky. A stiff wind streaks across the river. The forest along the shoreline moans. September's a horrible time to be stuck without a boat, with winter closing in.

"We'd better move," Mel says. "It's four miles to White Horse, the next set of rapids. It can't be much different from what we saw in Miles Canyon."

It's all we can do.

We walk side by side between the spruce and pine, the Yukon to the right our guide. The forest slows the wind that races from the river, but it don't help to cut the cold. Mel takes out his other pair of woolen socks and gives one to me. "Wear this over your hand," he says, "and keep your other in your pocket."

"What happens to us now, Mel?"

"We could build a boat," he says.

"With what? We don't got nothing more than Mama's washboard, two pairs of rubber boots, your knapsack, and that silly sled." I poke the sled runners Mel's looped his stockinged hand through. Why he keeps it, I don't know.

"Then we'll have to team up again."

"Who would want to take us on?"

"Oh, Jasper, I don't know. But what else are we going to do?"

Maybe this ain't the best time to tell him what I learned in Miles Canyon, that the claim we've hoped for since Mel bought that newspaper in July has probably been snatched up. But if One-Eyed Riley's mine truly is our only shot, I gotta win Mel over. He has to see.

"I heard something in the canyon," I say.

Mel kicks a pinecone from one foot to the next.

"It's about them Klondike claims."

"What about them?" Mel asks.

"Well"—there ain't no way to pretty this up, so I out and say it—"everything's been staked."

Mel stops, his eyes unsure. "How could that be true?"

"I don't know, but I believe it." The details ain't clear, but I'm certain that's what Albert said. There ain't no reason to tell my brother about what happened in the woods. He's got enough on his mind. "Them folks in Skagway and Dyea, them others on the Chilkoot and at Lake Lindeman, if this is true, they've come for nothing. But it ain't gonna be like that for us. That's why we gotta focus on Riley's mine."

Mel kicks that pinecone hard. It skitters across the snow. "I don't believe it."

"We can't know until we get there," I say, "but wouldn't it be best to be ready?"

Mel don't answer, but even so, I plunge right in. There's so many things I want to tell him, I can't hardly keep them straight. "Here's what I got so far. *Nine below's the way to go.*

*Gold on the bottom of the creek. Friday's the last chance to be lucky. Hunker down but not too much*—that's the one from Stanley."

We walk again, much faster than before. The wind no longer wails, it sounds more like it holds a thousand secrets I might learn if only I listen close enough.

Mel rubs that spot above his lip where he claims a mustache grows. "A creek, a number, a day of the week."

"I think nine below's a temperature."

"Could be," Mel says.

"And gold's found in creek bottoms." Not on bushes or trees, I know that now. "Hunker down. What do you think that means?" I squat to see if anything looks different close to the ground, but all I get is a good view of Melvin's rubber boots.

Mel's mouth quirks into a smile.

I jump to my feet, and the two of us keep on. It ain't long before the wind's beat out by the distant roar of water. The Yukon picks up again, gets moving faster than a stepped-on cat.

"We must be near White Horse Rapids," Melvin says. "Maybe there we can set things right."

Ahead the forest thins and boats cluster at the shore. Men drag them from the river a second time. "Them folks took a four-mile boat ride just to portage again."

Mel winks at me. "If the Therouxs are smart enough to portage this time, we could beat the two of them to the other side of the rapids."

Oh, it would be good to be ahead of them, even for a little while. Me and Mel break into a run. We just can't help ourselves.

We ain't able to hold that speedy pace for long before we gotta walk again. It's well into evening by the time we're past the rapids. Some folks load gear into their boats, some light out to travel a few more miles on the Yukon before darkness catches them. A few have set up camp for the night. The river flows around a pile of boards heaped on the riverbank. Closer up, I see exactly what they are: a smashed-up boat abandoned on the shore.

With all they lost, at least them Therouxs still got a way to travel. Me and Mel ain't seen them yet. I wonder if that means they were smart enough to portage. Maybe right this minute they're behind us on the trail, carrying a sack of soggy flour between them.

The thick clouds that hung low earlier have been blown away, leaving a brutal cold behind. In a clearing, tents huddle together, and from them comes the most delicious smell of bacon cooked up fine and fresh biscuits. My stomach growls.

"Let's find some supper," Melvin says.

We head to the first few tents, and Mel asks folks if they have any food to spare. No one does. Every tent we try, the answer is the same.

The last tent sits alone, on the edge of trees and

darkness. When they turn us away, Mel pushes deeper into the woods. He keeps on even when I call for him to stop. Only when the firelight from the last tent disappears does Mel slump to the ground, his head in his hands. "I don't know what to do. A meal's a small thing, and no one will share even that."

If they don't offer supper, there ain't no way anyone will give us a ride to Dawson.

But there's a couple things we still got. I settle next to Mel. A pinch of gold. Two pairs of boots, which probably won't get us far. And Pa's watch. "We could trade Pa's timepiece."

I can't see Mel's face in the coal-black night, so I don't know what he's thinking. And he don't answer for a good long time. "When Mama got sick and it was my turn to care for her, she told me about that watch. Do you know where it came from?"

Them ain't words I expected. "No," I answer.

"Mama gave it to Pa as his wedding present. It was hers to begin with, something that had belonged to Grandpa when she was a girl." Mel's voice dips low, and I can hear the sorrow he still holds inside. "Grandpa told her to use it if ever money got too tight, just like she said for us to do. She asked Pa to do the same."

All them times Pa spent the last of Mel's pay to buy some liquor, he never touched that fine gold watch. He could have, but he didn't.

In his own muddled way, maybe Pa was honoring her memory.

I gotta swallow to keep my throat from closing up. "It weren't only for me you left that watch behind."

"I guess I couldn't take it from Pa, either."

"We ain't gonna sell it, then," I say. "We'll carry on the best we can, even if we gotta walk from here to Dawson."

It ain't sensible in the least, but it's the choice we make. By the time the owl starts his call, me and Mel are wrapped up in that canvas to hold off the freezing night.

A layer of frost sparkles on the canvas next morning as sunlight slants through the trees. I push the cover off and am hit by air so cold, I break into a cough when I try to breathe. Mel packs the canvas in his bag, and I follow him to the shore.

Mist hovers over the Yukon, and beneath it, a thin layer of ice reaches from the riverbank a few feet across the water. It bobs in the current and creaks and groans most awfully. Them who camped at White Horse must first break through the ice to set out on the water. Soon their boats will sail down the river a hundred times faster than me and Mel will ever be.

Mel pulls his woolen stocking over his arm as far as it will go and grips his little sled. "You okay?"

He's a boy who's gone skinny, who sorely needs a bath, whose cap pushes too-long hair over his eyes.

Mel must see the same when he looks at me.

"As good as you are," I answer.

We pass through forests and clearings, the Yukon forever at our side. Our swift pace holds off the cold as long as we keep moving. The first day we find a couple shriveled berries still clinging to a snowy bush. Though they ain't filling, they're enough for us to push on till twilight. It's nighttime that's the worst. Without matches we can't make a fire. Rocks and trees and Mel's canvas are our only shelter.

The second morning, the Yukon's ice has changed. Some is soft, like the lumps of frozen foam that line the riverbank, some's shaped like blocks, as hard as wood or stone. The boats that pass must steer around them chunks of ice. In just a couple weeks the Yukon could freeze solid.

It's midmorning the third day when we see the boat that's run ashore at the river's edge. Ice encrusts its sides. Three fellows in long dark cloaks push and shove against the boat, but it don't budge. One sees us and waves for help.

"Come on," Mel says, and we take off running.

We get closer, and them men, they're the strangest I've ever seen. At first I think the hunger's got so bad I'm imagining the funny clothes they're wearing, sheets of black that fall from under their chins to the tips of their sturdy boots. Chains hang around their necks with golden crosses in the middle. Only their faces peek out.

"Hello, Sisters," Melvin says. "How can we help?"

Sisters? What's Mel on about? He don't got no one but me, and I sure ain't a girl.

Mel removes his cap, something he'd do only for a lady.

"The ice froze so thick last night, we can't get out," one says in a voice that's soft and gentle.

Then I realize why Mel's taken off his hat.

Those are ladies under there!

Mel taps my head, a reminder I'm to take my cap off, too. He acts like this is the most regular thing he's ever seen, three ladies dressed up like bats, tugging at a boat frozen in the Yukon River.

The five of us try to rock the boat, but it's stuck so fast, it don't even wiggle.

"Let's empty it," one lady says, "then try again."

I grab two heavy canvas sacks, but stumble when I reach the icy bank and piles of snow. Mel helps me to my feet again. "Who are these ladies?" I whisper.

"Nuns," he answers, as if that tells me everything.

The pile of goods grows on the shore, but it's a struggle to unload in the snowy drifts. Then I remember Melvin's sled. The runners slide smooth over the icy riverbank, and it don't take too many trips till the boat is empty. Then the five of us, we push that boat with all our strength. There's a loud crack, and it finally breaks free. It's left with a jagged hole the size of a dinner plate in its side.

The three ladies sink onto the boat's edge, tired and defeated.

There ain't no way it will ever sail again.

"Do you have a hammer and some nails?" Mel asks. "Because I've got an idea."

The tallest lady, the one with a pair of glasses, searches through their gear to find the tools Mel needs. He takes his sled apart and uses the wood to fix the hole. It ain't perfect, but it will hold.

"We can't thank you enough." The lady with the wrinkled cheeks smiles.

At first all three of them nun ladies looked the same in them odd clothes they wear, but now I notice they're all a little different.

One lady has eyes gray as a winter morning. "What are you boys doing out here all alone?" she asks.

Mel hangs his head. "Guess you could say we've run into some trouble."

"You hardly have any gear," the tall woman says.

"No boat, either," I add in. "We lost our partners in Miles Canyon. So we're gonna walk all the way to the Klondike." The tale is true as true can be, and oh, I see it pulls at their heartstrings.

"We're going to Dawson City, too," the wrinkled lady says. "Without your help, I don't know how we could have gone on. The three of us would be honored for you to join us."

Dawson. Just like us. They ain't the first ladies we've

seen traveling to the Klondike, but they're the first Sister-nuns, whatever that means. "You three are after gold, too?"

It's Mel who elbows me. "What Jasper means is we'd be awfully grateful," he says.

The lady with the gray eyes laughs. "No gold for us. We'll work in Father Judge's hospital. In Dawson City."

The wrinkled lady grasps Mel's hand. "I'm Mary Margaret. This is Mary Agnes"—she nods to the Sister with the kind gray eyes—"and Mary Elizabeth."

Mary Elizabeth is the lady who wears glasses just like me. She could be the tallest lady I've ever seen.

I ain't sure who this father is the Sisters have, but that don't matter. Who knows? Maybe all nuns got the same first name and are part of one big family.

"We're Melvin and Jasper Johnson."

Mary Margaret studies us with her sharp eyes. "You boys need some tending to. Mary Agnes and Mary Elizabeth, find Melvin and Jasper something to eat."

The other Marys shift around the piles of gear until Mary Agnes finds a tin canister. She lifts the lid, and inside there's six biscuits, light and airy and prettier than anything I've ever seen. Me and Mel eat every one.

Before I've swallowed my last bite, Mary Margaret turns to the shore. "Let's load our gear and get on the water," she says with real authority. She may be a little frail, but boy, is she in charge.

We clamber into the well-packed boat. Mary Elizabeth and Mel use the paddles to push off from the bank. They steer around the chunks of ice until we're in the middle of the river. From the back of the boat, Mary Margaret waves a wrinkled hand, directs me and Mary Agnes to unfurl the sail. We let it out, and the wind catches hold, pushes us through the water at a steady clip.

Traveling with the Marys is a hundred times better than with them Therouxs. For one, they work hard as any man, which is more than I can say for Stanley and the mister. Each hour we switch out rowers, me with Mary Agnes and Mel with Mary Elizabeth, whose strength matches his own. It saves our backs considerable. For another, they're right pleasant company. We pass the day without one ugly word.

Mary Agnes tells me stories when it's our turn at the oars, ones about her family at home. She has five brothers, two older and three younger, and oh, them boys were always in all sorts of trouble. One brother couldn't find a bucket when he had to milk the cow, so he used his pa's boots. Another ripped apart his mama's fresh-baked cake, because he'd lost his pocketknife and was sure it'd somehow fallen in the batter. How Mary Agnes laughed when she remembered, them gray eyes of hers dancing. Them brothers must miss her awfully. I ain't sure how old she is and it ain't polite to ask, but I bet it weren't long ago she was a girl herself.

She's a hundred times more likable than old Mr. Theroux.

None of the Marys knows about One-Eyed Riley, so I'll have to wait to get to Dawson to learn more about his mine. But just because they ain't after gold and are gonna spend their days cooped up in a hospital don't mean they have no interest in our surroundings. Mary Elizabeth knows every detail about where we've been and where we're headed. She says when we spy the Midnight Dome, a rounded peak that juts straight up into the air with a white gash on its side, we'll be near Dawson. The dome's where the Klondike River meets the Yukon, with Dawson City settled in between.

As we travel I've got time to dream about the things me and Mel might do with a mine worth millions. Things like sleep with feather pillows. Eat three square meals a day. Buy new shoes when we need them. It's almost too good to be true.

The sun hangs low on the horizon, ready to quit the sky. When we arrived in Skagway, the sun stayed up past nine o'clock. But now each night it sets a little earlier and stretches the nighttime darkness far into morning. Mary Agnes stops rowing. "Do you hear that?" We ain't sure at first what the thundering noise is on the shore and try our best to see in the slanting sunlight what's racing past the trees.

"Are they deer?" Mary Margaret asks.

But them giant animals ain't moose or deer.

"Caribou," Mel says.

They move as one, like an invisible rope binds them together. They run filled up with life, their powerful brown bodies and fine white beards as big and untamed as this wilderness that stretches from the river to the shore and straight up to the sun.

All of us, we watch in wonder until the caribou are gone.

An hour later, Me and Mel are tucked under two blankets near a crackling fire. It's the most comfortable I've been since we left home over a month ago.

"Mel," I whisper, once I'm sure the Marys are settled in their tent, "what's a nun? And how'd you know to call them Sister?" I've been dying to know all day long.

He rolls over to face me. "They're women who work for a church."

Mama took us to church a couple times. That one didn't have ladies who looked like the Marys, just an old codger who talked a lot, sometimes with his eyes shut.

"When you and Mama were sick, a woman stopped at our house dressed in the same black robes. She and others like her came from Seattle to help those with the influenza. She said if we ever needed help, we could ask the Sisters."

That's the memory I weren't able to place, of gentle hands and a cool cloth on my forehead when the influenza got real bad. I remember that argument Mel had with Pa the night after he brought the newspaper home, when Mel accused him of not caring for Mama when she most needed it. "Pa didn't want help, did he?"

Mel shakes his head. "He thought he could care for his family best. But then things got worse so fast that once he asked the nuns to come back . . ."

Mel don't finish, but I know what happened next. The nun's nursing healed me up, but for Mama it was too late. Sometimes I wonder if Pa wishes things had happened different, if maybe he wouldn't have sunk so deep if it was me he lost. Maybe now that I ain't around to remind him of them sad days, he'll heal up, like I did. I hope my leaving gives him that.

"Are you still mad at him, Mel?"

He's so quiet, I reckon Mel's fallen asleep. "Sometimes," he finally says, "but the farther we get from home, the more my anger fades."

Mel turns over and settles in, but my mind's still busy. There really are some on the Yukon who ain't after gold, folks who care about more than just themselves. Mama would have liked the Marys, how brave they are, how generous they've been. "Don't worry, Mama," I whisper, so quiet even I can't hardly hear myself. "There's people looking out for us. Your boys are doing fine."

Twelve days later, we wake to cold so deep, branches on the spruce trees break and snap, loud as a stick of dynamite. Mary Elizabeth says the sap's freezing up inside.

A thick fog wraps around the trees. "I don't know if we should leave yet," Mel tells us. "The ice is really bad."

We all walk to the riverbank. Hunks of ice big as wagons flow down the river. They crash and shove into each other, grind with a noise that makes my teeth ache. Even if we could get the boat out from the shore, there ain't nowhere to go. The ice shifts like clouds that race across a stormy sky, breaks apart, and rejoins in an ever-changing line.

First thing we need to do is free the boat from the ice along the riverbank. "I'll get the ax from the Sisters' gear," I tell Mel. "You grab the rope."

I hack the frozen slabs that grasp the boat as Mel unties it at the bow. I swing that ax so long, I'm sweating in the awful cold. We ain't got proper mittens, just Mel's woolen socks pulled over one hand. They freeze up solid fast.

I see the worry on Mel's face.

"My brothers pushed our wagon out of a muddy bog once," Mary Agnes says. "A boat in the ice can't be too much different. Here, let me try." Mary Agnes takes up the ax. Mary Elizabeth pulls the rope along with Mel. Mary Margaret gives the command, and we push and rock and chop and tug. One big shove finally sets it free. It scrapes across the ice, and oh, do we all shout. Mel pulls the boat as far out on the frozen river as he thinks is safe. From there we load our gear and do our best to shove into the part of the Yukon that still looks like a river.

All day it's a fight to keep the boat from slamming into islands of ice. Mel forces away what he can, the Sisters steer and paddle, while I hack ice from the oars. The sun creeps lower in the sky. We gotta set up camp before darkness falls, or else this boat will be crushed as easy as a hazelnut between these great heaving slabs.

Somehow Melvin pulls us close to shore. Mary Elizabeth finds a box of dried apples, and soon we're eating a kind of apple stew, sweet and soft and warm. Not since the Chilkoot Trail have I been so worn out. The fire snaps and crackles, brightens everyone with its light. I trace the calluses that line my palms right below my fingers. My forearms have grown brown, and my shoulders are right strong. Who knew so much could change in six weeks?

Mary Agnes's gray eyes smile. "I want you to know you're a good boy, Jasper. We couldn't have made it this far without you and Melvin."

Since Mama died, most grown-ups haven't cared much about me at all. I can't help how my arms reach right around that funny dress until I squeeze Mary Agnes in a hug. They loosen fast when I realize what I'm doing, but she won't let me pull away.

"If you and Melvin ever need help, come find us at the hospital in Dawson."

"Yes, ma'am," I say. And maybe on some quiet afternoon I'll stop by and tell her how me and Mel are faring. Just because.

• • •

If only we had known how close we were to Dawson City when we set up camp last night! Not an hour after we're on the Yukon, I spot a tiny bump on the horizon. I ain't sure what it is at first, but the nearer we come, the clearer it gets, a massive rock set against the frozen shore with a white gash through its middle.

"Midnight Dome!" Mary Elizabeth says.

I want to dance around, jump high as I can, and holler, but on account of the Sisters, I hold back. It wouldn't do to tip them overboard. It's Mel who shouts, a hoot so joyous, the Sisters break into applause, and oh, I can't help but join him.

Me and Mel have traveled two thousand miles with no sure proof we'd ever make it. And now we're almost at Dawson, right on the edge of the Klondike goldfields.

"We did it, Mel." I grab his hand and he squeezes tight.

Ahead the Klondike River reaches for the Yukon, like old friends who ain't seen each other in forever. It don't feel real, our being here, but it's as flat-out certain as the tents and scrubby pines that dot the hills near the dome.

I can't wait to get to those creeks and find Riley's mine.

# CHAPTER 10

A couple men onshore help drag our boat from the ice. Mel secures the boat and holds his hand out to the Sisters. The ground's a mix of snow and frozen mud, so thick along the riverbank, we've gotta hop from one tree stump to the next until we're level with the street. Like in Skagway and Dyea, a muddy road runs through Dawson's middle. Tents bunch up everywhere with a few snow-covered buildings in between. Men tromp about in hooded coats, dodge dogs that pull sleds through the muck or sleep curled together along the wooden sidewalks. Dawson City's crowded, dirty, and loud. On the Yukon, we sometimes passed other boats, but mostly we were on our own. I ain't used to all this up-close living.

Mary Agnes's gray eyes find mine. "Don't forget what I told you, Jasper."

Mary Elizabeth throws her long arms around me and Mel. "If ever you need us—"

"We'll be at the hospital." Mary Margaret squeezes my shoulder with her wrinkled hand. Melvin starts for their bags, but Mary Margaret waves him off. "Don't you worry about that. Father Judge will see to things. Best way you can help is to take good care of yourselves."

The Sisters cut a path straight through the muddy street. The Midnight Dome rises at the other end. Men step back to give them room, and even sleds pull aside. They're off to start their work in Dawson's hospital, and me and Mel, we gotta go find Riley's claim.

"Let's get on them Klondike creeks." I still ain't sure what them clues of Riley's mean, but surely things will come together now that we're so close to his mine.

"Not so fast," Mel says. "We've got to find a few supplies."

I ain't sure how we'll pay for them, but I still follow.

The scent of new wood seeps from buildings as we weave down the rutted street. Most storefronts ain't yet weathered gray. This town went up fast, slapped together quicker than two sides of a buttered biscuit. Like in Seattle, enormous signs are everywhere:

JOE'S RESTAURANT: OPEN DAY AND NIGHT

New York Saloon: First Class Liquors and Cigars
Waffles and Coffee $.25

We pass dance halls and cabins, a Mountie in a crisp red coat who watches over fellows as they chop wood. It looks like they've stacked enough logs near the North West Mounted Police station to keep fires burning clean through winter.

A man dressed neat and trim stands on the sidewalk in front of Pioneer Saloon. His arms are crossed against his chest. His little eyes stare down his sloping nose. Well, what do you know. Me and Mel made it to the Klondike as fast as Lord Avonmore.

"Boys." The lord nods crisply when he sees us. "Didn't expect to see you after the Palmer House."

"Me neither," I say.

"Are you mining, sir?" Mel asks.

"My men have explored every creek from here down to Solomon's Dome. They haven't found one open claim."

They ain't found a claim. That don't have to mean they've all been staked, but it don't sound good.

Mel's eyes dart to me and back to Lord Avonmore.

"I was told when we arrived that every claim along Bonanza Creek was staked two weeks after George Carmack and Skookum Jim discovered that thumb-sized nugget of gold."

Mel squints like he ain't hearing right.

Lord Avonmore sighs. “There aren’t hardly any mines left in all the Klondike. The best land has already been claimed.”

“It’s all been staked?” Mel says.

The saloon door opens, and out comes a fellow who holds a sack. “I’ll give you six pounds for twenty-four bottles,” he says.

Lord Avonmore grabs the bag. “That will do.”

“Champagne straight from England,” the fellow shouts through the doorway. “Fill yer mug for one pinch of gold!”

Lord Avonmore has made a trade. Champagne for an ordinary sack. It ain’t something ordinary in there, though, I can tell you that.

“That’s gold, ain’t it?” Six pounds of it, the fellow said.

Lord Avonmore sniffs. “Young man, it’s not polite to ask after another’s wealth.” But that lofty look of his fades quick. He can’t help saying more. “It isn’t how I hoped to find it, but this gold is mine.”

As we move on, Lord Avonmore’s words run through my head. There’s hardly any mines left in the Klondike. What Albert said in Miles Canyon really was about the claims. But how’d he know?

Mel stops before a freshly painted sign. “ ‘Turner and Company: Outfits Bought and Sold.’ This is what we’re looking for.”

There ain’t one supply that’s gonna change the fact

that most everything's been taken. What Melvin's after, I ain't sure.

We scrape our muddy rubber boots on the steps that lead to the door and push inside. In one corner, men warm themselves before a stove. Behind the counter a fellow sorts nails into piles. He wears a red striped shirt and a pair of gold-rimmed glasses at the end of his nose. His jaunty mustache ends in curls. All around him, row after row of wooden shelves stand empty.

"You're Mr. Turner?" Mel asks.

He shoves the nails aside. "Sure am. What are you after?"

Mel clears his throat and fixes his eyes on an empty shelf up high. "Nearly everything."

"Everything?" Mr. Turner shakes his head. "You must be new around here."

"We are," I say. What's wrong with that?

"Then you probably haven't heard Dawson's in bad shape right now. Food's scarce. Richest city in the world, but we can't get nothing once the Yukon turns to ice. We got gold aplenty, but you can't eat it. And it sure won't keep you warm through the winter." Mr. Turner flicks a strand of hair off his forehead. "Inspector Constantine of the North West Mounted Police posted a notice last week that said starvation stares us all in the face, and a man without his own supplies is a man who courts death."

Mel's cheeks have gone a pasty color. My belly pinches

like it's full of unripe cherries. This whole time I've thought that as long as we could get to Dawson City, we'd be safe.

"Best thing you two can do is turn around and go home. Find someone with a dog team who can take you to Dyea."

Home ain't something we got anymore. "Mr. Turner," I say, unhooking them Chilkoot rubber boots from Mama's washboard. "What could we get for these?"

He peers at me over his glasses before he takes them in hand. "Haven't had any sort of boots to sell since last spring. I'll give you twenty dollars for one pair or fifty dollars for both."

Fifty dollars. That's a whole bunch of money.

"Of course, I can't pay in cash," Mr. Turner says. "Hardly any of that around. We pay with gold dust and nuggets here. But I can make a trade."

"Food," Mel says, "if you've got it. And some mining gear."

"Gear's not a problem." Mr. Turner lifts a pickax from a pile stacked along one wall. "But you won't find a claim easily. Pretty much everything is staked. Most men who've just arrived in Dawson will have to hire themselves out and work another man's mine. It's food we don't have much of, but let me see what I can find." He ducks into his storeroom.

"Hardly any claims left," Mel mumbles to himself. "A man courts death without supplies."

For once, I don't got nothing to say. The space between us fills up with silence. It makes me want to drum my fingers on the counter or whistle a tune, anything to make this uncomfortable quiet go away.

Riley's mine. We need it now more than anything.

Mr. Turner returns a few minutes later, a near-empty sack in his hand. "These beans are all I got, about five pounds. If you're careful, you could make them last a couple of weeks if you caught yourselves a rabbit or two." He sets the sack on the counter next to the pickax, which seems useless now that them claims are taken. "There you go."

Mel's cheeks are pricked with red. "That's all you got? That's everything fifty dollars bought?"

"Prices around here ain't going to be what you had at home." Mr. Turner picks up a nail. "These sell for twenty-eight dollars a pound right now. 'Course, if you want variety, you can always try another shop." He grins, and his mustache lifts on both sides. "I hear the Alaska Commercial Company is swimming in ax handles and sugar."

Mel slides the pickax back across the counter. "I guess a cook pot and a tin of matches is what we really need."

Mr. Turner sets the pickax with the other mining tools.

"Matches cost extra. I'll sell you a pot someone traded last week so you can afford both." He hands Mel a cook pot with a broken handle. It's dented on one side.

Some deal that is. I grab the bag of beans, as light as a newborn kitten.

"Wait." Mr. Turner drops his voice and looks at Mel over the top of his glasses. "You see those fellows over there?" He tilts his head toward the men around the stove. "They're new in town. Some will try to stay and work for wages. Others will head back to where they came from, as soon as they get their bearings. A few have been here for weeks and haven't done much more than wander the streets or sit in my shop, staring with them vacant eyes. All their effort went to getting here, and now that effort's used right up. It's not too late for you to hire a sled and get out while you can."

"I appreciate your kindness," Mel says, "but we're staying."

"All right, then. Best of luck." Mr. Turner shakes his head as he spreads those nails across the counter again. "You boys will sorely need it."

Me and Mel, we stand on the steps in front of Turner's store. The road's less crowded than when we went in half an hour ago, probably because it's dinnertime, a comfort we can't afford.

I can't hold back my thoughts for one more second. "No claims means every Stampeder will be desperate for Riley's mine. And all those fellows brought supplies. They got food and tools and blankets and can search long as it takes." I kick against the wooden steps. "All we got is a measly sack of beans, a tin of matches, a sorry pot, and a worn-out piece of canvas."

Mel pulls me from the steps as new folks try to enter. "Jasper, I need you to listen." His cheeks are flushed like they were inside, but his brows are set in a determined line.

Through my busted lens, I spy shapes and colors and lots of busy movement. I close that eye so all I see is Melvin.

"Mr. Turner said these beans will last a couple weeks if we catch a rabbit, which we can't, since we have no way to hunt. If we eat one meal a day, I bet we could stretch the beans out for a week, maybe longer. So here's what we're going to do. We'll start at Bonanza and ask around if anyone knew Riley. Every creek we pass we'll write on your newspaper map. The whole time we'll try to figure out those clues. We got a week to learn as much as we can. After that . . ."

Mel don't finish, and I don't want to hear what comes next.

It takes only a few minutes to walk the mucky streets past tents and buildings to the south side of town. We cross the bridge over the Klondike River, right where it joins with Bonanza Creek. Both are smaller than the Yukon, and their ice is almost frozen solid. The cold out here tears straight through me.

Forests spread across a maze of hills and frozen swampland, a gray world of bare bushes and snow-covered evergreens. Mel don't move as quick as usual, so I get plenty of time as we walk to check if any nuggets cling to empty branches, then catch myself. That's just a made-up story.

Bonanza Creek runs in the valley below us. We step out from them pines and spruces into the strangest sight I've ever seen. Near the top of the hill where we stand, long wooden troughs propped up with spindly legs snake down to the creek bed. Tree stumps are everywhere. The hill's so torn up with holes, it's a wonder there's any room for the tents and cabins set up here and there. Men dig through mounds of dirt, climb out of pits, lift buckets of earth from deep underground. It don't look much different from a huge anthill with men standing in for bugs.

Mel nods to an old-time sourdough who sifts through a pile like the dirt's real special.

The sourdough nods back, not friendly, not otherwise.

We keep near the top of the hill close to the forest's edge, follow the curve of the creek below. Any space that ain't packed with tents or holes or them wooden troughs has got a prospector nearby. No one talks to us, but they sure do like to stare.

Down near the creek there's a clearing along the

bank. A willow tree droops its branches overhead. What was it Mr. Horton on the *Queen* said about willows and gold? Something, that's what. I hustle down the hill, push my hand through the ice, and dig into the creek's sludge.

A man with mud caked on his trousers and his tattered flannel shirt storms over. "What're you doing on my claim?" He taps a grubby piece of string tied to a willow branch. "See this? It means five hundred feet on both sides of the creek is mine."

I weren't gonna take it. I just wanted to see if I could find some gold. But maybe that ain't the best thing to say. "Sorry," I tell him instead. I let the mud drip from my fingers and wander back to Mel.

Mel touches a wooden stake marked FIFTY-FOUR ABOVE. "See this? It's his claim."

"I got that figured out."

A sourdough with a gray-streaked beard that hangs clear to his belly stops his shoveling. "Y'all are a year late. There's nothing here for you cheechakos."

"Cheechakos?" Does this old-timer think we're from that big city in Illinois?

"Greenhorns. Folks like you who've never spent a winter in the goldfields."

Beads of sweat gather on Mel's forehead. His eyes have got a peculiar shine.

"You okay?"

"I'm just a little hot."

That's strange. Since we've left Dawson, the cold has taken on a sharper edge.

"Do you know One-Eyed Riley?" Mel asks.

The old-timer takes up his shovel again. "Riley, that old cheat. When you find him, let him know Bill over on Bonanza's looking for him. He still owes me seventy dollars from a few years ago."

Me and Mel hike back up the hill. He checks the sun. "What time is it?"

"Almost three o'clock."

"Then we've got four hours of daylight left. Let's look at that newspaper map."

We move far enough from Bonanza we ain't on anyone's claim, find a place where the ground's flat and ain't too soggy, and spread out near some pines.

Mel smooths the newspaper across his lap. In the region labeled the Klondike, three rivers join together like a wiggly letter C. The Klondike River's to the north, the Yukon River's in the west, and the Indian River runs along the southern edge. The goldfields are everything inside those rivers, which includes a mess of tangled creeks. Could be every Klondike creek's got gold in it, or maybe not. Until a fellow searches, he ain't gonna know for sure.

"Here's where Bonanza runs into the Klondike." Mel marks the map with the pencil. "Here's where Eldorado runs into Bonanza south of here." His usually fine hand ain't nothing but a shaky scrawl.

"I ain't heard of Eldorado Creek."

Mel pushes his hair off his forehead. Somehow he's sweating in this cold. "Some of the men on the *Portland* mined on Eldorado. Bonanza's discovery claim is close to where the two creeks meet. We'll follow Bonanza to Eldorado and add in each creek we see to the map."

There ain't no talk about what we'll do once darkness falls.

On we go through the steep and muddy forest with no trail to follow, Bonanza on our left. Mel asks miners the name of every staked-up creek we pass. He writes in Trail, Pure Gold, 49, and Mosquito. A mountain rises beyond Mosquito Creek, not high and snowcapped like Mount Rainier back home or the peaks at the Chilkoot Pass. This mountain ain't so tall as it is broad and smooth on top.

"You see that?" I point across Bonanza. "Don't that mountain remind you of a rising loaf of bread?" My stomach growls just thinking about it.

Mel stares where I point, then rubs his eyes. "Do you mean the mountain in front or the one behind?"

"You see two mountains?" I stand exactly where he is and cover my eye without the lens to get the best view I can, but that don't change nothing.

Mel shakes his head. "I'll get those glasses fixed for you soon as I can."

In the few minutes we've been still, the cold's crept closer and clouds have crowded up the sky. I tug my muffler so it covers my chin. There ain't no time to dillydally.

We walk on a couple of miles. Usually Mel races ahead, but today he stays in back. "Them Riley clues," I say over my shoulder. "Three of them got words that are similar. *Below. Bottom. Down.* What do you think it means?"

"They fit with what we've seen today. Prospectors dig holes from the creek beds clear up to the hills. They search every shovelful of dirt for gold."

We stop nearby the next two creeks. Mel adds in Boulder and Queen.

"Queen?" I say. "Like our steamer? That's where I first heard about Riley." It feels like a chance we can't pass up. "Let's go take a look."

That means we gotta cross Bonanza, because Queen's on the other side. We find a sourdough who lets us over his part of the creek. It ain't easy, on account of the ice. Me and Mel, we balance on one rock to the next until we make it through.

Queen's a whole lot shorter than Bonanza but has the same sort of old-timers scooping dirt. "You heard of One-Eyed Riley?" I ask the first fellow we see. He wears a set of overalls and a kerchief around his neck.

The old-timer shakes his head. "You know someone named Riley?" he shouts to a miner one claim over. "He's only got one eye."

"I've heard his name, but I don't know him personally," he answers.

It takes almost an hour to walk the whole length of Queen. Either no one out here's familiar with Riley or they just don't want to talk. When we turn around, the sun has broken through them clouds. It lingers over the hills ahead. Day is fading fast.

"Why don't anyone know about Riley, Mel? I figured everyone would have heard his story by now."

For the longest time, Mel don't answer. All I hear are his footsteps behind me, the faintest trickle of water from the almost frozen creek. "I don't know," he finally says. "I'm not sure what to think."

The whole length of Queen Creek I go over what Mel said and what he didn't. I feel squeezed around the middle like I'm wearing trousers that have grown too tight. Mel ain't sure what to think. Because here's the thing: If One-Eyed Riley's mine is real, wouldn't folks here know about it? Or did the story of his claim grow bigger than it was ever meant to be?

Like when Cyril dared me to let that rooster loose. It was just a little prank thought up on the way to school. But whispers flew from desk to desk, and by the end of the day some kids were sure I'd bring a piglet the next morning and a big glop of mud for him to wallow in on the cloakroom floor.

Is that what's meant when they say Riley whispered his

riddles into the breeze, that a small story grew into something it weren't, passed from one man to the next?

As we near Bonanza, twilight's shadows stretch clear across the creek. Mel calls to a sourdough on Queen, a fellow we didn't see when we first passed through, with a washed-out beard pale as straw. "Did you ever meet a man named One-Eyed Riley?"

"No," the sourdough says, "but you could try looking for him in Grand Forks. It's a new town about two miles south of here, right where Bonanza veers to the east and Eldorado joins in."

My heart sits heavy in my chest. What if One-Eyed Riley's mine is just a dream?

This time me and Mel gotta cling to each other just to cross Bonanza's slippery ice without a lick of sunlight. Oh, I'm ready to stop, but where are we gonna go? We've already walked ten miles, easy, probably more. The sun is only a memory.

"How much longer, Mel?" I ask when we reach the wooded hill above Bonanza.

"Three more creeks, then we can quit."

I run through Riley's clues again, more from habit than anything. *Last chance. Nine below.* That number feels different now. "Wait a second. Tell me again what the claim on Bonanza was called?"

It's so dark with the trees and the clouds that cover

the moon, I can't see Mel, but I can hear him. "Fifty-four above."

Above what, I don't know. Could it mean fifty-four mines above discovery claim? "Maybe I've been thinking about *nine below* all wrong. What if it ain't a temperature, but the name of Riley's claim?" Hope flickers inside me. "That's it. What else could it be? Now all we have to figure out is the name of the creek and . . ."

I hear a thump. Then nothing.

"Mel?"

The silence stretches deep into the woods.

"Are you all right?"

It's like Frank's got me around the throat again, like he twists my shirt so tight, I can't hardly breathe.

"Melvin, answer me."

I race back through the shadows. Branches grasp my jacket, scratch my face, and there's my brother, slumped over on the ground, behind a thicket of trees.

# Chapter 11

Mel's skin is damp, and his cheeks burn hot as cinders. Why didn't I guess he'd been feeling poorly?

"Come on, Mel. Come on, wake up." I try to wipe his forehead like the Sister did when I had the influenza, but I ain't got a fresh rag or a basin of water, all I got is my sleeve, and oh, my hand is shaking fierce. Over one eyebrow Mel's skin is wet with something sticky.

Blood. He must have hit it when he fell.

Mel's sick and hurt, and there ain't a thing I can do about it.

I try to breathe, but the air don't go down right. It's like a needle's been jammed between my ribs.

"Come on, Mel, you gotta answer me."

The nighttime sky is flooded with clouds. Only the

faintest moonlight breaks through, outlining gnarled tree branches that reach like bony arms. What am I supposed to do, my brother sick and with his head banged up? I ain't even sure where we are, anyhow.

I ain't gonna cry like some little kid, I ain't gonna do it.

"It's gonna be okay," I whisper, though I ain't sure I believe them words myself.

My sleeve soaks fast with Melvin's blood, and now that we ain't moving, the cold sinks in, clean and deep. Mel's legs are kind of crooked, and his head's tilted to one side. I straighten him as best I can and cover him with my coat.

No one knows we're out here. The Marys said we could call on them anytime we needed, but they're in Dawson.

"Why'd this have to happen?" I shout to them silent trees. My brother's hurt. Everything is all staked up. We don't got much to eat and nowhere to sleep. And Riley's mine—if it's real at all—feels as distant as when I heard about it back on the steamer *Queen.*

"Mel?" I lean over him. "Can you hear me?"

Mel's head moves beneath my sleeve.

My heart beats swift.

"Jasper?" His voice rasps like it hurts to speak.

"I'm here. I'm with you."

But Mel don't say no more, and that's worse than anything.

He's breathing. I feel it in the rise of his chest, only it's like he's slipped away to a place miles from sleep.

A bitter wind snakes through the trees. Them empty branches scrape and groan.

What if Mel leaves, like Mama did?

I shake my head. She didn't leave. Mama died.

After the influenza, when I was strong enough, Mel took me to the cemetery. There was no special stone with "Abigail Johnson" written on it, not even a cross to mark her grave. Only a jagged piece of wood stuck in the ground.

Tears slip from my eyes, they splash on Melvin's face, but he don't move a wink.

"Don't you go. Don't die, Mel. You're everything I got."

I wipe and wipe his forehead clean. Mel's blood, my tears, the grime of six long weeks, it coats my sleeve and stiffens his hair.

I hum Mama's lullaby, the song that's soft as rippling water. It's the only comfort I got to offer. Then I do something I ain't done for years. I kiss my brother light on his cheek.

Maybe there are a few folks still out on Bonanza who could help.

I tuck my coat underneath Mel's chin. "I'm gonna go, but just for a little bit. I'll be back for you. I promise."

The wind cuts across my face and with it swirling snow. I try the best I can to run, but it ain't easy in the darkness. Maybe this swampy hill's gonna trip me like it did Mel, knock me down and claim two Johnson boys, easy as that. It ain't only sticks or rocks or snowbanks my feet gotta dodge, either, but them deep mine shafts that run from the creek bottoms up into the hills.

Fires smolder on the creek's far bank, left alone to burn down to ash. They blanket the valley in heavy smoke thick as the night sky. This whole world feels empty. Even if I shout for help, there ain't one living soul who would hear me.

I best push on. Long as I keep traveling south, I'm sure to come on one of them last few creeks that flow into Bonanza. The wind mixes up my ears, the snow confuses me, how it comes from all directions.

I wrap my muffler around my head, turn up my shirt collar at the cold, which pricks and lashes. Long as I keep moving, it can't get too bad, but that ain't true for Melvin. How much good's an extra coat gonna do him when he's burning up with fever in this snow?

Oh, Mel. I ain't gonna let you down. I promise you that.

For ages, them enormous pines have blocked the bit of moonlight that tries to escape the clouds, but suddenly between the trunks and smoke I glimpse the smallest flash of light. I run down the hill so fast, my feet fly out from under me, and then I'm up again, shouting with all I got. "Help! I need some help!"

"Where are you?" a voice calls.

Someone's there! "On the hill," I answer.

Boots crunch over twigs and snow, and I make out two dark shapes.

"It's a boy," one says. "What is it, son?"

"My brother." My chest is so tight, I can't hardly get the words out. "He's sick. I had to leave him." Then I do that thing more awful than any old kiss on the cheek. I bawl like a baby.

"Don't worry." The second man puts his coat across my shoulders. "We'll find him for you."

An hour later, me and Mel are wrapped in blankets inside a tiny cabin. I'm perched on a tree-stump stool, and Mel's asleep in the only bed. One of the men who rescued us is barely more than skin and bones. He feeds wood into a stove as the other tugs off his boots. Dancing flames shine on the strangest window I've ever seen, one made of glass jars stacked one on top of the next and stuck together with what sure looks like dried-up bits of moss.

Mel's face is as gray as the meat we got cheap in Kirkland, but these fellows have cleaned his wound, and he's breathing steady. "You better fight," I whisper, though he probably don't hear me. "You gotta beat this." Melvin's gonna be all right, because I can't lose him.

The skinny fellow pours something from a kettle into a dinged-up mug. His gray hair grows past his chin, but his face is shaved clean. "Want some?" he asks.

"What is it?"

"Boot broth." He tilts his head toward the other man. "Made special from Edwin's pair."

The man called Edwin has his feet propped near the stove. He runs his fingers through his thick brown beard as steam curls off his socks. Them boots ain't nowhere to be seen.

"Keeps you hardy," the skinny one says. "Out here we boil up a pair when the weather starts to change." My face must show I'd rather lick a beehive than try that stuff, because he laughs, his wide mouth full of gaps where teeth should be. He shuts the stove door, which cuts most of the room's light. "I'm only teasing," he says as he pours himself a mugful from the kettle. "This ain't a broth made from boots. It's spruce needle tea. I ran out of coffee a good while back, and it ain't a bad substitute."

Edwin nods. "Helps with scurvy, too. Last winter, Spare-Rib would have lost all his teeth if it weren't for his tea."

"I'll try a little." It'll be warm, at least.

The fellow called Spare-Rib pours me some.

The first taste of spruce needle tea is bitter, but oh, it goes down good. "Thank you." I must have said them words a hundred times since Spare-Rib and Edwin found me near a creek called Adams. They followed me back to Mel and didn't think nothing to scoop him up and carry him between them. He was awake by then, confused and feverish. We wandered past a couple cabins, dark and rough, until we reached this one.

"You don't have to thank us for doing what's decent," Edwin says. He pulls on his boots again. "I'm gonna go. You boys need your rest. Spare-Rib, I'll walk Little Skookum Creek one more time, see if I catch sight of that fellow."

The door slams shut, and me and Mel are left with Spare-Rib. His trousers are big enough for two of him, and he wears a cinched-tight belt to hold them up. Spare-Rib's one big jangly mess of bones.

"What's your name, son?"

I'm glad Mama ain't around to know I haven't introduced myself yet. "I'm Jasper Johnson, and my brother's name is Mel."

Spare-Rib offers me his hand. "I'm Jimmy Mackinson. 'Course, no one's called me that for years. I've been Spare-Rib since my Fortymile days, when my landlady wouldn't let me use her sheets on account of my pointy hips and elbows. Said I was sure to rip a hole clean through."

Fortymile, that mining town where Mr. Theroux claimed to live.

"Ever heard of Theroux?" I say.

"Thee-row?" Spare-Rib squints. "What's a thee-row?"

"A fellow me and Mel met on our way to Dawson. He said in Fortymile he was partners with Salt Water Jack and mined along with Buckskin Miller and Pete the Pig."

"Well, ain't that curious." Spare-Rib takes a swig of tea. "The Salt Water I knew worked alone. And never have I met two men who hated each other more than Pete and Buckskin. Pete swore he could smell Buck a mile off, on account of the fact he never bathed."

If a fellow named Pete the Pig gets stirred up about someone else's stink, it's gotta be real foul.

"Buckskin's partner was Two-Step Louie. Ain't never heard about a Thee-row."

Spare-Rib's story proves Mr. Theroux is a liar, one hundred percent. "But how'd Mr. Theroux learn them names if he's never been to Fortymile?"

Spare-Rib shrugs. "I heard Ol' Buckskin left the Klondike on a steamer a few months back. And Pete took a sled to Dyea last winter. Could your friend have run into one of them?"

"Maybe," I say, because who's to know? "But that Mr. Theroux ain't no friend of mine." Why he was so set on us believing he'd mined up here before, I don't know.

Outside the wind screams long and lonely. The fire, the blanket, the strong tea soak warmth clear to my bones. Apart from that night in the Palmer House Hotel, I've stayed in tents since that morning we left the *Queen*.

"You boys are lucky me and Edwin found you when we did. These last few nights there's been some thieving along Adams Creek, where we ran into you, and Little Skookum, this creek we're on right now. We planned to surprise the fellow if he came through again."

A shiver passes through me. What would that thief have done if he'd bumped into me or Mel?

Spare-Rib cracks the door, and cold air blasts into the cabin. "It's really coming down out there. When I saw them clouds roll in, I knew we were due for a good one." He shakes off the snow that blankets his boot and returns to the fire. "Not the best time to travel. I take it you and Mel have just arrived."

I nod, sort of embarrassed. "If we'd known the goldfields had been staked . . ." I stop right there. We did know, kind of, and still we didn't turn around. I ain't sure how to explain we got no home to go back to.

"Mining's about luck and timing, and, I hate to say it, neither are on your side," Spare-Rib tells me. "You hungry? I got moose-meat jerky, sourdough for biscuits, and plenty more spruce tea."

I remember what Mr. Turner said. "Ain't there a food shortage?"

Spare-Rib laughs, and I count seven teeth in that mouth of his. "Every year I've mined these parts, there's been a shortage of one thing or another. But as long as I catch me some rabbits or buy a moose from the Indians, it works out fine."

I tear right into the jerky. Spare-Rib pours me a second cup of tea. "We've got some beans we could share." Though it's all we got, it ain't right not to offer. Spare-Rib's been so good to take us in. I find the mostly empty sack and give it to him. Even if Spare-Rib keeps us on until Mel feels better, there ain't no way we'll make it through the winter with only a weathered piece of canvas and a week's worth of beans.

"Now that would be real tasty." Spare-Rib sets them on the table. "Thank you for that." He sits down beside me. "Might be you'll find a claim where Mel could earn wages, but with him sick, that won't be soon. The last three years the Klondike's frozen solid in the middle of October. That's just a week from now. After that, everyone hunkers down for the winter. Men work their diggings some, but not like in the summer, when the sun's up all hours. No one hires extra hands until the creeks and rivers break up in the spring."

Mel groans. I reach him as his eyes flicker open. "My feet hurt." His voice still scratches. The bump on his forehead has swelled up big and red and angry.

"Here, drink some of this." I offer him my cup. Mel makes a face as he swallows. Could be the funny taste or that his throat is raw. Then he settles back on the pillow. I hold my fingers to his cheek. It ain't as gray as it was earlier, but he's still awful hot.

Spare-Rib opens the cabin door and hurries outside.

"Where are we?" Mel says.

"In a cabin on one of those little creeks west of Bonanza. A fellow named Spare-Rib has taken us in." I tell him he's real sick, that he fell and we were rescued.

Mel shivers like he ain't wrapped in a blanket but is still out there in the cold.

Spare-Rib returns and brings in a bowl of snow. He lifts the blanket at the foot of the bed and pulls off Mel's socks. Spare-Rib studies Mel's toes, which are red and puffy. "Good. I don't see any white patches on the skin. Your toes ain't frostbitten, I can tell you that. Long as you feel pain, there's life in them yet."

Then he does a real strange thing. He takes a handful of snow and rubs it on Mel's feet. Mel don't pull away, like I expect. "Feel better?" Spare-Rib asks.

Melvin nods.

When Spare-Rib's done, he dries Mel's feet and wraps them in a cloth.

"You boys need some sleep." Spare-Rib tucks the blanket under Mel and gives me a lopsided grin. "I'd offer you the bed, but it's already occupied. How about we set you up in front of the stove instead?"

I lie down on the dirt-packed floor, my coat spread over me like a blanket, Mel's bed along my back. My head's against the tree-stump stool, and my toes reach to the wall. The cabin's so tiny, Spare-Rib's camped out underneath the table. I could walk the whole length of this place in five strides flat.

Pretty soon Spare-Rib's breath falls in line with Mel's. I'm glad Mel got to see that his Miner Code is going strong in this part of the Klondike. The fear that grabbed me when Mel fell and hurt himself, I've pushed it so far away, it can't touch me here.

I drift near the edge of sleep, but something Spare-Rib

said rubs like a pebble in my shoe. *Soon prospectors will hunker down for the winter. They'll work their claims but not as much as before.* Sounds like that Riley clue from Stanley Theroux: *Hunker down but not too much.* Maybe it ain't about getting low to the ground to hunt for gold, but about when to search for the claim. When everyone hunkers down, holed up in their cabins, maybe that's the best time to find it.

But I ain't even sure the story of Riley's mine is real anymore.

The fire pops in the stove. That funny whistle of Mel's starts in, and oh, I'm happy to hear he's resting easy. It ain't long before sleep comes for me, too.

Spare-Rib stokes the fire and moves about the cabin not much later. It's so dark, it ain't true morning, more like the backside of night. I lift Pa's watch to the firelight that spills from the open stove. It says it's a little past six.

"I didn't mean to wake you," Spare-Rib says as he buttons his flannel shirt.

"It's all right."

"Mel feels cooler than yesterday," he tells me.

I sit down beside my brother. Mel's cheeks ain't gray no more but are awful pale, with hollows deep as Spare-Rib's. A bruise now runs from the angry bump to his tangled mess of hair.

Spare-Rib sits at the table. A bacon-grease candle casts an eerie light over his biscuit breakfast. "You ready for some food?"

I nod.

"Come here, then."

I hold the cold biscuit Spare-Rib gives me in one hand, spread my map out on the table with the other, and with my pencil add in the creeks I've learned since last night. Edwin and Spare-Rib found me near Adams. Next to it is Little Skookum, the creek we're on right now. Must be named for Skookum Jim, one of the men who found the thumb-sized nugget last summer.

"What's that you've got?" Spare-Rib asks.

"A map. Me and Mel, we want to learn all the goldfield creeks."

He looks over my shoulder. "That's quite a map." Spare-Rib reaches for his boots. "Make sure Mel gets plenty of sleep, and fill him up with tea. I'll be out at my diggings if you need me."

Outside the window made of jars, it's still black as night. "Do you always start this early?" I ask.

Spare-Rib tucks his gray hair behind his ear. "Well, now, the last few years I have. I've been mining most of my life, and I ain't as young as I used to be. It takes me twice the time to do the things I did back then. And once my partner left, I had double the work to do alone."

I think of me and Melvin on a claim, what a great team

we would be. But the chance of that ever happening is slim now. "Is the work real hard?"

"It is. Some years have been better than others, but I ain't never found much gold," Spare-Rib says. "Still, I wouldn't give up this life, not for anything."

"Why not?" It seems like a whole lot of trouble without much reward.

"I'm my own boss in the prettiest place I've ever seen, where mountains scrape the heavens and creeks rush through narrow valleys, where snow's as soft and beautiful as it is mean, and the Northern Lights dance across the nighttime sky. Nothing beats it."

When Spare-Rib puts it that way, it makes more than perfect sense. Being in charge of myself in an untamed world like this, that would suit me fine.

Spare-Rib points to the edge of my newspaper. "What have you written there?"

"It ain't nothing, really. Just some things about a mine that probably ain't true. You ever hear about a fellow named Riley?" I ask.

"What's that?" Spare-Rib says. He looks at me real strange.

"One-Eyed Riley. Supposedly he gave up a mine worth millions."

Spare-Rib sinks onto the tree-stump stool. "That's what I thought you said." He sets his bony elbows on his faded blue jean trousers. "I ain't heard about Riley's mine since last October, about a year ago now. A big crowd searched for weeks."

The back of my neck prickles. Oh, this I can't believe. "The story's real?"

Spare-Rib nods. "It's real, all right, though no one ever found it. A few souls still poke around, but nearly all work their own claims again."

"Jasper?" Mel sits up. His eyes ain't glassy anymore, though that bruise over his eyebrow has darkened and spread.

I rush to his side. "How do you feel?"

"Better than yesterday."

Spare-Rib smooths Mel's blanket best he can. Icy snow plinks against the jam-jar window. "Sure is getting nasty out there," Spare-Rib says. "Maybe it's best I stay inside." He pours Mel a mug of tea. "The company in here's real fine."

He may be rough looking, but Spare-Rib's a good fellow. If Mama had met him, she'd have called him a gentleman.

Spare-Rib drags the tree-stump stool near the bed. I sit down with the two of them.

"Mel, Spare-Rib says Riley's mine is real. And no one's found it yet."

Mel's eyes grow big.

"Last time I saw him was about a year ago," Spare-Rib says.

"You know One-Eyed Riley?"

"Sure do. We were partners back in Fortymile."

"Partners?" I ain't sure about that, not after them stories from Mr. Theroux.

The cabin walls groan as the wind whips around.

"Me and Riley mined together a good three years," Spare-Rib says. "Then Riley set his sights on the creeks around the Klondike. He was one of the first to go, a year or two before the Bonanza discovery. Folks had figured for a while gold must be in these parts, but it wasn't until Carmack and Jim Skookum found that nugget in Bonanza that most of Fortymile up and left. The whole town emptied overnight.

"I left about a month later myself, lucky to find a claim so close to Bonanza still open. I set to work, like I'd always done, when I heard my old partner had been in Dawson, crowing that he had a claim worth more than anyone had ever seen. Fellows tried to follow him out of town, but he was clever enough to give them the slip."

"So no one ever tracked him down?" Mel asks.

Spare-Rib shakes his head. "But I saw him one more time. Last September there was a knock on my door. Riley stood on the other side, dressed in a heavy parka and moccasins, a bag over his shoulder. There was an early snow, the first of the season, with wind so strong it made his leather eye patch flutter. I invited him in out of the storm, but he said no. He was going 'round the dome, he told me, and was here to say goodbye. It was the last time I saw him. Then those rumors started that Riley had quit his mine and it was up for grabs. For a few weeks claims stayed empty as folks searched everywhere. But the frenzy died down when nothing was ever found."

Spare-Rib ain't fibbing. I can see it in his eyes.

"It's gonna pick up again. Lots of people me and Mel met while traveling to Dawson have heard about the mine. With no claims left, everyone will try to find it."

"That dome Riley talked about. What did he mean?" Melvin asks.

Spare-Rib leans forward on his bony knees. "Oh, I don't know. The man always talked in riddles. I figured since he said he was leaving, he meant Midnight Dome in Dawson City. You can't get out of town without passing it by."

"I have some clues about the mine, but I ain't sure what they mean. Maybe you could help me some?"

"Tell me what you got."

I read from my list so far. "*Nine below's the way to go. Gold on the bottom of the creek. Friday's the last chance to be lucky. Hunker down but not too much.*"

Spare-Rib studies the map. "That's a whole lot of creeks."

There's many me and Mel ain't labeled yet. It's plain discouraging. "I wish I knew all their names."

Spare-Rib trails his finger along the Klondike east

of Dawson. "There's Hunker and Gold Bottom and Too Much Gold."

That don't make sense. "What did you say?"

"Them clues of yours. They're a list of creeks." Spare-Rib writes in the names of those that up till now have been left blank.

Mel rubs his upper lip. "Those are far from the creeks we passed yesterday."

Too Much Gold, Gold Bottom. Those names fairly promise riches. They've got to lead to Riley's mine. I point to the map. "What if *Hunker down but not too much* means to follow Hunker Creek down a bit, but not as far as Too Much Gold?"

I imagine a line that runs the length of Hunker but not all the way to Too Much. It turns off at Gold Bottom Creek. "*Hunker down but not too much. Gold on the bottom of the creek.* Them two clues, they fit together."

"Last Chance is the first creek that runs into Hunker," Spare-Rib says, "but Friday and Lucky Creeks ain't close by at all."

"Maybe *Friday's the last chance to be lucky* isn't a real clue, then," Mel says.

"If I'm right about those first two clues, where do I go after Gold Bottom?"

Someone knocks at the door. "Spare-Rib. You in there?"

"Come on in," he calls.

Edwin opens the door. His shoulders are dusted with snow. Behind him, the sky is thick and gray. "You ain't going to believe this," he says.

Spare-Rib jumps to his feet. "You found the fellow who's stolen from the claims?"

"Not yet," Edwin says. "This is something else. Folks up and down Adams are talking about that old partner of yours again. Some fellows over on Queen Creek are selling clues to Riley's mine."

"You know I never bothered with all that," Spare-Rib says, "but it is awful strange. We were just talking about Riley and his mine."

"Why are they selling clues now?" Edwin says. "Riley left more than a year ago."

"Because plenty of new folks have heard about them, that's why." My eyes meet Mel's. "I gotta get to Queen."

I got four clues. At least one of them might be a fake. And here's a chance to learn one more.

Spare-Rib puffs out his hollow cheeks. "Sounds to me like a sham."

Spare-Rib's got his own claim. He can afford to think like that. But me and Mel have staked everything on One-Eyed Riley's mine. "I'll be back soon."

"Be careful," Melvin tells me.

I nod and with my coat and muffler race out the door.

• • •

Three miles north of Little Skookum, a line of men climbs Queen Creek Hill, then weaves through the trees. Them fellows wait real patiently, but I don't got time to waste. The snow comes hard and frigid, and I dash ahead to see what's going on. What my eyes take in at the front of the line I can't hardly believe. Behind a table made of crates stands them Therouxs.

Mr. Theroux hovers close to the man who's first in line.

"I knew Riley for a good ten years," the man says. "I was friends with all his friends. But I've never seen you before. So how is it you claim to have his clues?"

Mr. Theroux waves his hand. "Me and Riley met a long time before that. As for his clues, you can judge for yourself." Then he leans in and whispers something in the man's ear. Stanley pays careful attention to his uncle and writes something down.

Stanley's the one who'd heard some Riley clues at Lake Lindeman. Mr. Theroux didn't even know who he was back then. Now he's acting like Riley's an old friend.

Stanley hands over that paper to the man as soon as he's made his payment.

So this is why Mr. Theroux wanted people to believe he'd mined here before, to find a way to trick unsuspecting folks out of their gold.

I don't got to wait my turn. I can take some liberties, on account of all that time I spent with them Therouxs. I pass folks I ain't seen before and a few I recognize. A couple men from the claims along Queen Creek, that fellow from Bonanza with the gray-streaked beard, the one who said Riley owed him money—Bill, was that his name?—and a man in a derby pulled low on his forehead. Albert. Who somehow knew the Klondike was all staked out.

I elbow in near the front of the line.

"No you don't." The sourdough whose turn is next spreads his feet so I can't pass.

"I gotta talk to my uncle," I say, "the one who's selling clues."

I glance at Mr. Theroux. "Riley told me this one over supper when he visited me last spring," he says before he whispers to the first man in line.

I blow on my hands, try to warm them up. Sounds just like them lies he told about his Fortymile days.

"That'll be ten dollars." Stanley holds out a slip of paper for the man in front of the sourdough who won't let me by. "If you ain't got money, we'll be happy to take three pinches of your gold."

I poke my head around the sourdough, and that's when Stanley's eyes meet mine. In a flash he focuses on the man while he measures out his gold. The red spots on Stanley's face flame across his cheeks as he dumps that gold dust into a jar.

Boy, Mr. Theroux has drawn a crowd, and has he got everyone's attention. If I didn't know better, I might think he really was friends with Riley.

"What'd Riley look like?" someone shouts from the back of the line. "That'll settle if this man speaks true or if this is just a con."

Mr. Theroux's head jerks up. He looks around for the man who's asking, but the man don't make himself known.

The sourdough next to me spits a wad of tobacco into the snow. It lands inches from my feet. "Your uncle, huh? What's his name, then?"

"Theroux," I say. So what if he ain't family. There's a few questions I got, and something I want everyone to hear. Mr. Theroux's a fraud, it's as simple as that. "Uncle!" I dart around the sourdough. "It's me. Jasper!"

Mr. Theroux's eyes grow wide. His arms fall limp around his bulging middle. "How'd you get here?"

"On the Yukon, same as you. Those last two weeks on the river, me and Mel ate mighty fine. How'd your soggy flour hold up?"

Mr. Theroux smiles through his grizzled beard, the spitting image of an uncle right charmed to see his nephew. "Just fine. Now excuse me," he says. "I've got some important work to do."

The sourdough steps up.

Stanley shakes that jar of gold dust and studies it real close. He sharpens his pencil with a pocketknife the whole time his uncle talks. He does everything he can not to look at me.

I think about what Stanley told me on the raft. "Looks like you two got a good start on your gold," I say soft enough so only he can hear. "You gonna have that plate of eggs fried over easy you've pined for?"

It don't matter that there ain't any eggs in all the Klondike. It's the meaning underneath them words that I want Stanley to catch. He's better than this. He's got some dreams that don't involve his uncle's swindling.

Mr. Theroux whispers his clue to the sourdough, but Stanley ain't writing it down. "What is it you want, Jasper?"

"There's a couple things."

"Where's my clue?" The sourdough taps Stanley's arm. "Them other fellows got theirs on paper."

Stanley scribbles something quick and hands it to the sourdough. He fumbles as he unscrews the jar lid to collect the fellow's gold.

Stanley's occupied, but the mister's not. I best take the opportunity in front of me. With both hands spread on the table made of crates, I stare at Mr. Theroux, like Miss Stapleton would when she'd had enough of my talking. "I'm real curious how you met One-Eyed Riley, Uncle."

Mr. Theroux's nostrils twitch. Stanley's skinny fingers can't get the lid on right.

"Bet you were surprised when you got to Dawson and found gold don't grow on bushes and trees."

Mr. Theroux puts his hands right near mine and bends forward, till our noses almost touch. Puffs of frozen air float by me as he talks. "What are you doing, kid?"

"I want everyone to know you ain't Riley's friend," I whisper.

I back up a little and make my voice louder. "How do you like this snow?" It's coming down so fast, I can't hardly see where the sun's supposed to be. I ain't never been this cold before. "Is this winter as mild as the ones you lived through in Fortymile?"

Mr. Theroux moves from behind the crate box table, till he's right at my side.

Behind me, voices murmur. I peek over my shoulder and see the line of men ain't as straight as before. It's shifted and spread and moved closer, like a snake that's gotten riled.

I turn so I face everyone, so every soul will hear. "When did you meet One-Eyed Riley, Uncle Theroux? A couple weeks ago you didn't know a thing about him."

Mr. Theroux wraps his arm around my middle. "Shut that mouth of yours. Now." It might look like he holds me in a friendly hug, but that ain't what's happening. He crushes me against his chest and squeezes out every bit of air I got.

Black spots flicker in front of my eyes.

"I see you're all alone today," Mr. Theroux whispers.

"Keep up your foolishness, and it won't be hard to make you disappear. Who besides your brother will miss a scrawny brat like you, anyhow?"

I fight for air but can't hardly breathe. He's right. It would be easy for Mr. Theroux to get rid of me. Mel would never know what happened.

Mr. Theroux turns on his booming voice again. "Out in Omaha last spring, my old chum Riley paid me a visit. He said with all the time we'd spent together in Fortymile, I was the one who deserved his clues the most. Now, ain't it generous of me to sell them to you?"

"Your Fortymile partner," I barely choke out, "Salt Water Jack. He told me. He ain't ever. Heard of no Theroux." Those are Spare-Rib's words, not mine, but the mister don't need to know.

The frozen air fills up with shouts from the crowd:

"Buckskin Miller mined with Two-Step Louie! I know that for a fact."

"Riley ain't never been farther south than Montana. He can't abide the heat."

"These two are running a scam."

Mr. Theroux squeezes me so tight, I feel my ribs crack. Pain rushes through me, sharp and swift. I set my teeth onto his sleeve, bite as fierce as I can. That sure makes him scream. Dark blood seeps through the fabric. He shoves me hard enough that I stumble back.

Now every soul will know he's a liar, that he's here to cheat them out of their riches, men who've earned it fair and square.

"What'd Riley look like?" It's Bill, the old-timer from Bonanza with the gray-streaked beard. He moves in close to me and Mr. Theroux. "I'd know Riley anywhere, and I ain't the only one. So tell us about that Riley you know so well."

"Well." Mr. Theroux wipes his face with the bandanna around his neck, the one I'm sure ain't seen a bit of soap since I last washed it. "My memory ain't what it used to be."

"I said, what's Riley look like?" Bonanza Bill demands.

Mr. Theroux lifts his eyes to the snow-filled sky, considering. "Riley was a short man with a double chin. His hair was the color of cornsilk and his breath was something foul."

The old-timer puts his hands on his hips, where they're about level with the ends of his beard. "Some of you here today remember Riley. Was he like that?"

"The Riley I knew was as bald as a baby," says a voice from the crowd. Then others join in.

"The Riley I knew was knock-kneed and wore a green pair of suspenders."

"Last time I saw Riley, he had two eyes in his head."

"Riley's got long black curls that touch his shoulders."

"I thought Riley dropped dead years ago."

Everyone gets quiet, their thoughts on Riley and how he might have passed away. I stomp my feet to fight the cold as I try to figure something. How come not one person's talked about that leather eye patch Spare-Rib mentioned? How is it so many folks remember Riley differently?

"If anyone knows what Riley looked like, it's his old partner, Spare-Rib Mackinson," I say.

Mr. Theroux makes an ugly sound deep in his throat. "And how would you know that?"

I tap my chest and wince. My ribs burn like blazes. I hope they ain't broken. "Because me and my brother are staying with Spare-Rib, that's how."

Bonanza Bill sets his eyes on me. "How is it you're staying with Spare-Rib Mackinson? Ain't you that cheechako I met yesterday?"

"Enough talk," a fellow shouts. "If these clues are fakes, I want my gold back."

Oh, that sets off the crowd. Someone jabs me in my aching side, a set of boots tramp over my feet, which throb with pain and cold. Everyone's so close, I got to scramble over the table behind me. I bump straight into Stanley.

"He found them in the newspaper." Stanley watches the crowd, but he's talking to me. At first, I didn't know what he was on about.

"Found what in the paper? Who do you mean?"

"My uncle. Those miner names from Fortymile. He made up the story about living there."

"You better give us our gold!" someone shouts. "Or you'll have to explain yourselves to the authorities."

Mr. Theroux slashes his arm through the air and points a finger right at me. "My clues are real. It's this boy who's lying. He says he's my nephew, but I ain't ever seen him before."

"This boy," says a voice I've come to dread, "belongs with me."

Frank Hazard stands behind me. He clasps his big hand on my shoulder. "I've searched all over for you."

I look up. From his eyes to his drooping mustache, Frank's face is almost tender. "I thought I lost you." A tear slips down his cheek, and he pulls out a hankie and wipes his face, so that everyone might see.

I know what Frank's on about. He's softening the crowd. It's the same thing I tried with Mr. Smalley when I searched for a bunk on the *Queen.*

"I don't know this fellow—" I start to say, but I stop quick. Because something hard and pointy pokes my shoulder blade, and the way me and Frank face everyone, there ain't no one but him who can see.

Frank's got a revolver and he holds it to my back.

My heart goes fast as a jackrabbit.

I'm in a crowd, I tell myself. He won't dare hurt me,

at least not now. I swallow hard and lift my face to him. Whatever Frank's up to, I've gotta play along, because if I don't, he might try to hurt me later. "I didn't recognize you at first."

Frank shakes his head, sorrowful-like. "And me, your own dear pa."

My pa, he says.

"Let's go, son."

The crowd parts as we move forward. If anyone sees the gun, no one says nothing. Not Bill from Bonanza. Not Albert, who's got his hat tilted so far forward, it covers half his face. Not Stanley, who grips that jar of gold as we walk past. And certainly not Mr. Theroux. He only looks out for himself.

Melvin and Spare-Rib are clear over on Little Skookum. There ain't a soul out here who cares about what's gonna happen to me.

# CHAPTER 12

Frank forces me over Queen Creek Hill toward the woods that run high above Bonanza, his revolver still held firm to my back. My hands are cold and slick with sweat. I think through a million ways I could distract him, if only he didn't grip me with his other hand. Frank don't talk, and I don't dare anger him with that weapon right against me. All I can do is try to be ready for whatever he's got planned.

Once we're deep in the woods with no chance to be seen, Frank spins me around. My heart turns over when I spy the revolver, now pointed at my middle. All those awful feelings when he had me tied up in Miles Canyon come crashing back.

I shut my eye behind the broken lens to see if anyone

passes on the other side of the trees. What if I shout? Would someone come and help me?

"So," Frank says, his sour breath hanging frozen in the air, "you work with me now."

I don't know what he means, but I hope Frank sees I ain't gonna fight. I ain't gonna do anything that would cost my life.

The wind and snow have picked up and the cold has settled deep. With no sun to speak of, it ain't clear how late it is, but it's still afternoon. Soon Spare-Rib and Mel will wonder why I ain't back. Maybe Spare-Rib will tramp over to Queen Creek to search. But even if he gets that far, there ain't no way he'll find me.

"I know who you're staying with," Frank says. "One-Eyed Riley's partner. The man who knew him best of anyone out here."

"Spare-Rib and Riley ain't mined together for years, I promise."

He waves the gun. "Tell me your new clues. I know he must have given you some."

"I'm telling you, he didn't."

Frank grips the back of my head, holds that big face of his an inch from mine.

"What do you know about the creeks?"

So he knows them creek names run throughout the riddles. How I hate to tell him, but there ain't nothing else to do. "The clues I got have Hunker, Gold Bottom, and Too Much Gold. They're all east of Dawson along the Klondike River. That puts us pretty far from where we need to be."

If Frank already knows this, I can't tell from his stony face. "So Riley's clues could start in Dawson City and send a body east of town."

I nod. "From there you'd follow Hunker down a ways, continue south near Gold Bottom."

With one hand Frank keeps the gun trained on me. With the other, he pushes aside his fur coat and from his pocket pulls a thick piece of wood, maybe six inches long. The outside's covered in layers of bark, the inside's flat and even, a sturdy piece of log cut clean in half.

It's the wood he stole from Albert.

He shoves it into my hands. "Tell me what this means."

It really is a Riley clue. Words are neatly carved on the smooth side, smooth and even, like Riley took special care. " 'There are three sovereigns,' " I read aloud. " 'The middle one is Victory.' "

It makes no sense at all. "I don't understand."

Frank nudges me with the barrel of the gun. "Figure it out. Think through all them things Spare-Rib's told you about Riley."

"I said I don't know what it means!" *Watch your tongue, Jasper.* Them words of Mel's come to me quick. I can't argue or talk back, not with a gun pointed straight at me.

The wind lashes, sharp as broken glass.

Sovereigns. Where'd I hear that word before? Sheep Camp. That's where it was. At the Palmer House. The lawyer said something about Lord Avonmore and how many sovereigns it must have cost for them servants to lug that toilet paper and champagne.

I swallow hard. "The only sovereigns I've heard of are coins."

"Or kings. Sovereign's got a couple meanings."

Now that's interesting. I ain't sure what kings have to do with One-Eyed Riley's mine, but I'm gonna keep my mind open to the possibility.

"Three sovereigns. What could they be?"

"There's Queen Creek," I say, because a queen's as much of a sovereign as a king.

"And Solomon's Dome." Frank gazes at the trees, as though he can see something on the other side. "King Solomon was the world's richest king."

"Wait." I ain't never heard of a king named Solomon or his dome, but it reminds me of something. "Spare-Rib did say the last time he saw his old partner, Riley was about to head out of town. He said he'd go around the dome. I reckoned that meant Midnight Dome, the one in Dawson City, but it could've been another one." Maybe Riley meant to leave Spare-Rib with a clue.

Frank's eyes light up. I can tell he ain't heard this before. "Maybe it's Solomon's Dome, or that smaller one called Queen."

Two domes. One river. Two queens and a king. There they are, the three sovereigns from Riley's clue. But what's it mean that the middle one is Victory?

"Solomon and Queen Domes ain't far from here. Follow me." Frank unwinds the muffler from my neck and just like in Miles Canyon ties my hands in front of me.

That last bit of hope, the part that thought maybe Frank would let me loose when I told him what I knew, it's gone now.

Once when I was just a mite, I woke up scared. Mama got out of bed and lit the lantern for me, even though the brightness made it hard for everyone else to sleep. For the next three nights, she left that lantern near my bed, unlit but close enough to touch if I needed courage.

Oh, Mama, I need courage now. I pretend I got ahold of that lantern's polished handle.

Frank trudges south toward Little Skookum, one end of the muffler wrapped around his hand to guarantee I won't escape. We cover maybe half a mile, and every step, my boots sink deep in snowy drifts as I try to match his pace.

"There they are." Frank stops so quick, I nearly crash into him. "The domes." He points the gun to a mountain shaped like a loaf of bread on the other side of Bonanza. Even with a hint of darkness in the sky, I see the mountain now capped with snow, the same one me and Mel saw yesterday.

Except Mel saw two mountains and so does Frank. No matter how I try to see what they do, my broken glasses only show me one.

'Round the dome.

One dome, Riley said.

Maybe I don't need to spot what Mel and Frank say is there.

Maybe I only gotta see like a one-eyed man, like Riley.

If Riley only spied the one, that means Queen and Solomon Domes can't be separate sovereigns. They count as one. There's still two sovereigns left. That leaves Queen Creek as the second sovereign with one sovereign more, the middle one that's Victory.

Oh, my head is swimming with the notion.

If them clues send a fellow east of Dawson and then south down Hunker and Gold Bottom, where a body's supposed to swing around the dome, he wouldn't be too far from where we are right now.

"What happens if I find Riley's mine?" Will Frank let me go? Or will he pull the trigger?

"That ain't for you to know now, is it?"

If that's the best he's gonna offer, then the first moment I can, I've got to try to break away.

"Here's one last thing." The more I tell Frank, the better my chances of surviving. "Whatever creek Riley's mine is on, his claim is nine below."

"I know that," Frank says. "That's the first clue I learned."

"Below discovery claim, right?"

"Of course, what else could nine below mean?"

I shrug. The truth is I weren't completely sure what it meant until right this moment. "We gotta get close to the dome as we can to find the middle sovereign," I tell him, "the one that's Victory."

"What do you think the middle sovereign is?"

"I don't know yet, but that ain't gonna stop me." Since leaving home I've stowed away and tracked down Mel and climbed a mountain and traveled the Yukon on a flimsy raft, and tackled a whole pile of other things I ain't never done before. Now ain't the time to start believing I gotta have things figured out before I jump on in.

Dark's moved in, and no one's about. From where we stand, the dome is east of us, and Queen Creek is to the north. "Let's follow Bonanza past that little town of Grand Forks, where it meets Eldorado Creek," I say. "Over there, it looks like Bonanza runs near to the dome."

Frank unties the muffler wound about my wrists. "It wouldn't be right for a father to have his son tied up as we pass town. But no funny business now."

I move my hands, and a painful throbbing rushes through my fingers. The muffler held my wrists real tight, but it ain't that alone that makes them ache. The cold reaches clean to my bones. I've been outside since morning, and I forgot to bring Pa's woolen socks to wear over my hands.

Frank points his gun straight at me through the pocket of his long fur coat. "Not a soul in Grand Forks will know I got you at gunpoint."

We leave the woods and scramble down the hill to Bonanza. Darkness wraps itself around us. The snow's gotten so thick, it's hard to lift my feet. My sore ribs twinge with every breath, and the cold makes my toes hurt something fierce, but I remember Spare-Rib said the ache is good, it means blood's still moving through them.

Soon we're near Grand Forks, and just as soon we're past. The only thing in that tiny town is a couple of shacks. I ain't ever been on this part of Bonanza. Me and Mel didn't make it this far last night. Claim fires along the river burn down to coals, lining the creek in pockets of red. They thaw the ground for tomorrow's diggings, but they don't offer much light.

Then a stream joins with Bonanza on its far side. It's the first one we've seen since Grand Forks. The cabins along it are sparse and tucked away, the darkness blindfold-thick, but the snow has slowed a bit. "I gotta ask a question," I say.

"So do it."

"It's for someone on that creek. We ain't gonna find Victory unless we ask."

We gotta cross Bonanza to reach them cabins. The ice is smooth in some parts, in others thin and brittle. And what feels solid ain't no guarantee it truly is. Frank shoves me on in front of him. I scramble to keep from falling and gotta creep across the moaning surface, where just below, water still trickles. Frank's right in step behind me. He holds the muffler like a lead. If I fall through, he's far enough behind me to be safe, close enough to pull me out, if he had a mind to.

I inch closer to the creek bank, near enough to leap to solid ground. Pain shoots through my feet as I land, so awful, I have to bite my lip to keep from bawling. Just as he takes his final steps, Frank's foot pierces a weak spot in the ice. He shouts and stumbles, the muffler tight between us. When he lifts his foot, even through the darkness I can tell his leg is wet almost to his knee. In just a few short steps, Frank's limping. He ain't only soaked—he's hurt, too.

We near the first cabin. Frank pushes me forward and waits out of sight, near a patch of spruce trees. I bang and bang on the door, but no one answers. Even though the gun ain't rammed against me anymore, I feel it, like it's still pressed to my back.

Out along the stream again, I trek deep into the darkness while Frank limps along behind. The night is big and cold and empty, but at least the snow has stopped for now. Mel's got to be real worried. Is Spare-Rib wandering

Queen Creek in search of me? We've only stayed with Spare-Rib for one night and a morning, but even so, his tiny cabin feels homey with its jam-jar window and tree-stump stools and his pot of spruce needle tea.

Maybe this is my chance to run. I spin around, look to see how close Frank is behind me. But I can't tell exactly where he is. If I took off, he might shoot. Even if I got free, there ain't no way I'd make it to Little Skookum on my own.

I got no choice but to continue on. The cabin up ahead is a small dark lump set far from the creek bank. I pound at the door until it swings open.

"What do ye want?" The man inside holds a lantern that casts a golden ring of light. He wears a coat made from a blanket. Black curls brush his shoulders.

"Riley?" Could it be?

"Who's that?"

I shake my head to clear it. This man ain't Riley. He left a year ago. "Please, do you know about Victory?"

The man squints at me strange-like. "What are you on about? What's Victory?"

"I think it's a place," I say, and oh, I hear how strange that sounds.

"I ain't ever heard of Victory. This here's O'Neal Creek."

Riley left five clues. I know for certain *nine below*'s the last, and I got a real strong feeling the Victory clue falls right before it. Don't victory come at the end of battle, when the winning's sure? These clues have been a load of work, but I've put up a real good fight. Frank may get the gold, but he can't take finding the claim from me. I ain't gonna get this close just to be defeated.

"Any chance there's a creek named for a king nearby?"

He holds that lantern close to me. "What are you doing, son? You got me out of bed just to ask ridiculous questions?"

Everything inside me wants to tell him about Frank Hazard covered in the black of night, the gun he points at my back.

"Please. I need your help. Do you know a creek named for a king?"

"Well, I don't know about no kings. But come to think of it, there's Victoria, a little creek not much bigger than O'Neal, and mostly dried up, anyhow. I suppose it was named for the queen." He points over his shoulder. "It's out that way."

Victoria. That could be it! The English queen Miss Stapleton talked about. She's got a name like Victory. Guess one of them lessons my teacher gave counts for something after all.

When the door shuts tight, Frank grabs my wrists to tie me up again. We travel back along O'Neal. Frank's slower now. He lunges forward like that foot of his is stiff.

I bet he twisted it when he stumbled like he did. The wet and cold must make it hurt a whole lot worse. My feet ain't got much feeling left, but at least they're dry. They burn each time they hit the ground. That's good. It means there's life in them, there's life in me. I ain't gonna give up yet.

"How did Albert get that Riley clue?" I've been wondering about him for a real long time. Maybe it ain't smart to ask, but I figure since Frank's forced me to work for him, I got a right to know.

"That fool. He still came to the Klondike even though them Mounties kicked him out last spring."

Kicked out by the Mounties? No wonder he was so cagey about the law. He must have stole here, too. It ain't exactly an answer to my question, but I know better than to push for more.

"Which way did that man say the creek was?"

"Over there." I wave my hand, but now that we're out in the middle of nothing, I can't quite remember which direction we're supposed to go.

Frank wanders left, then veers to the right, a tangle of footprints trailing behind us.

The heavy clouds have thinned enough that moonlight brightens the snow. Strange green lights float across the sky, shoot up like waving banners, shift and twist in silence.

"You see that?" Frank says.

Who could miss it? I stop for just a moment. They must be the Northern Lights Spare-Rib talked about.

He shoves my shoulder. "Not in the sky. Over there."

I can barely make out the shell of a cabin, half burned and abandoned. We walk over and step through the wall, where the door should be. Snow's piled in one corner, a rickety bed's against the other standing wall. It's been empty a good while.

Frank turns around. "This must be Victoria." Frank moves faster now.

I spy two old mining troughs and a couple more empty cabins tucked up in the hills.

"Folks must have left the creek when it went dry."

Whatever I imagined Riley's creek to look like, it sure weren't this.

"What are you waiting for?" Frank says. "Find nine below."

"Please, how about you let me go. You can find the claim yourself. You don't need me anymore."

Not even finding Riley's claim matters to me now. It's living that's important. This life I've got I want to last.

Frost clusters on Frank's eyebrows. Icicles droop from his mustache. He strikes the revolver's barrel on my shoulder, and pain rings through my bones. "Find nine below," he says again.

That's when I kick him in the shin, the one that's already banged up good. He howls and grabs his leg. I try to run along Victoria's dried-up creek bed, but it's real dark. My hands are still tied together and the snow's right deep. I make my way as best I can, passing cabins along empty and abandoned mine shafts. Then I reach a claim that's different from the others. The cabin sits closer to the creek bed than the ones behind me did, but that ain't what feels peculiar. This claim feels bigger. Double the size, I reckon. It must be discovery claim. Every gold creek's got one. The first place gold's found, the prospector's rewarded with two claims joined together.

Frank lumbers like he's hurting, but it don't take him long to catch me. He grabs the end of my muffler and yanks me close. The revolver presses against my back. "I should shoot you now, to get it over with."

I shake as bad as when me and Pa traveled in the wagon down that old rutted road that ran behind the wool mill. "Please don't. This is discovery claim. I'll get you to Riley's from here."

All that's left to find Riley's place is count off nine more stakes downriver.

Frank kicks my heels. "Get moving, then."

My heart thuds painfully inside my chest. Why's he keeping me around? Frank could find Riley's mine real easily on his own. He don't got a need for me.

He counts the claims as we pass through, searches for markers to show where one starts and another ends.

"One."

The moonlight shines on a bandanna tied around a branch.

"Two."

A bit of wood wedged in the ground.

"Three."

A pile of rocks.

"Four."

An awful feeling rises in my throat.

"Five."

Since the Palmer House, Riley's mine is what I've dreamed about.

"Six." Frank jerks the muffler. "Hurry up."

But once Frank's got the gold . . .

"Seven."

. . . what's left for him to do . . .

"Eight."

. . . but shoot me dead?

"Nine."

A shiver creeps across my shoulders, and it ain't from the biting cold. I'm really here, at Riley's mine. Mel's the one who's meant to be with me. If things had been a little different, maybe we would have found this place together. The mine ain't like I pictured it back on the Chilkoot, a cabin stocked with all them tools I imagined

Riley left for the lucky soul who found it first. If there was ever a cabin here, it's long gone. Rusty tools are scattered everywhere. Three mine shafts line the creek bed.

Frank loosens the muffler around my wrists, points to the first hole. "Get in there and look around."

"Yes, sir," I say, hoping to buy his favor. He'll get nothing but sweetness from me now.

I dangle my feet over the edge of the first mine shaft. It ain't much wider than my shoulders. Them dirt walls are as smooth as the shaft is cramped. Now I know why Frank kept me around. A man the size of a grizzly bear ain't gonna fit inside. He needs me to do the work for him. With a deep breath I jump and land a good ten feet down in a mess of snow. There ain't no way to see but by the faintest moonlight.

I run my hands over every inch of the shaft, careful as I can. "I don't see nothing," I shout. "Don't feel nothing, either."

Frank reaches in. I got to dig my toes and fingers in them smooth shaft walls and climb until I grab his hand. "Where'd he stash it?" he says. "Where'd he hide the gold?"

Even though he sees my hands are empty, Frank makes me turn my pockets out, like I might have tucked something away while he blinked.

The second shaft is much the same—dark and narrow without nothing inside.

At the bottom of the last shaft, half buried in a drift of snow and tucked behind a rock, I feel an old tin can. It's light and kinda squashed, the only thing I've found on this whole dern claim. I stuff it in my pocket and climb up as best I can.

Frank don't even notice when I'm out. He's too busy searching under fallen branches and scanning every inch of the dried-up creek. He mumbles about how much he deserves Riley's gold, that with all his years of steady mining he should be filthy rich. He kicks at rusty tools and scattered logs, madder every minute.

I lift that can to the moonlight. A small white square's inside. It could be Riley's hankie or a letter from back home. It ain't soft like fabric when I pull it out. It's a folded piece of worn-out paper. I close my eye behind the broken lens and tilt the paper toward the light.

If you made it here, you've got your wits about you. I worked this claim for three years and all for nothing. No more than an ounce or two of gold did it ever yield. But that ain't the way I want to be remembered. So I made up this little story, see, of my wealthy claim.

Keep this worthless place if you want it, or curse my name. It don't matter to me. I've had my fun.

Riley

I grab a broken pickax and dash it to the creek bed.

Riley's a liar. He ain't no better than them Therouxs. His mine was only a story, a big joke on everyone who heard it and believed. All those weeks I dreamed of this place, the new home meant for us Johnson boys, they were for nothing.

It was a hoax, an awful trick made up by One-Eyed Riley.

I pick up a rock and slam it to the ground.

Frank stops his searching. "What's wrong with you?"

I don't say nothing, just hold out Riley's letter.

Frank's curse words tell me he's read it to the end. He lobs stones at a tree trunk, picks up more, and hurls them at the creek bed. "You cheat! You liar!" He shouts loud enough I bet Riley, wherever he is, feels deep in his belly that he's been found out.

Suddenly, a shot fires, then two more.

I dive for the ground.

Pain tears through my leg.

Then darkness overtakes me.

I'm propped against a pine tree when I come to, tired and cold except for the fire raging in my leg. My muffler's wound around my calf, where a thick patch of blood's begun to spread. Frank shot me, then he doctored me up? My mind ain't quite right yet, but it's good enough to know that's strange.

Frank pries off his boot and pulls down his sock, which crackles with ice. Even in the faint moonlight I see how red and swollen his foot is. His toes have them white spots Spare-Rib mentioned, the ones that mean frostbite has settled in. I can't feel my toes no more, but at least I didn't step through a sheet of ice. Frank's in a real bad way.

Truth be told, I ain't much better. I got a bullet in my leg, and I'm trapped with the man who did it, who threatened me all afternoon and had me think I wouldn't last the night.

But the green muffler's knotted firm below my knee. What am I to make of that?

Frank pulls a tin of matches from the pocket of his long fur coat. He tries to set a pile of damp branches alight, but so far he's only managed loads of curling smoke. He grabs that tin of matches and throws it at the dry creek bed. The matches fly in a hundred directions.

"How I see it, I got two choices."

Two choices. My belly tightens. Frank ain't talking about his sorry fire. What decision has he got left to make but leave me all alone or finish me off quick?

Far away the strangest sound drifts in, a wailing like a wolf, a whole pack of them.

"I can pretend I never found the mine, or I can say I never looked for it at all."

The pain's real bad. Maybe that's why I don't understand. "Why would you do either of them things?"

Frank turns his head so quick, his icicled mustache swings like willow branches stirred up in a breeze. "I ain't gonna be called a fool. If others learn about Riley's trick, that's what folks will think of me."

"Folks think what they want to, anyhow." That I know for sure.

The wailing becomes barks, and it's a whole lot louder now. Frank pulls himself to his feet, puts all his weight on the leg that didn't crash through the frozen river. "What's out there?"

I try to look, but it ain't so easy to move.

How I long to ask Frank what he's got planned, but I ain't sure I want to hear what he'll say. "Where do you think Riley is now?" I ask instead.

"That I'd like to know."

Behind us comes a scraping sound, like something slides across the snow. I shift to see what's going on, and my leg smarts with jabbing pain.

A dog team races from the direction of O'Neal Creek. Lantern light dances across the drifts as the sled behind it slows. Two fellows ride along, one in red and one in black. The fellow in red pulls out a rifle and aims it straight at Frank. "You're under arrest for kidnapping and possession of a firearm."

Frank breaks into a clumsy run and the Mountie follows after. His coat flaps like some hairy wing, but he ain't quick enough on his bum foot. The Mountie pins him in the snow, a tussle of red and furry brown. With his knee on Frank's back, the Mountie cuffs Frank's wrists behind him, then hauls him off the ground.

Everything happens so quick, my head can't quite keep up.

The fellow in black rushes to my side, and I see it ain't no fellow but Sister Mary Agnes. She wraps me in a blanket, folds me in a hug inside her long dark robes, and oh, I yelp with pain.

"What is it? What happened to you?"

"I'm hurt," I say.

"Did that man injure you somehow?" Her eyes are fierce.

I nod. "His gun went off, and I felt an awful burning in my leg."

Mary Agnes spreads the blanket on the ground and eases me down.

How come after a night as Frank's prisoner, it's the kindness of a Sister that gets my eyes to watering?

"It's going to be all right," Mary Agnes says. "I'll be right back."

I let what's happening sink deep as I breathe in the scent of the snow-damp blanket, feel its itchy wool pressed against my cheek. I'm out from under Frank's control. "I'm safe," I say to the black night, to Mama's memory. "I'm gonna be okay."

Mary Agnes returns with the lantern and unties the

muffler from my leg. "Oh, Jasper." I feel the searing cold of snow as she cleans it. "You must be hurting dreadfully." I gotta bite my lip while she pokes around. "The bullet's gone, but you've got an ugly graze." She tears a portion of her long black robe and fastens it around the wound.

Soon as she's tied that ragged bandage in a knot, Sister Mary Agnes storms over to Frank while the Mountie leads him to the sled. She tells him he should be ashamed of how he's treated me. I ain't never seen a lady as mad as she is.

That Frank won't even look my way. "It was an accident," he tells the Mountie. "I dropped my gun and it went off."

As I hear Frank say it, his words strike me as true. Why else would he have bandaged my leg?

That don't sway the Mountie none, and it shouldn't. "Like it was an accident you took this boy and pretended to be his pa."

Pa. A heap of thoughts comes flooding back, a mix of bad and good. But something shifts inside me. Them awful moments the last two years, they can't be erased, but they also don't deserve to be the first place my mind goes when I remember him.

Mary Agnes helps me sit again. She holds me close. "How'd you know?" I whisper. How'd the Mountie learn Frank had taken me? How'd Mary Agnes figure where to search?

"All of Dawson's heard about you," she says. "Last evening a fellow walked into town, straight for the Mountie station. He said a boy had been kidnapped by a man with a revolver. The last he'd seen, the two of you had headed to the woods above Bonanza."

My middle warms, and it ain't just from Mary Agnes's robe. Someone knew I was in trouble and tried to help me.

Mary Agnes goes on. "Not long after, a prospector from O'Neal Creek raced to Dawson in a sled. He said a boy had come to his cabin all alone and full of questions about Victoria Creek. It didn't sit right with him.

"By then the whole town was astir. I ran to the Mountie station. As Inspector Constantine set out to leave, I told him I knew two boys without a father, that if anything happened to them . . ." Mary Agnes clears her throat. "I persuaded him to let me come along on the chance the boy was you or Melvin. Because of the prospector, we knew to search Victoria Creek. Thanks to the smoke, we found you."

"That's Inspector Constantine?" I watch the Mountie as he forces Frank into the sled, a regular fellow, same as anyone. "He's the man in charge of the entire Klondike?"

"That's him," she says.

I can't quite believe it. Inspector Constantine's worked through the night, come all this way. For me. Who was the first fellow who went to the Mountie station? It had to be someone who was at Queen Creek with them Therouxs. Could it have been Stanley? It weren't the mister, that's for sure. He ain't high on morals, but Stanley could be, if he got a chance to try some out.

Maybe Mel and Spare-Rib heard the news that I'd been found and are waiting in Dawson City. "My brother, have you seen him?" I ask. My voice wobbles a little.

Mary Agnes shakes her head.

Inspector Constantine approaches. "Let's get you settled in." He scoops me up in his arms. It hurts so bad I got to hold my breath to keep from crying out. Him and Mary Agnes tuck me in the sled as gentle as they can. "What is this place?" he asks.

"This is One-Eyed Riley's mine," I say.

Frank wears an ugly scowl.

The inspector blinks once. Twice. "Sounds like you've got a story to tell us between here and town." He straightens out the dogs' leads, and they yap and sing in their excitement. Then smooth as gliding down the backside of the Chilkoot on Melvin's sled, we race across the snowbanks straight for Dawson City.

The trees blur past and the wind whips the blanket wrapped around my shoulders. I tell my story, and it's a good one. It starts with two boys who set out to find some gold. It's got clues and creeks and the promise of a wealthy claim, some folks who weren't decent and others who were right kind. It ends with the discovery that Riley was a sneak, his mine not worth a thing.

Frank keeps silent till the very end. "Who's the one who turned me in?"

Inspector Constantine stands on the back of the sled. The ride's real swift, but he holds himself steady, the lantern bobbing at his side. "A man I kicked out of Dawson a few months ago for stealing another man's gold. I sent him away on the steamer *Portland.* Didn't recognize him at first, as he'd shaved his mustache and his head. But I remembered him when he started talking. He confessed once he reached Seattle he left again to come back here with hardly anything but a few meager supplies." Inspector Constantine's dark eyes watch Frank carefully. "Seems he was anxious to get back to search for Riley's mine. But you already know that. You and your friend will get a lot of time to catch up when you're shipped out of town together."

Frank grumbles under his breath.

Albert? He risked getting caught himself to turn Frank in?

"I want you at the hospital as soon as we reach Dawson," Mary Agnes says.

"If Mel's there, please, could I get a few minutes with him first?"

Mary Agnes squeezes my hand. "I'll allow that."

The sled wheels to the right, and up ahead I spy a couple buildings, their lights blazing inside and out. Soon we're on a street lined with tents and stores, cabins and saloons. I reckon every lantern in Dawson City's been lit tonight. The Midnight Dome keeps silent watch on the far end of the road.

A crowd welcomes us as the sled slows. The other Marys are in front, but even closer are Mel and Spare-Rib, who rush to meet us before the sled even stops. Mel stumbles as he reaches for me, but rights himself quick. He don't let go until he lifts me in the air.

My brother, who's nearly a man, he's got tears on his cheeks. "You're safe."

"You're better." Our words run together.

Spare-Rib pats my arm. "You had us worried."

Mel starts to set me down.

"Be careful with him," Mary Agnes says. "He's been injured."

Mel's eyes fill up again. I ain't ever seen him like this before.

"I'm gonna be okay," I tell him. Soon enough Mel will know everything. I don't want to worry him no more, if I can help it.

Mel gently helps me stand on my good leg. I rely on the sled to keep me steady. I study Mel, his ugly bruise, his weary face, them shoulders that have got so strong since we left Pa. He's worth more than a thousand gold-filled mines.

Inspector Constantine forces Frank to stand.

"Give him a blue ticket straight out of town!" a fellow shouts.

"Don't you worry," Inspector Constantine says. "This man will get his due. It's the boy over there you should concern yourselves with."

Everybody turns to me, their eyes curious. What does the inspector mean?

"He's got quite a story to share. But first, someone fetch him a hot drink."

A fellow hands me a scalding cup of coffee, which burns my tongue but tastes real fine.

"Go on, Jasper," Mary Agnes whispers once I'm finished. Mel and Spare-Rib look real curious.

I clear my throat and nod to the inspector. "Some of you knew Riley."

A couple fellows nod and murmur.

"And some of you just heard about his riches." I lick my cracked lips. Everyone waits like I hold the answers to all their questions, which I do. "Well, I've been to his mine."

"You found—" Melvin starts to say, but Spare-Rib shushes him.

"And I can tell you there ain't nothing there."

"What do you mean, nothing?" a man says. "Did another fellow beat you to the gold?"

"Nope." My eyes are glued on Frank. His grimace

ain't changed since we learned about Riley's trick, but I ain't scared of him no more. "It was all just a prank, one cooked up by Riley."

"How do we know that's true?" another fellow asks.

"I'll let Riley tell you himself." I take that letter from my pocket and read it in the lantern light. Spare-Rib shakes his head, like he ain't a bit surprised. But Melvin's face is drawn. It's so quiet once I finish, I hear the latch on the Mountie station door as Inspector Constantine leads Frank inside.

Then someone laughs, but not with merriment. His long gray beard fairly quivers. "Of course," he says.

It's Bill. The old-timer from Bonanza Creek.

"Of course it was a prank. That fool Riley. That ridiculous old fool."

The crowd begins to move along, abuzz with all that's happened.

"I'm sorry, Jasper," Melvin says. "You wanted Riley's mine so badly. And now you're hurt and—"

"We're gonna be fine," I tell him. Of anyone, Mel best understands why I chased so hard after Riley's claim. Even though I ain't sure what's to come, my brother will be with me. We've done pretty well so far.

Mel nudges my shoulder. "Look who got three months on the woodpile." He points to the Mountie station.

A Mountie stands guard as two men swing axes above

their heads without a lick of skill. It's them Therouxs. They can't seem to split the wood scattered at their feet no matter how they try.

"Careful," Mr. Theroux shouts. "You 'bout sliced through my kneecap."

"Then move aside," Stanley says.

"All this work, it stirs up my rheumatism." Mr. Theroux sets down his ax. "I best rest a spell."

"No you won't." The Mountie hands him the ax again. "You'll rest when I tell you to."

It's just how them Therouxs acted in the saw pit during our Lindeman City days, except the Mountie won't take none of their lip.

"They didn't only sell fake Riley clues," Mel says.

"They were the thieves me and Edwin tried to track," Spare-Rib continues. "Before they set up that hoax of theirs on Queen Creek, they lifted gold from nearby camps."

"You know what else?" Mel brushes his hair off of his bruised forehead. "Their thieving didn't start in Dawson. Stanley confessed he saw his uncle take the gold stolen at Lake Lindeman."

"Old Joe's gold. Mr. Theroux stole it while we lived with them?" We sailed for a week with that crook and had no idea at all.

Spare-Rib shakes his head. "The woodpile's too good for them, if you ask me."

I lean heavy into Mel. "Are you okay?" he asks.

I shake my head. Even though I only got my weight on one leg, the pain's still bad.

Mary Agnes turns from the Sisters. "It's time for the hospital, Jasper, and you won't tell me otherwise."

"The hospital?" Mel's eyes grow wide.

"Melvin, help me with your brother," Spare-Rib says. They lift me in the sled and tuck the blanket gently beneath my legs.

Mary Agnes rides up front, and Spare-Rib's in the back. Me and Mel are in the middle. He wraps his arm around me. "I thought I'd lost you," he says.

"You can't get rid of me that easy." I shove his shoulder playfully. "I made you a promise I'd stick with you. For always. It's as simple as that."

The dogs lean forward in their harnesses, eager to begin their journey.

# Epilogue

I swirl the laundry water 'round and 'round, so fast some swishes over the pail's rim. Though the light in the cabin is weaker than Spare-Rib's spruce needle tea, there ain't no way I miss the glimmer everyone north of Skagway hopes for. Along with the sludge collected in the bottom of the pail are streaks of gold more beautiful than anything, just like Spare-Rib said there'd be.

"Now pour off most of the water into this tub," he says, "and swish what's left around again."

I try to hold the bucket firm, but water splashes across the floor. I don't know how to pan so good as Melvin does. He's learned a whole lot from Spare-Rib in the month we've stayed with him. Spare-Rib took us in once I left the hospital and says we can stay until the sun returns next spring. After that, me and Mel ain't sure what will happen next, but we don't gotta have that figured out just yet. We can just take each day as it comes.

"Gold's heavier than dirt," Mel says, "so it doesn't matter if you spill. The gold will settle on the bottom."

"Let me show you, Jasper." Spare-Rib lifts the pail with one hand and snaps his wrist. I move in closer, and Spare-Rib holds me steady. That night out on Victoria left me hurting for a while. I ain't too strong on my feet just yet, but it will come. That's what Spare-Rib says, and I believe him.

"Did you see it?" Spare-Rib asks.

I nod. As long as he keeps the water moving, a flicker of sparkling gold streaks around the bottom like a comet's tail.

This gold is mine to keep, rinsed from the folds and pockets of Little Skookum's miners, a payment on top of what I charge for laundry, earned fair and square. Fellows here ain't too clear on what it means to keep clean. They think they're set if they change their underdrawers every two weeks. Some would rather toss a dirty shirt than have it laundered.

I guess you could say I've got my work cut out for me, but I'm right fine with that.

Last night I wrote a letter I've thought about for weeks, since I spent those days resting in the hospital in town.

Dear Pa, it said:

Don't worry none. Me and Mel are happy here.

Then I wrapped it around the pocket watch. Come spring, once the Yukon's flowing, I'll send it back to Washington.

Because that watch is his, a wedding gift from Mama.

He deserves a chance at happiness, same as anyone.

# Author's Note

On August 17, 1896, George Carmack and Skookum Jim found a thumb-sized nugget of gold while panning in Rabbit Creek, a southern tributary of Canada's Klondike River. Word of their discovery quickly spread, and within two weeks of staking their claim, the Rabbit was renamed Bonanza (Spanish for "source of wealth" or "stroke of luck") and the entire creek was staked.

The Klondike gold rush, one of the world's largest, was well under way.

Most men who staked a Bonanza claim were from two neighboring mining towns along the Yukon River: Alaska's Circle City and Canada's Fortymile. The mining town of Dawson City, which sprang up in the swampland where the Yukon and Klondike Rivers intersect, was about twenty miles northwest of Bonanza's discovery claim.

It wasn't until a year later that the rest of the world learned of the discovery. On July 15, 1897, a steamship named *Excelsior* pulled into San Francisco, full of weary, run-down prospectors with suitcases, jam jars, and sacks that overflowed with gold. Two days later, when the *Portland* arrived in Seattle, the city was prepared. Journalists rowed out to the *Portland* to get the story before the steamer even docked. The first copy of the *Seattle Post-Intelligencer* was available by the same time those on board were able to disembark. The newspaper's headline read as follows:

**GOLD! GOLD! GOLD! GOLD!**

**SIXTY-EIGHT RICH MEN ON**

**THE STEAMER *PORTLAND*.**

**STACKS OF YELLOW METAL!**

For five years, the United States had been in the grip of an economic depression. The hope of easy riches in a land not too far off but distant enough to promise adventure appealed to many. Like San Francisco, the city of Seattle caught gold fever. Businessmen left their jobs immediately. People emptied their bank accounts and told their families to expect them back with riches in a few years. Even the mayor of Seattle quit his job to start a company connected with the goldfields.

Information—and misinformation—rapidly spread: Gold grew on bushes and was so plentiful, it could be scooped from the ground. A bicycle could easily carry a man the two thousand miles between the Pacific Northwest and the Klondike. Even newly minted guide-books contained questionable information. Bona fide Klondike outfitters sprang up overnight in large cities along the United States' and Canada's west coasts, selling clothes, dehydrated food, and mining gear. People were encouraged to take with them a ton of goods, called an outfit, which consisted of a year's supply of food, tools, and clothing.

The enthusiasm, stories of incredible wealth, and rapid ability to relay information through newspapers led to the frenzy known as Klondicitis. Those who left for the Klondike became known as Stampeders, for it was a huge number that rushed across the continent from not only North America but around the world. All sorts of people came, from those down on their luck to those well established in their fields. Barons and princes, farmers and doctors, and prospectors from goldfields in Nevada, South Dakota, Colorado, and other corners of the world joined with prospectors from California's gold rush days in the race to the Klondike. And although not so many in number, women and children came, too.

Most heading to Canada traveled to the saltwater ports closest to the Klondike, the Alaskan towns of Dyea and Skagway. The two communities, less than ten miles apart, were almost nonexistent only months before. Those who passed through Skagway faced Jefferson "Soapy" Smith and his gang, who'd come to Alaska with the plan to swindle Stampeders. The con men posed as prospectors, barbers, and outfit packers. Even the local authorities were under Soapy's power. From Skagway, the Stampeders entered Canada on the White Pass Trail, roughly thirty-seven miles of switchbacks (trails with winding turns) that ran between swamps, boulders, and hills. Thousands of packhorses were worked to death on the White Pass Trail because of its harsh terrain and the Stampeders' unrelenting drive. It was so awful, Stampeders nicknamed White Pass the Dead Horse Trail.

Those who docked in Dyea traveled into Canada on the shorter but steeper Chilkoot Trail, which ran about twenty-six miles and included a 3,500-foot climb. It took the average man forty trips up and down the steep mountain to get his goods across. Unlike Skagway's White Pass Trail, which was sometimes closed because of heavy rain, the Chilkoot was open year-round. Once it was covered in snow, Stampeders carved footholds into the mountain's side. Stampeders swarmed these Golden Stairs day and night, hauling their gear.

The two trails joined at Canada's Lake Bennett, where Stampeders built boats to sail the last six hundred miles down the Yukon and into Dawson City.

Like Jasper and Melvin, only a few people who left in August made it to Dawson City by the fall of 1897. They had all traveled light, ignoring the advice to bring their ton of goods. By February 1898 Canada's North West Mounted Police began collecting taxes at the Chilkoot and White Pass summits on goods brought into the country. A ton of goods for every Stampeder was no longer a recommendation but a requirement enforced to protect

Stampeders from starvation. The Mounties turned back all who tried to enter Canada without it.

During the winter of 1897–1898, twenty-two thousand Stampeders traveled through the Chilkoot Pass alone. By the time the majority of people who'd left the West Coast in July and August had made it over the passes, it was already October. Winter was well under way. Prospectors were forced to wait out the winter until the spring thaw along the banks of Lakes Lindeman and Bennett.

The California gold rush, which started in 1848, was known for its lawlessness, but the Mounties in the Klondike kept firm control. Those who broke the law were either given a blue ticket, which forced criminals to leave the territory, or made to do heavy labor on the Mountie woodpile.

Those seeking gold weren't the only ones affected by the gold rush. With the arrival of the Stampeders, indigenous peoples such as the Tagish, the Tutchone, the Tlingit, and the Hän-speaking people who lived close to the area around Dawson created new economic opportunities for themselves. They worked as packers, guides, or hunters. Women contributed to their family's income by making and selling clothes to Stampeders ill-prepared for Yukon winters. The rapid influx of people who came during the winter of 1897–1898 hastened the spread of disease and the decimation of indigenous homelands and hunting grounds, and disrupted ways of life.

Additionally, the Klondike gold rush forever altered the environment. Streambeds, forests, and surrounding habitats, including even mountainsides, were damaged by those who uprooted and destroyed anything that hindered them in their quest to find gold.

The Klondike gold rush lasted only three years. By the summer of 1899, gold had been discovered in Nome, Alaska, and many mining in the Klondike abandoned their work to seek gold there.

Of the hundred thousand people who set out for the Klondike, thirty to forty thousand reached Dawson City. Half of them actually looked for gold. Four thousand found gold. A few hundred found "quantities large enough to call themselves rich." And "only the merest handful"[1] kept their wealth.

Although most of the characters in this story are a product of my imagination, a few were true historical figures:

- Seattle's mayor William Wood quit his job to start the Seattle and Yukon Trading Company, a steamship company that carried men and freight to the Klondike goldfields.
- Jefferson "Soapy" Smith was a con man who arrived in Skagway at the end of August in 1897, just a few days before Melvin and Jasper. It wasn't until the

1 Berton, Pierre. *The Klondike Fever.* New York: Carroll and Graf, 1985, p. 417.

fall that he had control of Skagway. I've altered this for the sake of the story so that Soapy's scams are in full swing before the Johnson boys arrived.

- Clarence and Ethel Berry mined on Bonanza and in one year made $130,000 (that would be thirteen million dollars today). Ethel carried $100,000 worth of gold in her bedroll as she and Clarence left the Klondike on the steamer *Portland*. The Berrys were said to be so wealthy, Clarence kept a coal oil can full of nuggets at the door of their cabin with a sign that read "Help Yourself."
- Arizona Charlie Meadows ran a portable bar on the Chilkoot Trail that he set up in places like Canyon City and Sheep Camp.
- Lord Avonmore traveled to Dawson City with ten thousand pounds of gear, including tinned turkey and folding tables, as well as one hundred pounds of toilet paper and seventy-five cases of champagne. Because the real lord's champagne froze along the way, it sold for only twenty-five cents a case.
- Salt Water Jack, Buckskin Miller, and Pete the Pig were all men who mined in Fortymile. Two-Step Louie was from Dawson.
- Three Sisters of St. Anne, all named Mary, arrived in Dawson by steamer in 1898 and worked in the Klondike's first hospital, aptly named St. Mary, which Father William Judge opened in August 1897.

- There really was a Jimmy "Spare-Rib" Mackinson in Dawson who wasn't allowed to use his landlady's sheets because she was sure his bony hips and elbows would tear them.
- And although there was a man in Dawson named One-Eyed Riley, he never had a hidden mine. He was a gambler who was always broke. But one night he won twenty-eight thousand dollars and was so determined to leave the Klondike rich, he paid a thousand dollars for a dogsled ride out of town. In Skagway, someone persuaded him to try a dice game, and in just three rounds, One-Eyed Riley was broke again.
- Inspector Charles Constantine was sent by the Canadian government to the Yukon goldfields in 1894. He served as the Yukon's magistrate, judge, land agent, gold commissioner, and customs officer and was the most powerful figure in the entire territory.

Because of the Klondike's inaccessible location, much of its gold rush was "shrouded in mystery . . . leaving the most famous event in the last decade of the nineteenth century wide open to . . . exaggeration and hyperbole."[2] The ideas of mystery, exaggeration, and hyperbole were

2 Adney, Tappan. *The Klondike Stampede.* Vancouver: UBC Press, 1994, p. xvi.

fun to play with as I wrote *Jasper and the Riddle of Riley's Mine.* I hope the story has left you with a flavor of not only the gold rush itself but how the rest of the world came to imagine that far-off distant land, a place of risk and gamble and life-changing experiences that for some were worth more than any gold.

For those interested in reading more about the Klondike gold rush, I highly recommend the middle grade nonfiction book *Call of the Klondike: A True Gold Rush Adventure* by David Meissner and Kim Richardson.

# Acknowledgments

The idea for *Jasper and the Riddle of Riley's Mine* began with a simple question from my sons. "Mom, when are you going to write a book about a boy?" Going in, one of the few things I knew about my main character was that he'd be based on Mark Twain's immortal Huckleberry Finn. So it feels right that Noah, Caleb, and Mr. Twain get first thanks and top billing in this list of folks who've played a role in Jasper's story.

I am indebted to Stacey Barney for demanding of me my very best (and her unshakable belief that I can pull it off), Kate Meltzer for her careful attention to detail, and Tracey Adams for being my literary cheerleader. Thanks to the entire Penguin Young Readers Group team for their tireless devotion to children's books, to Richard Amari for a map that could have come straight from the goldfields, and to Craig Phillips, whose cover captured the story's energy and sense of adventure perfectly.

A special thank-you to Karl Gurcke, Historian for the Klondike Gold Rush National Historical Park, for vetting my work and answering endless questions; to Jody Beaumont, Traditional Knowledge Specialist for Tr'ondëk Hwëch'in, for the insight she gave about the impact the gold rush had on First Nations Peoples; and to Steve

Bramucci, who kindly allowed me to read *Huck's Legacy: The Complex Nature of the Humorous First-Person Storyteller*, his Master of Fine Arts thesis for the Vermont College of Fine Arts.

Carolee Dean walked me through story structure when *Jasper* was no more than a vague idea. Donald Burge, Terry Lynn Johnson, and Anna Catherine Ingwersen graciously gave feedback during various stages of the writing process. And my critique partners Valerie Geary, Uma Krishnaswami, Stephanie Farrow, Vaunda Micheaux Nelson, Katherine B. Hauth, and Mark Karlins read and reread portions of this book with enthusiasm and so much helpful insight.

Years ago, when I was researching pioneer women for the manuscript that eventually became *May B.*, my mother lent me a book called *Women of the Klondike.* Thanks, Mom, for introducing me to such a rich setting, and for the love you and Dad have always lavished on me.

I'm so grateful for the countless people who have asked after this book, including my faithful blog and newsletter readers; my dear friend Jamie C. Martin; my sister, Christine Casey; the fine people of High Desert Presbyterian Church; and my running partner, Beth Benham, who brought my family dinner more than once while I was on deadline. For readers young and old who've told me they can't wait for my next book, you are so appreciated.

I can't forget to thank my husband, Dan, launderer extraordinaire, who reminds me in tough moments that things are going to come together because he's seen the whole book-making process play out a couple times before. Here's to our year in Skagway sometime in the future!

Poet Robert Service described the Stampeders and sourdoughs alike as those who "Hear[d] the challenge, learn[ed] the lesson, [paid] the cost . . . , [who] suffered, starved and triumphed, groveled down, yet grasped at glory." I've learned so much from the stories of these everyday people who pushed themselves to remarkable lengths. Their grit and determination are inspiring indeed.

*© 2010 Crystal Sanderson Photography*

Caroline Starr Rose spent her childhood in the deserts of Saudi Arabia and New Mexico, camping at the Red Sea in one and eating red chile in the other. As a girl she danced ballet, raced through books, composed poetry on an ancient typewriter, and put on magic shows in a homemade cape. She's taught both social studies and English in New Mexico, Florida, Virginia, and Louisiana. In her classroom, she worked to instill in her students a passion for books, an enthusiasm to experiment with words, and a curiosity about the past. She is the author of the critically acclaimed novels in verse *May B.* and *Blue Birds.* Caroline lives in New Mexico with her husband and two sons.